LIKE A
HOUSE
ON FIRE

LIKE A HOUSE ON FIRE

a novel

Lauren McBrayer

G. P. PUTNAM'S SONS | NEW YORK

PUTNAM
— EST. 1838 —

G. P. PUTNAM'S SONS
Publishers Since 1838
An imprint of Penguin Random House LLC
penguinrandomhouse.com

Excerpt from "I Did Think, Let's Go About This Slowly" from *Felicity* by Mary Oliver,
Published by The Penguin Press New York
Copyright © 2015 by Mary Oliver
Reprinted by permission of The Charlotte Sheedy Literary Agency Inc.

Library of Congress Cataloging-in-Publication Data

Names: McBrayer, Lauren, author.
Title: Like a house on fire : a novel / Lauren McBrayer.
Description: New York : G. P. Putnam's Sons, [2022]
Identifiers: LCCN 2021053555 (print) | LCCN 2021053556 (ebook) |
ISBN 9780593331828 (hardcover) | ISBN 9780593331835 (ebook)
Subjects: LCGFT: Novels.
Classification: LCC PS3613.C2756 L55 2022 (print) | LCC PS3613.C2756 (ebook) |
DDC 813/.6—dc23
LC record available at https://lccn.loc.gov/2021053555
LC ebook record available at https://lccn.loc.gov/2021053556

Printed in the United States of America
1st Printing

Book design by Alison Cnockaert

I did think, let's go about this slowly.
This is important. This should take
some really deep thought. We should take
small thoughtful steps.

But, bless us, we didn't.

—MARY OLIVER,
"I DID THINK, LET'S GO ABOUT THIS SLOWLY"

LIKE A
HOUSE
ON FIRE

one

ATER, THEY WOULD argue about who saw the other first. As Jane would tell it, Merit was sitting in one of the ridiculous green acrylic chairs in the lobby, pretending to read a five-month-old issue of *Architectural Digest* with such feigned intensity that Jane stopped in the doorway of the conference room to admire the act. Merit, meanwhile, fully aware that Jane was watching her, had, up until the precise moment her future boss stepped out of the conference room, actually been reading the magazine, savoring every elevated, multisyllabic word. So what if it was the April issue in mid-September? Merit hadn't read a magazine in months, not since Nash was born, maybe even longer than that. She was devouring this one, with its slick, glossy pages and its clean sans serif font, enchanted by its organized, elegant calm.

It'd been a rough night. Nash had woken up four times, and when Merit finally lost her cool and whisper-hissed in her nine-month-old's face with as much venom as she could muster, "Mommy has an important interview tomorrow, go to sleep *RIGHT NOW*!!!" her son laughed so loudly he woke up his older brother, who then demanded water and cough drops. The morning that followed had been a shit show on every possible level (had Merit known that excessive consumption "might have a laxative effect," she might've thought twice before giving a four-year-old an entire bag of sugar-free lozenges to take back to bed with him). And even though Merit had told Cory over a week ago that her big interview was that morning at nine, her husband had neglected to mention that he had to be at work early and couldn't take Jude to school. Consequently, Merit spent the entirety of her morning trying to get her sons bathed, fed, dressed, out the door, and into the bird-crap-covered Subaru she meant to have washed before her interview, and zero time preparing for the interview she was lucky to have gotten and really didn't want to fuck up.

So, as luxurious as it might have felt to be sitting alone and reading a gorgeous magazine in a temperature-controlled room that didn't smell at all like bodily fluids, Merit wasn't relaxed. She was so tired her eyes felt like they'd been washed in bleach, and she was nervous. Partly because she needed a job more than she wanted to admit, but mostly because she'd spotted Jane in the conference room a good ten minutes before Jane came into the lobby and saw her.

("Imagine being me in that moment," Merit would say when they'd tell the story later. "I'm trying to stay calm and I see the woman who holds my fate in her hands and she looks like *her*.")

Jane's work had been featured in all the major design magazines, so Merit had seen plenty of photos of her potential new boss leaning across ten-thousand-dollar dining tables in spectacularly staged homes. But none of these images had done Jane justice. Watching her that morning, head tilted back in a laugh, blond hair falling away from her face to reveal the sharp, precise features that had seemed too severe online, Merit decided that the problem with all the photos was that Jane wasn't smiling in any of

2

them. She looked striking and stylish in every shot, but not beautiful. The woman in the conference room, by contrast, was fucking gorgeous. Warm and radiant, glowing the way that attractive women who drink enough water and sleep more than four hours at a time often do. Merit felt like a homely, dehydrated teenager in her ill-fitting black pants and stretchy striped T-shirt, which that morning had seemed like a hip fashion choice but clearly was a wild lapse in judgment. Jane Lodahl was a ravishing adult woman (*Scandinavian! From Denmark!*) who probably didn't own T-shirts. (In fact Jane possessed no fewer than two hundred of them, all white, black, or gray.)

The day of Merit's interview, Jane was wearing a black A-line midi dress with gold buttons down the front, the kind that costs five times what you think it should and only looks good on women with tiny waists and curvy hips. Merit's own body resembled a stretched-out unitard on a coat hanger, droopy and mostly shapeless except for the sad little sacks of skin where her tits and ass used to be. Nothing about Jane was droopy, shapeless, or sad. At fifty-six, Jane had phenomenal tits and an enviable ass. The body of a woman who'd never had children, Merit told herself, to make herself feel better.

(It made her feel worse.)

Merit couldn't have described the very particular sensation in her stomach as she watched Jane hop up on the slab table in the conference room, legs dangling, while the four men she was meeting with stood around awkwardly in their skinny pants and stiff shoes. Jane was always sitting on tables and leaning on counters, putting her full weight on things the same way she liked to bear down on people, as if to see what they were made of. It would take a long time for Merit, who was typically quite perceptive, to understand that Jane's oppressive self-confidence, finely calibrated to elicit unease in others, was an affectation she'd cultivated to get ahead in a profession dominated by men.

But Merit didn't know any of this the day she interviewed at Jager + Brandt. All she knew for certain as she followed Jane into her office that morning was that she desperately wanted this extraordinary woman to hire her. As she perched nervously on one of the many chairs clustered around Jane's desk—not a single one acrylic; Jane didn't oblige any of that high-design bullshit in her personal space—it occurred to Merit that she'd been so preoccupied with coming up with the right story to explain the three-and-a-half years she'd taken off from architecture to pursue fine art that she'd neglected to ask herself whether she actually *wanted* the job she was there to try to get.

Sitting across from Jane, she felt as if she wanted it more than she had ever wanted anything in her life.

"So you took some time off to paint," Jane said, one eyebrow arched as she began to doodle aggressively on the copy of Merit's résumé lying on the desk. She had a slight Danish accent and a nearly imperceptible overbite, which Merit might not have noticed had she not been staring exclusively at Jane's mouth, which was decidedly less intimidating than her eyes.

"I did," Merit said, and was pleased at how un-defensive her voice sounded.

Jane obviously already knew this. Merit had explained the clear gaps in her résumé in the cover letter she'd fired off after three too many glasses of rosé the previous Monday night. The wine wasn't her savviest move, but if she was going back to work, it would be on her terms. "Unconventional" was the word she'd used in the letter, despite the fact that Cory had told her it was code for "weird" and that she should call her career path "entrepreneurial" instead. Merit didn't see how spending three years trying to make enough art for a single gallery show could properly be called "entrepreneurial." Plus, trying to frame her failed creative pursuit as a clever career move made her feel desperate and pathetic, and she was neither of these things. Technically, this job was the only real possibility she had, and, yes, their mounting credit card bills demanded that she start getting a paycheck, but she had a B.Arch. from Cornell and a master's from Berkeley. She had to be at least as competent as ninety percent of the architects at her level. So, if she didn't get this particular job at this particular firm, there would be another one. There was no need to panic yet.

"And?" Jane asked, leaning back in her chair and propping her feet up on her desk. She wrapped her dress around her legs and tucked it between her knees. Merit wondered if she was wearing underwear.

Merit lifted her eyes to Jane's. "Utter failure," she answered. "I only sold one piece, which was barely enough to cover the gallery's costs."

"So here you are," Jane said.

"Here I am."

Jane studied her for a moment. Merit forced herself not to look away. Jane's eyes were very blue. Merit sensed that Jane was trying to make her uncomfortable. Instead, she felt uncommonly alive.

"You have the credentials, obviously," Jane said. "But are you any good?" She hadn't bothered to open Merit's portfolio.

Merit didn't hesitate. "I wouldn't waste your time if I weren't."

Jane arched an eyebrow. "And you're sure you're ready to come back to the grind?"

"Definitely," Merit lied. "I'll always love fine art, but I'm hardwired for the faster pace of architecture and design." She cringed a little at this last bit. It'd sounded less cheesy in her head.

"And I'm apparently hardwired to get fucked in the ass by incompetent middle-aged men who keep falling up," said Jane dryly. She crossed her ankles. "You have kids?"

Merit hesitated, in part because her mind was still stuck on the transition from ass-fucking to children, but also because she knew that a woman without kids asking another woman about her children in a prospective employment situation rarely turned out well for the one with kids.

"A girl's allowed one lapse in judgment," Merit heard herself say. "Or two, in my case."

Jane didn't say anything, but Merit saw a hint of a smile.

She leaned forward in her chair and put her palms on Jane's desk. She couldn't have said what came over her. It was unlike her to be so crass. "Please hire me, I need to get the fuck out of my house."

Jane laughed uproariously, and Merit knew she had the job.

CORY, THAT NIGHT, was ecstatic.

"I'm so proud of you, babe," he said, pulling the cork from a bottle of red wine. "You're back in the game!"

"What game?" Jude asked. Merit was wondering the same thing herself.

"Mommy got a job," Cory told him. "She's going back to work." He slid Merit's glass across the counter.

"I'm going back to work in *architecture*," Merit corrected. "I was always working."

"And now you won't be doing it for free." Cory grinned mischievously and raised his glass. "To Mommy!"

Merit felt like punching her smiling husband in the face.

"To Mommy!" Jude echoed, milk sloshing out of his metal cup. A few weeks before, Merit had purged her kitchen of plastic in a frantic attempt to convince herself she still existed. Replacing everything was a completely unnecessary expense, but the woman she'd always understood herself to be cared far too much about the planet, cytotoxicity, and aesthetic design to serve her children milk in fogged plastic drinkware. Sure, the stainless steel tumblers she'd replaced them with were much too heavy and made a horrible clanging sound when they were dropped, but their presence in her kitchen asserted that Merit was still there, that she hadn't lost her entire identity in motherhood.

She wondered now if her decision to go back to an office job that would require a daily shower and eyeliner was a variation on the same theme.

Merit resisted the urge to wipe up the spilled milk. The table was covered in water spots anyway. She took a long sip of wine.

"How're you feeling about it?" Cory asked, heaping *cacio e pepe* onto her plate. Despite her husband still not knowing the difference between being funny and being an insensitive jerk when it came to her career, he'd brought home her favorite dish from her favorite Italian place, and he'd called in the take-out order all by himself. On the whole, Merit was feeling great.

But Cory was asking about her new job, and her feelings about that were much harder to pin down.

The truth was, she'd never really *wanted* to be an architect. She'd picked it as a major because she was afraid she'd never make it as a painter, and she told herself that designing houses was creative enough. She threw herself into it at first. It was nice to not think about the future anymore, to be carried along by the momentum of a well-worn path. The decisions just sort of made themselves.

In a way, architecture had led her to Cory. When they met in a GRE prep class their senior year at Cornell, he was an ambitious environmental engineering major who thought grad school in California would help him get into tech. She needed a master's degree and zero chance of snow. Berkeley was on both their lists. They both got in. They both went. They moved in together the summer after their first year.

"Do you think we're moving too fast?" she asked him over beer and cheap noodles the night they signed the lease.

"Nope." He was unequivocal and calm and that had been the end of it.

The next day, he showed up at their apartment with a sack of oil paints and an old poem Merit was pretty sure he'd ripped out of a campus library book. She asked him to read it aloud to her, and he did, stammering uncharacteristically in a few places, his cheeks pink with his awareness of it, which seemed to Merit like the purest expression of love.

the problem scrunched into her forehead;
the little kissable mouth
with the nail in it.

It was an odd little poem about a woman hanging a wind chime, but Cory seemed moved by it, and Merit was moved by him, by his conviction that they were meant for each other and his recognition that even though she hadn't painted since college, oil paints were the surest salve for her fear. He got down on one knee after that, and she said yes before he could even get the question out. Of course she wanted to marry him. He was smart and handsome and made her laugh when she was stressed out. It didn't occur to her to expect more out of love than that. She put the sack of paints in a closet and resolved to be a really good wife.

They graduated the following summer and got married that fall. By then they both had jobs in the city, so they traded their tiny apartment in Berkeley for a loft they couldn't afford in San Francisco, where they commenced living as they imagined young, debt-laden urban newlyweds should. They worked long hours for bosses they didn't like and went out every night with people they barely knew and drank overpriced coffee every morning to fight the hangovers they swore they'd never have again and always did. Her parents said they were praying for her. Her college roommate told her she was living the dream.

But, as the years passed, it stopped being fun. Merit wasn't sleeping well, and her stomach hurt a lot of the time. She missed painting. She hated her job. Sometimes in the middle of the night, she woke up short of breath. What was she actually *doing* with her life? When she'd left home at eighteen, her only goal was escape; she'd wanted to get as far from her conservative parents and their suffocating world view and the humidity of

Northwest Florida as she possibly could. Fourteen years later, she wondered what she'd been running *to*.

She started seeing a therapist, who told her she should meditate and get back into art. So one Sunday morning, hungover and shaky, she pulled out the oils Cory had given her and painted for the first time since college. When Cory woke up and found her in the bathroom, a canvas propped up on the shower ledge, she was crying with relief.

"This is who I want to be," she told him, and he nodded like he understood, and for the first time in a long time everything seemed all right.

She got pregnant with Jude that night.

The fact that they hadn't been trying made it feel like providence, and that was good, because Merit wasn't sure she was supposed to have kids. Mostly she worried she wasn't cut out for it. She wasn't a horrible person—she'd always been kind to strangers, a conscientious houseguest and an avid recycler—but if she were honest (and she was, back then, always honest), she suspected she wasn't selfless enough to be a truly great mother, and that's the only kind she wanted to be. But then she got pregnant while she was still on the pill, on a day that already felt like an inflection point, and she decided not to question fate.

Cory turned the loft into a baby's room and bought her nontoxic paints.

To be clear, he wasn't suggesting that she try to make a career out of her art. Not that morning in the bathroom, when they sat side by side on the ledge of the tub and she finally told him how unhappy she'd been. Not later, when she was pregnant and miserable and spending sixty hours a week in a cubicle drafting toilet partitions on a computer screen. Not even when she was on maternity leave and painted *Discord*, the piece that got all the attention and earned her a real gallery show. Cory was supportive of her art as long as it remained a side hustle, something that made her interesting and a little quirky but didn't affect the balance in her 401(k). It was the central unspoken tension in their marriage; the fight under the surface of every argument about something else.

It was still there now. Five years after that morning in the bathroom. Three and a half years after she quit her job without telling Cory she was going to. And six months after the owner of the gallery where she'd had her show called to say he didn't expect to sell any more of her work, could she please come get her pieces? Except it wasn't a fight anymore, just a knot of mutual resentment they'd become good at pretending wasn't there. It was the real reason she'd decided to go back to architecture, but she'd never admit it. That would feel too much like defeat.

"You're at least a little bit excited, right?" Cory asked, and frowned. Merit still hadn't answered his question about the new job. "I hope you don't feel like I pressured you into this."

"Don't be silly," Merit said, leaning forward to kiss his cheek. "It was my idea."

And it had been. In fact, she'd called the recruiter without even telling him, just in case she changed her mind. It wasn't until after her first interview was set that she mentioned she was thinking about going back to work. By then she'd convinced herself that a full-time job in architecture was something she genuinely wanted for her own identity and sanity, not something she felt compelled to do because her husband liked her better when she was employed.

After dinner, Cory took his laptop up to their bedroom. Merit caved and let the boys watch TV while she loaded the dishwasher by herself. God, she hated the fucking dishwasher. The relentless cycle of loading and unloading. The greasy plates and cups that were left, night after night, on the mid-century dining table she'd found at a flea market when she was pregnant with Jude, back when she thought having nice furniture was possible for people with kids.

She caught a hint of her reflection in the window over the sink as she muttered to herself about gender inequity and poor table manners and barely recognized herself. When had she become a disgruntled thirty-seven-year-old nag who talked to herself in the kitchen while schlepping dishes to the sink? What happened to the bubbly, vivacious person she'd been in college, the girl who dropped her shoes and her bag and sometimes her bra on the floor just inside the front door and left art supplies all over the place? Cory was the neat freak, the boy with Minnesota manners, the one who knew which vacuum attachment was appropriate for the carpet and which one to use to clean the couch. He was the one who was supposed to keep them unfilthy and organized, yet he'd somehow managed to opt out of this side of himself when they had kids. Or did it start when Merit quit her job without running it by him first? Cory had always been so polite. Merit suspected that this sustained housecleaning strike was his passive-aggressive fuck you.

Well, he could get over it now. She was going back to work, with a salary that wasn't fantastic but was apparently high enough to bring his libido roaring back. They hadn't had sex in nearly two months, but the morning after Jane offered her the job on the spot, Cory pulled Merit into the shower with him, and they did it twice before the kids woke up. The surge of his desire was so transparent it annoyed Merit, but only mildly. So what if her husband's hard-ons were tied to her career? The girl he'd wanted to marry was teeming with ideas and ambition. For the past several years his wife had been perfectly happy painting in her pajamas all day, sometimes without ever brushing her teeth. As she mounted him on their bed for round two that morning, still wearing her bra because she hated what breastfeeding had done to her tits, Merit wondered if she'd lost her edge.

Cory grabbed her butt and flipped her over. She'd come easily enough in the shower. It felt like a lot of work to try to go again. She moaned believably, then made a grocery list in her head.

Cory left for work, and Merit went to Union Square, where she rapidly spent eight hundred dollars she didn't have on three new work dresses. She didn't love the way they fit, but buying them made her feel like a professional person who would know better than to wear a stretchy striped T-shirt to a workplace. And although she would never look as fabulous as Jane in a working woman's frock, her arms at least were toned, and her legs were tan from sitting outside on the roof deck above their building with the boys. She took them up there when she got back from shopping that afternoon. Was she really ready to go back to an office job? She'd occasionally fantasized about driving down the coast while her sons were napping and never returning, but now that she had a legitimate excuse to leave them for nine hours a day without endangering their lives, she felt like crying at the prospect of doing it.

She let herself wallow in nostalgia as she watched them play in the sandbox she'd bought off Craigslist at the start of the summer, when it was clear she wouldn't sell any more of her art and she was trying on the idea of being a full-time mom. She'd told herself it was a relief not to be striving anymore, that she didn't need a splashy career, that building towers out of Legos was the most satisfying activity on Earth. Some days she believed this. Most days it took effort not to stand in the center of her living room and scream.

Not that she blamed her children for how things had turned out with her art. But it certainly hadn't helped that she'd been sleep-deprived and hormonal as she tried to speed-paint fifteen large-format canvases for her first and only gallery show, without any childcare because Cory insisted they couldn't afford it with only one salary coming in. Her pieces weren't awful, but they weren't particularly good, either. She didn't disagree with the sole critic who'd bothered to give her a review. He'd called them "proficient but sterile." It described how she'd felt as she painted them.

So, yes, she was ready to go back to architecture, to straight lines and graph paper and the chance to do something she was less likely to fail at while not worrying whether they would be able to pay their rent. She was even more ready for her husband to stop sighing heavily every time he walked in the door and found her sitting unproductively on the couch. Still, she had a pit in her stomach, the pang that always accompanied the last day of any vacation, even the shitty ones. Mostly, she hated finality, and her decision to go back to work full-time felt like something she could never undo.

She put the boys down for a nap and tried on her new dresses again. Standing in front of her full-length mirror in the blue one, she wondered why she'd bought it. She wasn't a dress person. She looked better in pants.

What she should've gotten were groceries. She didn't have anything to make for dinner, and they were out of the vanilla coffee creamer Cory liked.

Her phone buzzed on the nightstand.

JANE: Hi.

Then:

JANE: I neglected to cover a crucial topic in your interview. It bears on my decision to hire you.

Merit frowned and picked up her phone. She wrote back with three question marks but then deleted all but one.

MERIT: yes?

She waited. The three gray dots appeared. She imagined Jane on the other end, effortlessly put together, feet up on her oversize desk.

The text popped up.

JANE: dear god please tell me you drink.

t w o

J ANE TOOK HER to lunch on her first day, to a trendy restaurant down the street from their office. The sidewalk patio was packed with attractive millennials in denim and white sneakers having conversations that involved a lot of aggressive smiling. Merit felt ridiculous in her new work dress, in no small part because her new boss was wearing skintight shredded jeans, a black T-shirt, and steel-toed stiletto boots. Apparently, the frock Jane had worn for Merit's interview had been a one-off, on loan from a stylist for a magazine shoot at a house in Nob Hill later that afternoon. Except when forced to pose for aspirational photographs in six-million-dollar homes, Jane exclusively wore jeans.

(Merit regretted ripping the tags off her new dress. Could she somehow reattach them and take the hideous thing back?)

Despite the crowd at the restaurant, the hostess signaled for them as soon as they walked in and took them to a corner table out back.

"The scene's a bit obnoxious, but the food's pretty good," Jane said as they sat. "And there's zero chance of running into Lars or Erik here, which is the real win."

"What are they like?" Merit asked. She was dying for more intel. All she knew about the two men who owned the company that now employed her was what she'd managed to find online; namely, their ages (forty-six and forty-seven), their origin story (they met in business school at Stanford), and their reputation for being "disruptors" in the very niche world of historic preservation design. She'd also learned that despite the fact that their last names were painted in oversize letters on the side of the warehouse they'd bought to house their new architecture firm, neither Lars nor Erik was a licensed architect. That's what they'd hired Jane for, to be the architect of record on every permit application they filed with the city.

"Peter Pan and his middle-aged golden retriever," replied Jane. "It'll be obvious from your first conversation with them which one is which."

"Is it weird that I got this job without meeting them?" Merit asked.

Jane shrugged. "Who cares? Lars said specifically that I should bring someone onto my team, and I didn't want to give him the impression that he had any say over who I chose."

"So they could meet me and decide to fire me," Merit mused. She was oddly elated by this. Not so much at the prospect of being fired but at the subtle rebellion of her hiring.

"They could," Jane said. "But they wouldn't. You're too attractive."

Merit nearly laughed at the absurdity of this.

"So they like the tired-mom look?"

"Oh, stop," Jane said, rolling her eyes. "Nothing about you says tired mum."

"You asked about my kids within the first five minutes of meeting me!"

"I only guessed you had them because you seemed like the type of person who would."

"What type of person is that?" Merit asked. She was suddenly acutely aware of her nipples. She'd stopped breastfeeding Nash when she first made the decision to go back to work, but she was still producing random bursts of milk. A pins-and-needles sensation erupted in both breasts. It didn't escape her that she'd just answered her own question. *The type of person who lactates at the first mention of kids.*

Merit saw Jane's eyes flick from Merit's face to her chest, and she knew without looking that one of the breast pads she'd shoved in her very ill-fitting bra that morning had migrated to her armpit and she was leaking through her new dress. *So much for taking it back.*

"I'm going to run to the restroom," Merit said quickly. She slid an arm across her body and felt wetness against her wrist.

"Shall I order for you?" Jane asked, keeping her eyes averted.

"I'll have the tuna melt," Merit heard herself say, even though she was quite certain she had never ordered a tuna melt in her life. She hurried toward the bathroom, arms folded across her chest.

Fortunately, the bathroom had a hand dryer. Unfortunately, it was mounted at waist level, forcing Merit to crouch over it awkwardly with her nipple jammed into the narrow opening. Though "jammed" was a stretch. After sputtering out half a tablespoon of milk, her left boob had resumed its normal postpartum shape, which resembled an overripe peach dangling in worn-out pantyhose. It slid right in.

This is why there is gender pay disparity, Merit thought as her breast was pelted with air.

Jane was absorbed in her phone when Merit got back to the table.

"Everything okay?" she asked, glancing up as Merit sat.

"Yep!" Merit felt an urge to say something scandalous, if only to distance herself from the lactating woman in the dorky work dress who'd just aerated her nipple in a bathroom hand dryer. She chewed on her lip and waited for Jane to finish her text instead.

"We have a pitch tomorrow morning," Jane said finally, setting her phone on the table.

An exuberant *fuck yeah!* flew through Merit's head. She felt mildly maniacal and immediately blamed her hormones. "What's the project?" she asked in a civilized voice.

"A house in Sausalito," Jane replied. "A neighbor of mine, actually. The woman who owned it died last year and now her granddaughter wants to gut it."

"You live in Sausalito?"

"Second home." Jane grimaced. "Which makes me sound awfully bougie, doesn't it?"

"I think *wanting* a second home is bougie," Merit replied. "Actually having one just makes you rich."

Jane laughed. Merit felt a jolt of pleasure.

"I bought it before I got married," Jane explained. "And I would've stayed there, but my husband decided that Sausalito was a 'suburban cesspool.' So, we bought a condo on the bougiest of bougie streets in the Marina, and I cry myself to sleep every night instead."

"What does he do?" Merit asked.

"Owns a restaurant. Yours?"

"Engineer," Merit said. "He works in tech."

Jane nodded, like this fit. Merit supposed it did.

"So you're coming with me tomorrow," Jane said then. "To the pitch."

Merit appreciated that it wasn't a question. "Does it matter that I don't know anything about the project?" she asked.

"I'll send you the proposal when we get back to the office," Jane said with a wave of her hand. "But it doesn't matter, you won't have to speak. I just need your trustworthy face."

"Again with my appearance," Merit joked. "I thought you hired me for my skill."

Jane smiled indulgently. "Honey, I'm an architect. Everything is an aesthetic choice."

The waiter arrived with their food. Jane had ordered a very civilized steak salad. Merit stared at her tuna melt with deep remorse. The cheddar was aggressively orange and only half melted. The sandwich as a whole was awkward and messy, which made Merit herself feel awkward and messy.

This sandwich is not a metaphor, she told herself.

She lifted it gingerly toward her mouth. A hunk of tuna plopped down on her plate.

She set the sandwich down and picked up her knife and fork.

"So the pitch should be fun," Jane said, slicing her steak.

"Will you wear jeans?" Merit asked.

"Most definitely."

"So . . . should I wear jeans?"

"You can wear whatever you want." Jane stabbed a piece of meat with her fork. "But if I were you, I'd go with a different bra."

"Noted," Merit said, and felt her cheeks flush.

"Not that I don't love a leaky tit," Jane added, smiling. "Especially over lunch."

MERIT SPENT THE afternoon going through Jane's proposal. It was artfully done, but basic. There weren't any animations in the slides, which Merit thought was a missed opportunity. She popped into Jane's office to tell her this and offered to add some in.

Jane arched a brow. "You know how to do that?"

"Well, yeah," Merit replied. "It's kind of the reason people use presentation software in the first place? Otherwise you could just build this as a PDF."

"How old are you?" Jane demanded.

Merit smiled. "Younger than I look."

Jane leaned back in her chair and put her feet on her desk. "Ugh, Tony is always offering to 'jazz up' my presentations. He thinks they're boring, too!" Tony was Jane's assistant, an architecture student at California College of the Arts. He wore bifocals and had a tattoo of a cactus on his biceps, and he only spoke when spoken to. Merit hadn't determined whether this was by direction or choice. Merit's offer letter had said that she'd have "access to an assistant," but she'd never had an assistant at her old firm, and Jane seemed very territorial over Tony, so Merit had already decided to answer her own phone.

"Tony!" Jane was yelling at the hallway. Ten seconds later, Tony appeared in her doorway.

"What's up?" Tony asked nervously.

"Merit agrees with you that my presentations are dull."

Tony looked horrified. "I never said they were dull."

"Only because I'm your boss and I'm very intimidating."

Tony didn't argue with this.

"I never used the word 'dull,' either," Merit pointed out.

"Oh, you didn't have to," said Jane. "It was implicit in the gentleness of your tone. Which I appreciated, by the way." She looked from Merit to Tony. "So is this who I am now, Tony? A person whose presentations are 'jazzy'?"

Tony looked like a deer in headlights. Was this a test? Was there a wrong answer?

(Did everyone ask themselves these questions when looked at directly by Jane?)

"Couldn't hurt?" he said finally. Merit felt the urge to give him a hug.

Jane turned back to Merit. "You heard the millennial," she said. "Go make our presentation jazzy."

"You got it," Merit said. It wasn't lost on her that Jane had used a plural possessive pronoun. In the span of this conversation, *her* presentation had become *theirs*. It also wasn't lost on her how much delight she took in this.

"You're not scared of her," Tony whispered as they were leaving Jane's office.

"Sure I am," Merit said. (She wasn't.)

Jane left the office at seven, stopping in Merit's doorway on her way out. "I'll bring us coffees in the morning," she said. "What's your drink?"

"A latte," Merit told her. "But I'm happy to get them. Just tell me where you like to go."

"Don't be silly," replied Jane. "Despite the fact that I've forced you to do monkey work on my presentation, you're not my errand girl. I'd send Tony, but he gets very stressed out about my order being wrong, and invariably that results in my order being wrong."

Merit laughed. "Is your order very complicated?"

"I like a drop of hazelnut syrup in a macchiato," Jane said.

"Seems simple enough."

"Right?" Jane smiled. Merit was struck again by how pretty she was. "I'll see you in the morning, then?"

Merit smiled back. "Yep."

Jane disappeared into the hall and then popped her head back in. "Oh, and so far I feel really good about my decision to hire you. Don't fuck up my deck." She didn't wait for a reply.

Merit listened to the *click* of Jane's heels on the hardwood floors, then the *ding* of the elevator, the *whoosh* of the doors. The whole building felt empty now that she was gone.

Merit stayed another forty-five minutes, triple-checking her changes before emailing Tony the revised slides to review before she sent it on to Jane. Attention to detail had never been her strong suit, but there was no reason her new boss had to know that.

It was already dark by the time Merit made her way down Market Street toward the BART station. She found the experience of walking on the sidewalk by herself exhilarating. Yes, she wanted to get home and see the boys, but the nanny she'd found on Craigslist—who had a list of references Merit promised herself she would eventually check—was feeding and bathing them, so technically she didn't have to rush back. She'd originally intended to be one of those working moms who said upfront that she had to be home for dinner or bath time or whatever other aspect of her kids' daily routine she'd deemed essential to oversee in person every day. But then Jane made motherhood sound like a professional defect, and Merit did not want to seem in any way defective. Besides, her children refused to eat most of what she cooked, anyway, and bath time always ended with someone screaming and a vague sense of guilt that she'd used too much water. Plus it wasn't like her husband had ever hurried home. So she told herself she'd revisit her priorities later and asked Sierra to do everything but put her children to bed.

She expected to feel bad when she came through the front door that first night. She'd been bracing for it, the gut punch of regret expressed on Instagram by deeply conflicted working moms everywhere. But when she walked into the living room and saw Jude and Nash already in their pajamas, bellies full with food she didn't have to cook, hair still wet from a bath she didn't have to oversee, Merit's heart felt as if it might burst with joy.

"Mommy!" Jude yelled, scrambling off the couch. "You're home!" He tumbled into her, pressing his face into her chest. Nash squealed from his bouncy seat on the floor.

"I'm home," Merit said, breathing him in. Minty shampoo, strawberry toothpaste, the distinct little boy scent underneath. "I missed you guys," she said, and wondered what it said about her as a mother if she liked her children more now because she'd been away from them all day.

"I missed you so much, Mommy," Jude said, his face buried in her neck. She heard his little voice catch.

"How'd everything go?" Merit asked lightly, flicking her eyes across the living room to Sierra.

"Everything was great!" Sierra said brightly. "Jude didn't seem psyched about fish nuggets for dinner, so I made them *keftedes* instead. I hope that's okay?"

Merit felt herself nod, but this information was very confusing. First, she had no clue what *keftedes* were. Second, unless *keftedes* were gummy worms, Merit didn't understand how this girl had gotten her sons to eat them.

"They're really yummy meatballs, Mommy," Jude offered helpfully.

"I know, sweetheart," Merit lied. "Did you like them?"

"They're my favorite food," said Jude, as if Merit was already supposed to know this.

"Awesome, buddy. I hope you thanked Sierra for making them." This last part was laughable.

"Do you like your new job?" Jude asked.

Merit nodded. "I do."

Jude's face crumpled. "You like it better than us?"

"Of course not, sweetie," Merit said, rubbing his back. She refrained from pointing out that he'd never asked his father that.

Merit heard the knob turn behind her. Cory was home.

"Daddy!" Jude fell over himself to get to the door. "What are those?"

Merit turned.

Cory was holding a grocery store bouquet. He hadn't removed the orange sticker with the price in bold type—$6.99.

"So pretty!" Merit heard herself say. One of the pink carnations was already dead.

Cory handed her the bouquet. "You look great. I like that dress."

"Flowers and compliments! I should've gone back to work sooner." She kissed him on the lips and tasted the cold brew he always drank on his drive home to help him power through whatever work he would stay up late to finish. With her heels on, she was exactly his height. She liked being at eye level. For the past several years, she'd lived in slip-on sneakers and had always been looking up at him. And he, down on her.

Enough with the fucking metaphors, she told herself. God, she was tired.

"So . . . how was it?" Cory asked when Sierra was gone and the boys were asleep. They were alone in the kitchen, eating leftover *keftedes* and drinking a truly awful bottle of red wine.

"It was great," Merit said. "Really fun."

She knew he was expecting more details, but she didn't feel like getting into it. What she felt like doing was eating one more delicious meatball and then falling asleep. Without loading the dishwasher. Maybe without washing her face.

"What's the office vibe like?" he pressed.

She yawned. "It feels pretty chill? I get the sense Jane does her own thing."

"And you like her?" Cory asked.

"So much."

"That's great, babe. I'm really happy for you."

Merit nodded and popped the last meatball into her mouth. They really were exceptional. She silently congratulated herself for having such excellent taste in nannies. And without using an agency at that! She chewed her food slowly, watching Cory gather their empty dishes and stack them in the sink. It seemed to her the sexiest activity a man could undertake. She couldn't remember the last time he'd cleaned up the kitchen. If she'd known this was on the other side of her going back to work, she might've done it ages ago.

She swallowed the last of the meatball. She didn't want the wine.

He turned and saw her watching him.

"Whatcha thinking?" he asked.

"Nothing. Just that I had a good day."

Cory grinned playfully as he wiped his hands on a dish towel that definitely needed to be washed. "Wanna make it a great one?"

Sex felt like a lot of effort, but he looked so cute and hopeful, and he'd done the dishes, after all. She stood up and unzipped her dress.

His eyebrows went up. "Just like that?"

Merit pushed the fabric down over her hips, delighted that she'd had the foresight to wear new underwear. "I'm a working girl now," she said, reaching for Cory's belt. "I don't have time to mess around."

SHE MET JANE at the ferry terminal the next morning. Jane insisted they stand at the very front of the boat.

As they pulled away from the dock, Merit sipped the latte Jane had brought her and felt the frenzy of her morning recede. First, Jude refused to put on underwear, and then Nash busted his chin on the coffee table, and then her mom called to wish her a good first day of work, despite the fact that Merit had told her mother at least five times that she was starting the day before, on a Monday, the obvious day for a person to start a new job. Undeterred by the fact that both her grandsons were scream-crying in the background, her mother then launched into a very long and very convoluted story involving spiritual warfare and plastic skeletons, until Merit finally feigned bad service and hung up.

"I sometimes think this boat ride is the only thing that keeps me from slitting my wrists," Jane said, tilting her head back to get some sun on her face. There were baby-fine hairs sprouting at her hairline, like little blond blades of grass. She didn't have a single strand of gray.

"You might have mentioned that *before* I took the job," Merit said easily. She was wearing vintage jeans and a black silk blazer and felt decidedly more like herself.

"Oh, I couldn't have," Jane said, opening one eye. "You seemed so damn earnest."

"You don't like Lars and Erik," Merit heard herself say.

Jane gave her a look she couldn't read. "What's not to like?"

"Maybe the fact that they take all the credit for your designs?"

Jane smiled. "There is that." She closed both eyes again, soaking in the sunlight. There were freckles on her nose Merit hadn't noticed before, faint lines above her lip, a tiny scar on her chin. "But I knew what I was getting into."

The sun went behind a cloud.

Jane opened both eyes and leveled her chin. "Have you ever been to Copenhagen?"

Merit shook her head.

"It's cold there, by now," Jane said. She sounded wistful. "Colder than it ever gets here."

"Yikes," Merit said, and made a face. Her mind went to the winters she'd spent in Ithaca, the way her toes would freeze from Halloween to spring break. Cory used to tease her for leaving her socks on every time they had sex. She'd cling to him under the covers of her twin bed, his body hot like a human radiator, until they were both damp with sweat. Now he slept with the windows open, the blankets flung off, on the other side of a California king.

"Yeah, it's brutal," Jane said. "Though I've decided it's the reason Danish women don't age. The cold is like six months of cryotherapy every year." She tugged on the sides of her face with her fingertips, smoothing out wrinkles she didn't have. "California has turned me into a leathery old hag."

"Is this when I point out how completely ridiculous you are?" Merit asked.

Jane smiled. "You catch on quick."

The sun emerged from behind the clouds, bright and hungry and warm. Merit looked over at the Golden Gate Bridge, glittering like a burning ember across the bay, and wondered whether fewer people jumped when the sun was out.

"How long have you lived here?" she asked Jane, her eyes still on the bridge.

"Twenty-nine years," replied Jane. "Which seems impossible, honestly. I was only supposed to be here six days."

Merit turned her head. "What made you stay?"

"I fell in love with an American."

"Your husband?"

"God, no," Jane said. "Edward came fifteen years later, after the sun damage and cynicism set in." She smiled a little. "The first guy was another architect I met at a conference. He had the body of an action figure and knew how to fix things. All the Danish men I'd dated before him were slight and ineffectual. By the time I realized that my hunky American was actually a nasty drunk, I had a job I loved and a fucking amazing tan. So I didn't go back."

"Is your family still in Copenhagen?" Merit asked.

"What's left of it."

Merit wasn't sure what to say next. She'd had too much coffee. She felt shaky and had to pee.

"And yours?" Jane asked. "Where are they?"

"Florida."

Jane shuddered. "Talk about *yikes*. Do you go back there a lot?"

"Not really. My parents take a lot of cruises, so that lets me off the hook." Merit didn't mention her parents' deplorable politics, or their religious views, or the country club they belonged to that still didn't admit Jews.

"Dear god," said Jane. "The only thing that sounds more hellish than being in Florida is being on a cruise ship filled with people from Florida."

Merit looked over at her new boss and cocked her head. "How about being on a ferry boat with one person from Florida?"

Jane smiled. "Totally different. Heaven on earth."

THEY TOOK AN Uber from the ferry station to the property, a powder blue Victorian with decorative pediments and dormer windows that stood out in a row of ultramodern homes. The owner hadn't arrived yet, so they stood on the driveway to wait.

"When I bought mine these were all hundred-year-old houses," Jane said. "Now only a few are left."

"Where's yours?" Merit asked.

Jane pointed up the street. "Five houses up. It's an Edwardian, built fifteen years later than this one, so it was inherently less hideous at the outset. Plus, it's white so it doesn't immediately make you think of a gay funeral." Jane saw Merit's shock. "What? I can appreciate historical design without *liking* it."

"Um. A gay funeral?"

"My kid brother's funeral was a sea of powder blue. Though maybe that was a Danish thing? It's admittedly a small sample."

"Gay Funeral is an excellent name for a shade of paint," Merit said to say something, and immediately felt like a jerk.

"It is!" Jane said without missing a beat. She did a little pirouette and started toward the house.

"I'm sorry about your brother," Merit heard herself say as she followed Jane up the driveway. "And I'm sorry I made that stupid joke about the paint."

Jane looked back at her. "You're hilarious."

"I'm serious!"

"So am I. And my brother would've loved your joke about the paint." Jane started up the stairs to the front door. "Ugh, my thighs are killing me," she moaned, and squeezed the backs of her legs. "My trainer kicked my ass yesterday."

Merit was two steps behind, exactly eye level with Jane's ass. She felt her own butt sinking into her upper thighs, her skinny jeans bagging at the seat.

You're not competing with her, she told herself as she joined Jane on the landing. *So what if she's nineteen years older? She can have the better ass.*

"What?" Jane asked, eyeing her.

"What?" Merit said back, and immediately tripped over her feet.

Jane reached back to help her up. "If you're nervous about the pitch, don't be. With your jazzy presentation and my undeniable charm, we've got it in the bag." Jane nudged her with her hip, and it seemed impossible to Merit that they'd only been working together for one and a quarter days. "Just maybe stay off the spiral staircase in those boots?"

A white SUV turned into the driveway. The woman in the driver's seat was Merit's age, and through the windshield Merit saw two little boys in car seats in the back seat.

Jane waved as the woman got out.

"Sorry," the woman called as she shuffled her sons out of the car. Her name was Chloe, Merit remembered from the proposal. "My sitter canceled at the last minute." Chloe pushed her sunglasses off her face and smiled the defeated smile of a woman who had been forced to accept the

29

fact that in lieu of the hours of progress and productivity she thought she was going to have, her day would be a raging dumpster fire instead.

I know how you feel! Merit wanted to cry out. *I've been there!*

But standing next to Jane in suede booties and black silk, her kids with a full-time nanny on the other side of the bay, she was somewhere different now.

Chloe mounted the front steps, dragging a squirming child with each hand. "Thanks so much for coming all the way out here," she said wearily. "I know it's a hike." Merit wondered if she'd been close with her grandmother, if she'd spent Christmases opening presents at this beautiful old house. Merit still missed her own grandma terribly. Her dad's parents passed away before she was born, but her mom's mom used to come stay with her when her parents would go on vacation. They'd play Scrabble and drink cherry limeade on the beach, even when it was cold, and they'd talk for hours about grown-up things like art and death and sex. It was at her funeral that Merit decided to go as far away as possible for college and never come back.

"We should be thanking you," Jane was telling Chloe. "We love a midmorning jaunt. This is my colleague Merit, by the way. She's a much better architect than I am, but she brings me along for laughs."

It was endearing and kind and complete bullshit and all three women knew it.

"I'm so glad you're here, then," Chloe said to Merit.

Merit remembered the mornings she'd spent crying in her closet while Cory was at work, when her paintings weren't selling and Nash wouldn't sleep.

"You and me both," she said.

three

"LEMME GET ON top," she whispered.

Cory nodded, breathing heavily, and rolled over onto his back. Merit didn't particularly *want* to get on top, not at 7:16 on a Sunday morning, not when her parents were right above them on the pullout in the loft and sunlight was streaming through their bedroom window with such ferocity it reminded her of a gynecologist's headlamp. But this impromptu romp was taking longer than she'd anticipated, and this would speed things up. She pulled her hair out of the ponytail she'd slept in, trying to channel the sexiest version of herself. She suspected it wasn't all that sexy. Maybe that's why her husband still hadn't come.

She rocked her hips faster. The boys would wake up soon. She should've locked the door.

"I'm gonna come," Cory said breathlessly. "Did you . . . ?"

If you have to ask if I came, then I probably didn't. . . . "I'm good," she said, in a way she hoped communicated immense pleasure and not annoyance that it was taking so long. She almost added, *Please hurry, my parents are still on East Coast time,* but thought better of it. She reached back and squeezed her husband's balls instead.

Her parents had flown in for Nash's birthday party that afternoon. Or, rather, her parents had planned a trip to come visit them the week after Thanksgiving and "suggested" that it might be nice if they could celebrate their youngest grandson's birthday while they were in town. Nash's actual birthday wasn't until December 17, but her parents were going on a cruise to the Galápagos Islands the day after Christmas and coming to California that close to their departure was just "too much" for them. Having them in town for five days was too much for Merit, especially now that she was working fifty-hour weeks, but she wasn't cruel enough to deny her mother a grandchild's first birthday party, particularly after delivering the news that there would be no christening (she'd caved when Jude was a baby, but only because her mom had bamboozled her with a shotgun ceremony at their church in Pensacola on Christmas Eve). The birthday party was her mom's consolation prize, proof that Merit and Cory were still participating in mainstream society and hadn't become fringy left-coast liberals for whom nothing was sacred.

Merit had woken up at four-thirty that morning and hadn't been able to fall back asleep. She didn't know if it was the party that afternoon or the inevitable inquisition she'd get from her parents when she told them they were going to brunch that morning instead of church, but she spent the next two and a half hours tossing and turning and fantasizing about various illnesses she might feign to justify hiding out in her bedroom all day. When the sun came up and Cory pulled her against him, already hard, she was grateful for the distraction and channeled the energy she might've put into faking a sickness into pretending to be turned on.

"I'm gonna hop in the shower," she said when Cory finally finished. "Don't forget we have a reservation at Central Kitchen at ten." She pecked his cheek and ignored his groan. She didn't want to have sixteen-dollar eggs Benedict with her parents, either, but that's what you did when you were trying to convince your parents that your chaotic and disorganized life was, in fact, aspirational because you lived in a city with Zagat-worthy brunch. It wasn't her fault that her husband didn't possess whatever gene was required to let his father-in-law pick up the check.

Miraculously, the six of them managed to get out of the apartment that morning without anyone yelling or crying. Jude didn't even complain about having to wear shoes. Things were going so well that Merit was almost enjoying herself, until she made the mistake of answering an email from Jane at the table, prompting a nonstop commentary from her mother on the necessity of observing a Sabbath and the perils of being a working mom.

"I really enjoy my career," Merit told her mom, pointlessly. The woman was the definition of "out of touch." She'd been the bookkeeper for her father's dental practice for thirty years, which had apparently given her the impression that she'd had a demanding career that she'd expertly managed to "juggle" without sacrificing her weekly Bible study or the PTA. Her only child, in her view, was not being assertive enough with her new boss.

"You said she's a woman," her mother said. "Is she a b-i-t-c-h?"

"Oh, Merit loves her boss," Cory piped in.

Merit kicked him under the table. Having her mother think she idolized Jane wasn't better.

"What do you love about her?" her mom pressed.

"I wouldn't say I *love* her," Merit said, shooting a look at Cory. "I respect her because she's great at what she does."

"Well, make sure you're establishing your boundaries," her mom said. "Not all women are allies, dear."

Merit hadn't engaged after that.

"Why do you let it get to you?" Cory asked on the drive home. Her parents were behind them in their full-size rental car, which was impossible to park in the city and irritated Merit every time she looked at it.

"I don't."

"You barely spoke at brunch."

"I didn't like the food."

"Mer."

"She's my mom, Cory. I can't help it. I care what she thinks. And apparently she thinks I suck at establishing boundaries."

"She didn't say that," Cory said. "She expressed some worry that you might be working for a b-i-t-c-h. That seems like a reasonable motherly concern."

"It's not funny."

"C'mon. It kind of is. Wait until she finds out Jane doesn't have kids!"

"What's a b-i-t-c-h?" Jude asked from the back seat.

"A very powerful woman who people are afraid of because she's so good at her job," Merit said, turning in her seat to look at him. There was dried mac and cheese in his eyebrow and marker all over his hands.

"Like you," Jude said. "Right?"

She reached back to ruffle his hair. It was lighter than Cory's, and curly, like hers used to be. "I'm not that powerful," Merit said.

"Will you do my dinosaur puzzle with me when we get home?" Jude asked.

"I'd love to, sweetie, but I have to set up for Nash's party this afternoon. Maybe Daddy will?" She glanced over at Cory.

"Can't," he said. "I'm gonna ride down to Mount Sutro and do the loop a couple times." He looked at Jude in the rearview mirror. "But I bet Grandma would love to do your puzzle with you, buddy."

"You're going on a bike ride *now*?" Merit asked. "The party starts at four."

"I'll be back by three." Cory looked over at her. "That's okay, right?"

She knew if she told him that actually, no, it wasn't okay for him to leave on his mountain bike right before the forty-person party they were hosting in their home, he wouldn't go. But she didn't want to. She didn't want to *have* to.

"Totally," she said.

Of course it didn't occur to her husband that she might need help setting up for the party she'd planned by herself during the first months of a very demanding new job. When her piece-of-shit Civic broke down on the side of the road at midnight during a snowstorm after their second date, Merit waited by herself for three hours for the tow truck instead of calling Cory to pick her up. When she was pregnant with Jude and got so sick with the flu the doctor told her to go to the ER, she took a taxi there and back because she didn't want to bother Cory at work. In each case, Cory had brought it up afterward, and both times she'd shrugged and said it wasn't intentional, it just hadn't occurred to her to ask for his help. This wasn't remotely true; each time she'd wanted to call him first thing. But then she'd asked herself if she really *needed* him. The answer was always no.

She wasn't trying to be a martyr. She handled things on her own because she liked being the sort of person who could, and because it made her feel less like her mother, who routinely asked other people for help just so she could judge the extent of their affection for her based on their willingness to give it. Merit didn't need her husband to prove he loved her by setting up chairs for a party, or taking out the trash. And it wasn't like Cory did nothing. He was responsible for bike tune-ups and signing the kids up for team sports.

The bike tune-ups, at least, he'd never fucked up.

"Mommy?" came Jude's voice from the back seat.

Merit turned around to look at him. "Yes, sweetie?"

"Since Daddy is so busy today, can I just do the puzzle with you?"

MERIT WAS ARRANGING mini cupcakes on a platter when Cory blew into the kitchen in his bike shorts, his dark hair mussed from wind and sweat, at three forty-five.

"Part of the trail was closed," he explained when her eyes went to the oven clock. He gave her a sheepish grin. "I had to improvise and might have misjudged how long it would take me to get home."

"You're forgiven," she said easily, leaning over to kiss his sweaty neck. "But please don't do the thing where you disappear for the first thirty minutes of the party and force me to entertain everyone by myself."

"It'll only take me five, tops, to shower," he promised, pulling open the fridge. The door was blocking his face, but she intuited his frown. "Is this all the beer you got?"

"I bought a dark and a light, like you said."

"But how many bottles?"

"Twelve of each."

"How many people are coming to this thing?"

"Around forty."

"So we have a total of twenty-four beers for forty people?"

"More than half of them are kids."

Cory shut the fridge. "I'll run to the corner and get another case."

"Great," Merit said. She didn't point out to him that only six of the people who were coming to the party would even want beer because everyone else preferred wine, or that no one besides her mother would have more than two drinks anyway because it was four o'clock on a Sunday afternoon.

"What else do we need?" he asked.

"Nothing I can think of," Merit said breezily. She felt the opposite of breezy but an airy tone was the key in conversations like these. "I have a big platter of grilled vegetables, some hummus, and three salads. Twelve bottles of wine. Kid food for the kids." She didn't mention the four dozen cupcakes, or the photo booth she'd put together, or the giant pin-the-tail-on-the-dragon she'd painted by hand.

"Should I get some meat?" Cory asked.

"Get whatever you want."

"I just want to make sure we have enough food."

"So do I, babe. That's why I spent three hours and four hundred dollars at Costco yesterday. But I didn't get any meat, so if you want some, knock yourself out." Merit did her best to smile in a way that did not seem upset. *Remember the lovely morning sex!* she told herself. She didn't need to remind herself that only one of them had gotten off.

Cory sighed. "I appreciate all the work you put into this party, babe. This isn't a criticism of you."

"Understood," Merit said. There was nothing she wanted to do less in this moment than have this conversation. "Just go to the store, okay? Get whatever you want. It's fine, babe. Really."

"I'll just get the beer," Cory said, and left.

Merit's dad ambled into the kitchen. "Your mom sent me for some chardonnay."

"Wine fridge," Merit said. "Under the bar."

Watching her dad muscle the cork out of a bottle of Costco chardonnay so his wife wouldn't have to get off the couch, Merit wondered if her parents were happier than she and Cory were. She doubted her father had ever questioned his wife's menu choices fifteen minutes before a party was supposed to start. And her mother had certainly never screamed the words "mental load" at her husband after being asked by him for the seventh time why their four-year-old was still using a pacifier at night. Merit wasn't sure she'd ever heard her mom scream *anything* at her dad, except possibly during sex (there was one night in high school when she came home an hour before curfew and overheard some soul-scarring dirty talk she spent the next twenty years trying to block out).

"Somebody pooped his pants before his party," came her mom's voice from the living room as her dad finally got the cork out of the wine.

"Be right there!" Merit yelled. "Let me just pull out the rest of the food!"

"Can I help you, sweetheart?" her dad asked.

"No, it's okay. I got it. And besides, Mom needs her wine."

"I heard that," her mom said, appearing in the kitchen with Nash in her arms. "Lucky for you, I can pour my own wine, and I can multitask." She filled a glass to the brim with chardonnay. "Come on, Nashy, let's go get clean pants and leave your mama to stress about your party all by herself." She took her wine and her grandson and headed up the stairs.

Merit looked at her father. "I'm not stressed."

Her father nodded.

"No, seriously," Merit insisted. "I'm not."

"Okay, sweetheart," he said. "Do you want some wine?"

"No," Merit said. (She did.)

"Mommy!" Jude yelled at the top of his lungs from the boys' bedroom. "Nash pooped all over his clothes! It's disgusting!"

"Fantastic," Merit muttered, annoyed at herself for making the rookie move of putting an eleven-month-old in his brand-new birthday party outfit more than three minutes before the birthday party was scheduled to start. Her father went to the cabinet for another glass and poured her some wine.

"It's supposed to be fun," he said as he handed it to her. In high school it'd been Hershey bars. He'd slipped them under her bedroom door every time she had a bad date. It was the closest he'd ever gotten to engaged parenting. At the time, it felt like a lot.

Merit gulped the chardonnay like it was water, aware as she was doing it that she had officially become the kind of mom who pounded white wine before her kid's first birthday party, which is to say, a total fucking cliché. Merit set the empty glass down. Her head was starting to ache.

"I'm having fun," she said, going to the fridge for the rest of the food. "Can't you tell?" She pulled the foil top off the pan of grilled vegetables and felt a jolt of panic that she hadn't bought enough. Speed-counting charred strips of eggplant, she did the math in her head. Nineteen adults, five kinds of vegetables, two dozen of each. She'd thought this through.

"It doesn't have to be perfect," her dad said.

"Believe me, Dad, I'm not striving for perfect," she said, slopping hummus into a serving bowl. She should've gotten the yogurt dip, too.

"How about I open more wine?"

"Excellent," she said as Cory came in with three cases of beer and a log of salami the size of her arm.

"It was on sale," he said, handing her the meat.

There was a metaphor here, surely, in this giant hunk of salami that her husband had just thrust into her hands to deal with despite the fact that she hadn't asked him to get it, and it didn't at all go with the rest of the Lebanese menu she'd painstakingly planned. Vegetarian on purpose, because her dad's cholesterol was through the roof.

The phrase that came to mind was "dick move."

"I'll go hop in the shower?" he said.

She looked at her husband and seriously considered bitch-slapping him with the meat.

"Take your time," she said instead.

THE COLORED BUBBLES were her idea.

Yes, Nash was only turning one, but their couple friends all had older kids and she'd wanted to give them something fun to do. She'd mentioned it in the invitation—"wear clothes you don't mind getting stained!"—and she'd organized all the mini bubble containers by color so the kids could enjoy the civilized experience of making a sudsy rainbow in the sky. Why she hadn't recognized that children under the age of five who'd just shoved cupcakes in their faces couldn't possibly have a civilized experience of anything, she didn't know. She wasn't a first-time parent. There was no excuse for this.

Since she'd orchestrated it—and been the one to painstakingly add drops of food coloring into one hundred and forty mini bubble containers so that each kid could have a complete ROYGBIV—she had no one but herself to blame when her youngest party guests started slinging rainbow-colored soap suds at the building's new deck furniture, which the landlord would absolutely make her pay for.

At least they had extra beer.

As she stood in the center of the mayhem in her favorite gray sweater, now speckled with food dye that would definitely not wash out, surrounded on all sides by children shrieking at full volume and the excessively peppy chatter of their lightly intoxicated parents, Merit began sweating profusely and briefly considered hurling herself off the roof to make all of it stop. Had there really been a time when she looked forward to a gathering like this?

"How's the new job?" her friend Leena asked. She was holding a napkin containing a chewed-up carrot and hummus combo that one of her twin daughters had spit out and was smiling at Merit in a way that appeared genuine. Maybe because she'd had the foresight to wear all black? "Is it as horrible as you thought?"

"Hm?" Merit was having difficulty concentrating. She was preoccupied with trying to remember why she'd ever thought it was necessary to throw a party for a human who was too young to form memories. Parents everywhere did this. Why? Parents were adults. The parents at this particular party were highly educated adults. Why did they keep falling for this shit?

"The new job," Leena repeated. "Do you hate it as much as you thought you would?"

Merit remembered being a woman who dreaded going back to work, but only vaguely. That same woman must've planned this party. A woman whose life didn't involve sharp delineations between workday and weekend, which is the only reason she could come up with for why she'd selected a Sunday evening for this godawful event. "Uh, no, actually. It's been great."

"She works too much," her mother piped in.

"Mom."

"You do!"

"I think she works a perfectly appropriate amount," Cory said, sliding his arm around Merit's shoulders.

"And still manages to throw kick-ass parties! With bubbles!" Leena shook her head. "I don't know how she does it."

Merit couldn't fathom how anyone could call this cramped, chaotic gathering "kick-ass." Then again, it was coming from a woman with an MFA from Stanford who seemed perfectly content holding a four-year-old's chewed-up food in her hand. Merit's sweater began to itch.

"She's tired," her mom said. "I can see it on her face."

"I think she looks great," Leena said.

"I agree," Cory said, and gave her shoulder a squeeze.

(Merit wondered: Since they'd taken to discussing her in third person, did she still have to stand there and participate?)

"I'll grab some more beer," she said abruptly, and left.

Down in the kitchen, Merit stood with her hands on the island and told herself she was being an asshole. No one liked kid birthday parties. None of the people on her roof deck were *actually* having fun. They were just pretending to have fun because that was the social contract among families with young kids. She was lucky to have friends like these—kind, caring moms with part-time jobs they did from home, who'd blown out their hair and worn lip gloss to come stand on her cramped roof deck for two hours and make small talk with the same group of families they saw at every gathering like this. Nice, friendly dads who hadn't used work as an excuse not to come to a party at four o'clock on a Sunday afternoon even though they probably had demanding perfectionist bosses with impossible expectations just like Merit did, bosses who would expect them to show up on Monday morning with all their tasks completed, just like Merit's would, even though she knew Merit was hosting a child's birthday party that weekend and that her parents were in from out of town.

There were downsides to working for a badass, Merit had learned. Jane lowered her standards for no one, and she never let up. It helped that they'd gotten over the hump of a new work relationship by the end of Merit's second day, facilitated in part by the impromptu champagne and oysters they'd had in Sausalito after Chloe hired them on the spot. But Merit still wasn't entirely sure where she stood with her new boss. She wondered now if the completely unnecessary email she'd gotten from Jane that morning at brunch had been a test. She was glad she'd responded so quickly. She checked her email again now and felt a flicker of disappointment that Jane hadn't written back.

Where was Jane right then? Someplace fabulous, Merit decided, doing whatever stylish Scandinavian women without children did from four to six on Sunday afternoons. Merit wished, suddenly, that she was doing whatever Jane was doing, with Jane, instead of hosting a party she didn't even want to attend. Then again, Jane was probably with her husband. A man who owned restaurants and boats and who would never think corner-store salami was appropriate party meat.

"Babe?" came Cory's voice from the door that led to the deck. "Can you bring up some extra paper towels and a trash bag? One of Leena's twins just threw up."

Merit stared at a crusty lump of hummus on the island and considered running out the front door. "Coming!" she called.

The remainder of the party was a game of group delusion in which ten couples with advanced degrees pretended that Leena's feverish four-year-old had eaten something that didn't agree with her instead of acknowledging that they'd all just been exposed to the stomach flu. Or maybe they were all just drunk, a distinct possibility since Cory was forcing IPAs on everyone like a cosmetics saleslady at the mall. Merit didn't know whether he was being a good host or trying to prove that he was right about needing the extra. By the time the party was over, she didn't care. She thanked him for being so thoughtful, ate a giant hunk of sweaty salami, then loaded the dishwasher by herself.

Jane texted her later that night, after the boys were in bed and Merit was doing the only task she hated more than loading the dishwasher: packing Jude's lunch. She was in the middle of an internal debate about whether it was okay to give her child hummus that had been sitting outside for three hours and likely manhandled by flu-infested kid fingers when the message came through. Late-night texts from a boss would normally have sent her into an instant panic spiral, but this time all Merit felt was relief.

JANE: how was the party?

Merit grabbed a beer from the fridge and hopped up onto the counter to write back.

MERIT: best party ever obvs. how
was ur wknd?

Jane responded with a string of thumbs-up emojis, which might've been sarcastic or sincere. Merit smiled at her screen.

> MERIT: lol. that good, huh?

> JANE: i tried to work on a pitch and fucked up
> the deck. don't hate me but pls fix!!!!

> MERIT: u need tonite?

> JANE: no no tmrw fine. enjoy ur nite. xx

Merit was still smiling as she put down her phone and went back to packing the lunch. She was in such a good mood that she decided to throw out the hummus and make Jude ants on a log instead. So what if she still had a soils report to review and a zoning summary to write before calling it a night? In twelve hours, Sierra would show up, and her parents would leave for the airport, and she'd go to the office, where Jane would be hilarious and demanding and no one would ask her what elementary schools she was looking at for Jude or whether Nash was using a sippy cup yet. It would be hectic and stressful and, gloriously, she would feel exactly like herself.

"SO THE PARTY was a success?" Jane asked. It was Monday afternoon and they were in the conference room sketching plans for a new renovation in Pac Heights. At Merit's old firm, they did everything on computers. Jane insisted on doing all her initial drawings by hand.

This was their new afternoon routine, sitting side by side at the conference table, taking turns with the drafting pencil, Jane in her black-framed readers, chewing on her lip as she moved the graphite over the paper with strong, decisive strokes, Merit beside her watching every move. She would catch herself staring sometimes, taken by the artistry of it, mesmerized by this woman who brought entire houses to life. She'd worked as an architect for seven years before she quit, but Merit had never experienced the process quite like this. Sitting next to Jane, architecture wasn't the client-serving slog she'd once decided it was; it was an intricate, untethered art.

"Define success," Merit replied, watching Jane freehand a Victorian hallway. Her lines were impossibly straight.

"Did people show up? Did they have a good time?"

"Yes, and yes. I think?"

"Everyone except you," Jane said.

Merit smiled. "It was fine. It was a kid's birthday party."

Jane stopped drawing and pulled her glasses off. "Don't lie. You hated it. I'm interested to know why."

"How do you know I hated it? Maybe I had a great time."

"I know because your eyes sparkle when you're talking about something you're happy about, like the second bathroom you're so determined to fit in this house—which, by the way, I still maintain won't work."

"My eyes are brown," Merit pointed out.

"I am aware," Jane said.

"And the bathroom will fit. How do brown eyes sparkle?"

"I don't know. Yours just do. And when I asked about Nash's party, they stayed boringly dim."

"Really? Hm." Merit was touched that Jane remembered her son's name.

"Merit!"

"Sorry! Okay, fine, I didn't have fun. I didn't feel like myself. Or, maybe I did, and that was the problem?"

"Elaborate," Jane said.

"Can I not?"

"No. Out with it."

"My friends are all work-from-home moms," Merit said finally. "And they're great. But being around them yesterday . . . I dunno. I think it made me realize how much I hated being home full-time with my kids? Which I could never say to anyone other than you."

"Yeah, no judgment from this barren bitch."

"*So* not what I meant," Merit said, cheeks flushing.

"You're very adorable when you blush."

Merit covered her cheeks with her hands. "You're relentless."

Jane smiled. "But wouldn't you rather be here, in this windowless conference room, being tormented by a childless monster, than home with your kids?"

Merit smiled back. "Give me that drafting pencil, you barren bitch."

Jane handed it to her.

"I get it, you know," she said as Merit started to sketch. "It's not the same, obviously, but I have an out-of-body experience every time I go back to Denmark. It's not unpleasant exactly. But more the realization that you're not the person you thought you were. And maybe never were."

Merit stopped drawing and looked at her. "Yes. Exactly."

"And then you ask yourself, so who the fuck am I? And you start to spiral a little, because maybe the person you are is not the one you set out to be. So then you have to decide if you even *like* this person you've become." Jane shuddered. "It's all very taxing."

"It is!"

"But here's where I've landed on all of it," Jane said. "Since I'm centuries older than you, allow me to impress you with my wisdom and insight."

"Please do."

"It's not us, it's them."

"And who's the them?"

"The lemmings who decided that women are supposed to be one thing or another instead of everything at the same time."

"So . . . men."

"Not just men," Jane corrected. "Women, too. In fact, women may be the worst. The only people who understand us are gay men."

Merit bit back a smile. "I guess we shouldn't fuck up this house, then." The owners were an early-thirties gay couple both she and Jane adored.

"Exactly." Jane put her readers back on and looked down at their half-drawn plans. "What next?"

"The upstairs bathroom."

"You and this bathroom! I'm telling you, there isn't space for it. Not within the existing footprint, anyway. And not if we want to keep the fire-place in the master, which we absolutely do. The master will be too small if you put it where you've just drawn it. And the bathroom will be too big."

"Not if we create a king-size-bed nook next to the fireplace in the mas-ter," Merit said, pointing. "Where the bay window is."

Jane was already shaking her head. "No. There won't be any light in the bathroom. That outside wall isn't exterior. There's a hallway on the other side."

"Which is why," Merit went on—she was sure her eyes were lit up now—"we put a transom window above the bed." She drew it as she was talking. It was unconventional, but she knew in her gut it would work. "There will be plenty of light coming through it because the bay window is right there, and plus it's west-facing, so the bathroom won't feel dark, even late in the day."

"I'm not sold," Jane said plainly.

"Okay," Merit said. She wasn't ready to give up. "Why?" She was aware that this was the first time she'd ever challenged Jane. She had a fleeting second thought about having just called her boss a barren bitch, but then decided it improved her position. Giving no fucks was the only way she'd win this.

And she wanted to win.

"Other than the fact that it reeks of trendiness?" Jane asked.

"Um, Thomas Jefferson had an alcove bed at Monticello."

"He had an alcove bed*room*," Jane corrected. "Not a bed built into a corner."

"And what's wrong with a bed built into a corner?" Merit was so enjoying this.

"It's a master bedroom," Jane said with only a touch of impatience. "The bed is typically the center point of the design, and you've put it in an alcove, which means the clients won't get to buy their pretentious turn-of-the-century frame."

"Yes, but these particular clients said specifically that they wanted the space to be 'inventive' and 'low-key,'" Merit reminded her. "And if we put their bed in a nook, they can do a his-and-his reading area in front of the fireplace, which I think they'll dig."

She saw Jane wavering.

"And if we put it in the plans and they hate it?" she asked.

"You can blame it on me."

"Except they didn't hire you. They hired me."

"Okay," Merit said, and shrugged. "So no second bathroom, then." She bit her lip and waited.

"Don't be barbaric." Jane took the pencil from her hand. "A bed nook it is."

four

I N M A R C H , J A N E proposed a double date. "Let's go to Edward's restaurant," she said, tearing open a package of turkey jerky, one of the many bizarre snack options in their office kitchen and Jane's latest breakfast of choice. "You, me, and our handsome lesser halves."

Merit was reheating her latte for the third time. She hadn't slept well the previous night. She was managing six of their projects, and all of them were behind schedule. None of the delays were her fault, but still.

It'd been a tough couple of months. Lars and Erik had been on the cover of *Veranda* in January, and now everyone in the greater Bay Area wanted them to renovate their very expensive and structurally problematic one-hundred-year-old homes, not realizing that neither Lars nor Erik had any meaningful architectural skills, or that their sole contribution to the design process would be to fire off incomprehensible emails containing words like "ideate" and "align" while Jane and Merit did all the work. Not that Merit minded this arrangement in theory, but there were times when she wanted to tell her exacting and inflexible superiors to please care about their projects twenty percent less. It wasn't that Merit didn't appreciate the high standards, it was more that she was becoming less and less certain of her ability to meet them, and disappointing Jane gave her stress dreams at night.

"So . . . dinner?" Jane pressed.

"That sounds fun," Merit said. But, really, it didn't.

Jane hopped up onto the counter. "Let me know what night works, yeah?"

Merit nodded. "Sure. I'll check with Cory."

"You okay, little bird?"

Merit looked at her. "You have a nickname for me now?" Jane had a nickname for everyone. None of them were nice.

"I was trying it on for size."

"You think I'm birdlike?"

"A bit?"

"So mean!"

"It's not a commentary on your physique," Jane promised. "It's that sometimes you remind me of a tiny bird trapped in a small space, crashing into things. *Adorably*," she added with emphasis.

"This is a hostile work environment."

"Cheer up, little bird. Have some jerky." Jane held out the bag. Merit shook her head. The microwave dinged and Merit took her latte out. She'd overheated it, making the milk lumpy on top.

"I have to get back to work," Merit told Jane. "My boss is a bitch."

Merit sent Cory a text when she got back to her office.

MERIT: jane invited us to dinner

As she waited for his reply, Merit tried to picture the four of them sitting at a table, making conversation, eating tapas, drinking wine. Why was it so hard to imagine? Part of it was that she wasn't sure how she was supposed to act at a dinner like that. The other part, she suspected, had to do with what Jane would think of Cory.

CORY: sounds fun

MERIT: is it weird?

CORY: why weird?

MERIT: bc she's my boss?

This wasn't exactly it, but it was as close as she could get. She couldn't tell Cory that Jane had opinions about everyone and would instantly form one of him, or that she was worried Jane would decide her husband was boring or unattractive, even though Merit knew Cory was neither of these things.

But also: Why did it matter to her what Jane thought of Cory?

CORY: not weird

Merit realized she didn't care at all what Cory might think of Jane.

She put her phone away and pulled up the construction plans for a creepy Gothic Revival in Telegraph Hill the owners had decided to gut. There were structural issues she had to solve, and the electrical, though not her problem, was a mess. She gulped her lumpy latte and resolved to finish her next pass by lunch.

She was so engrossed in the work that she didn't hear Lars come through her door until he dropped into the chair across from her desk.

"So," he said. Merit was so startled she knocked over her empty cup.

"Hi," she said, when she wanted to say, *What the fuck!*

She could count on one hand the number of in-person interactions she'd had with Lars Jager in the six months she'd worked at his firm. Two staff meetings, the Christmas party, and a semi-awkward exchange in the hallway on a Wednesday afternoon that involved his complimenting her shoes. It'd been clear, in each of these encounters, that he had a very short attention span. And that he liked being in charge.

"How's it going?" Lars asked, putting his feet up on her desk. Merit wasn't sure if he meant her employment in general or the project she had up on her screen.

"Great," she said, because it seemed like a safe answer to both.

"So enthusiastic," Lars said. Merit had the sense that he was making fun of her. She told herself not to care.

"How's Jane?" he asked when she didn't say anything.

"Uh, fine, I guess? I think she's in her office."

"I meant what's it like to work for her," Lars said.

"It's great."

Lars laughed lightly. "Now I know you're lying."

"Not at all," Merit said. "Jane's . . ." *amazing / incredible / infuriating / hilarious / so fucking intense.* There was so much she could say, but she didn't want to say any of it, not to Lars. Even the most generic adjective would give too much away.

"Great?" Lars offered.

"Exactly."

"You forget I've known her longer than you have."

Merit realized she had no idea how long Lars and Jane had known each other, a fact she'd never considered before but which bothered her tremendously now.

"Sounds like I should be asking you for the intel, then," she said.

Lars seemed to be studying her. "What made you want this job?"

The state of my marriage. My credit card bills. My diminishing sense of self.

"That feels like a trick question," Merit said.

Lars grinned. He had very small teeth. "You're funny. How old are you?"

"Um."

"What, am I not allowed to ask that?"

"Pretty sure you're not," Merit replied. This conversation was stressing her out. She wanted to get back to work. *His* work, which she was being paid slightly under market to do.

"I'm guessing you're at least thirty-five," Lars said before she could say anything else. "Jane likes minions of a certain age. Which is why you're doing a job someone five years younger could do."

Merit felt herself go still.

Don't do it, was the thought that shot through her brain as Lars waited for her to respond. *Don't ask what he means.*

She made herself smile. "Lucky me."

Lars dropped his feet and stood up. "This was fun."

Merit couldn't resist. "Was it?"

This made Lars laugh, which felt like a victory Merit didn't want.

"You should do something with this space," he said then, glancing around her tiny office. "It's really fucking bleak." His eyes landed on the one personal item she had, a framed photograph of her with Cory and the boys. "Cute family, though," he said.

It felt like too much work to smile. "Thanks."

"You should bring your kids in sometime."

"I'll do that," she said. There was literally no chance in hell she would ever do that.

"Cool," he said, and walked out.

"HE WAS CLEARLY fishing," Merit told Cory that night. They were at a restaurant in their neighborhood, without the kids. They'd been doing that more, meeting for dinner after work, now that they had a nanny they could afford to pay to stay late. She'd overheard Cory tell his sister on the phone the day before that their marriage was "better than it'd been in years," which was comforting if Merit thought about it a little, and incredibly annoying if she let herself think about it a lot. It seemed pathetically unnuanced to be a woman whose marriage problems boiled down to the fact that her husband liked her better in heels.

"Fishing for what?" Cory asked.

"Details. About Jane."

"Okay. So?"

"So it's bizarre."

"Why?"

"You don't think it's weird that my boss's boss snuck into my office to grill me about my boss?" She hadn't told him about the minion comment, or the thing about her age.

"It doesn't sound like he was *grilling* you," Cory said. "You said he asked what Jane was like to work for. And now he *snuck* into your office? This story is getting more exciting by the minute."

"Don't be a dick."

Cory blinked. "Wow."

Merit reached for her wine. Admittedly, the dick comment was a bit much, but she didn't feel like apologizing for it.

She set her glass down and rearranged the napkin in her lap.

"I'm sorry I called you a dick," she said finally. "But I felt like you were being mean."

"Mean?"

"I don't need you to challenge every detail every time I tell a story."

"I'm not *challenging* you, Mer."

"This is what I'm talking about! You're like the fucking word police."

She saw him bristle at the f-word. *When did he become such a prude?*

She sighed. "Let's not make a thing out of this. All I was saying was Lars came into my office to ask me about Jane, and it felt weird."

"Got it," Cory said.

"How was your day?"

"My day was fine."

"Cory."

"Merit."

"I don't want this to derail our entire evening."

"Then don't let it," Cory said. "My day was fine. I had a series of increasingly frustrating phone calls, capped off by a series of even more frustrating emails about a product we were supposed to be beta testing six months ago that still isn't ready."

"I'm sorry," Merit said. She wanted to rewind to the beginning of this dinner, before they had the same fight they'd been having for a dozen years. When they were in grad school, it took the form of Cory teasing her about her tendency to embellish the details in the stories she told. Now it was this constant fact-checking; his treating her like an unreliable narrator who couldn't be trusted to tell the truth. Maybe she *was* an unreliable narrator. Maybe she *couldn't* be trusted to tell the truth.

"It is what it is," Cory said, and picked up his beer.

They were quiet for a few minutes, drinking their drinks.

"So the kindergarten lottery is next week," she said finally, to have something to say.

"You still feeling good about it?"

Merit forced herself not to be irritated by the question, not to fire back, *How does one feel good about a random process over which one has absolutely no control?*

"Yep," she said instead. She put on a sanguine smile. "It is what it is."

Cory, unexpectedly, laughed.

The waiter arrived with their food, giving them something nonconfrontational to do for several minutes. Merit's scallops were delicious. She wished she'd had more wine, but now that she was eating, drinking more felt pointless. She had to get up early, anyway. Working for a woman in her fifties who exercised religiously had shamed Merit into buying a month of unlimited classes at a nearby Pilates studio, which she was now forcing herself to use three mornings a week. This was in spite of the fact that whatever endorphin high she achieved from these six A.M. workouts evaporated the moment she came through her front door at seven-twenty to find her sons still in their pajamas demanding breakfast and her husband in noise-canceling headphones sipping coffee on the couch.

"So, this dinner with Jane and her husband," Cory said when the waiter came back for their empty plates. "Did you schedule it yet?"

Merit shook her head. "She asked me to give her some dates."

"How about next week?"

"Sure," Merit said. She didn't understand why Cory was so keen on making the dinner happen, but to make a thing of it would force her to interrogate her own ambivalence. Not that her feelings about it were of any consequence; Jane wasn't going to let it drop.

Minions don't get to call the shots.

"You seem like you're on the fence about doing it," Cory said, studying her. "I would've thought you'd be looking forward to it. You love a group dinner."

"I *am* looking forward to it," Merit lied. She flagged over the waiter and ordered another glass of wine. "But this isn't supper club. It's dinner with my boss."

"A boss you love working for."

"I wouldn't say I *love* it," Merit said testily. The only thing worse than being an over-thirty-five minion was enjoying it. "It's fine."

"Mer. You *hum*."

"I hum."

"Yes."

"Like, metaphorically?"

"How does one *metaphorically* hum?"

It was an interesting question, one that made Merit think of the last orgasm she'd had. Two Wednesdays ago, after a dinner out that had gone much better than this one. She'd enjoyed it, but she wouldn't go as far as to say her body *hummed*. Maybe if she'd let Cory go down on her? He'd tried, like he always did, and she'd pulled him up with two hands, like she always did, until he'd sighed and given up. Was it her fault their sex life had been so lackluster lately? Was she not adventurous enough?

"So you're saying I *literally* hum?" she asked, putting sex out of her brain. She was on her period this week, anyway.

"Yes."

"When?"

"Mostly when you're getting ready in the mornings." Cory smiled. "It reminds me of when you used to stay over at my apartment senior year, when you were taking that art lab you really liked. You hummed so much Dan started wearing earplugs, remember?"

Dan was Cory's roommate at Cornell and the best man at their wedding. He was an anesthesiologist now and still very sensitive to noise. Merit hadn't thought about that art lab in years. It was when she'd first learned how to paint alla prima and became obsessed with layering and light.

"You seem really happy," Cory said.

It was nice, the way he was looking at her now. She twirled a piece of her hair. "Well," she said, shoulders rising and falling quickly. "I guess I am." The happiest she'd been since that art lab, maybe. She thought better of pointing that out.

A happy little minion. She felt her smile fade.

"I wasn't trying to be a dick before," Cory said then, quietly.

"I know," Merit said.

"And as far as your story goes," Cory added, signaling for the check, "you don't know what you don't know."

"Meaning what?"

"Maybe Lars was trying to find out how much you knew."

Merit frowned. "About what?"

Cory looked at her like it was obvious. "Whatever Jane hasn't told you yet."

JANE WANTED TO do the dinner on a Saturday night, because she said Edward would be more relaxed if the restaurant was busy.

"He gets all butt hurt when there are empty tables," she explained to Merit over take-out sushi the next day. They were eating in the conference room, working through lunch.

"Um. I'm pretty sure you can't say 'butt hurt' anymore." Although it struck Merit that "butt hurt" was a fairly apt description of how she'd felt since her conversation with Lars. She still hadn't mentioned it to Jane, and wouldn't, not after what Cory had said at dinner. The idea that she might not have all the information made her want to keep some information to herself.

Jane rolled her eyes. "My brother was the queerest bottom in all of

Denmark. I can say 'butt hurt' all I want. Fred, by the way, was always butt hurt. Figuratively speaking."

"That was your brother's name—Fred?"

"Frederik," replied Jane. "He hated when people called him Fred. Which is why I used it exclusively his entire life. Is there more soy sauce?"

Merit tossed a packet across the table. "Poor guy. His sister was so mean."

"She really was," Jane said. "Although she did buy him his first car." Jane grinned. "Which I gave to him with a vanity plate that said IM-FRED. I would've had it say BUTTHURT but lucky for him, Danish plates only have seven spots."

Merit smiled. "What was the age difference?"

"Seven years," replied Jane. "He died the week after his twenty-ninth birthday. Of complications from AIDS."

Merit felt her smile fall. "Oh, Jane. I'm so sorry."

"Yeah, it was brutal. Particularly since HIV treatment in Denmark is so easy to get, and free. Basically nobody dies of AIDS in Denmark anymore. But Fred was always sort of sickly, ever since we were kids. He always had really shit luck."

"It's just so awful. I don't know what to say."

"You don't have to say anything, little bird. Just tell me Saturday works for our dinner, and I'll make sure we get the table I like. Seven o'clock?"

THE SMALL RESTAURANT was packed when Merit and Cory walked in at four past seven on Saturday night. The timing was intentional, and precise. Jane was always on time, and Merit didn't want to get there first.

She'd spent the entire ride over obsessing about her outfit. She hadn't wanted to ask Jane what she was wearing, and Cory was zero help. She'd decided at the last minute to wear a navy silk romper she'd bought herself at an after Christmas sale, a questionable choice for a dinner with Jane, who would probably show up in jeans.

But Jane had dressed up, too. Merit saw her as soon as they arrived, standing at the end of the bar in a white cashmere sweater, a leather skirt, and over-the-knee suede boots. She looked phenomenal. Merit squeezed Cory's hand and wondered if he thought her fifty-seven-year-old boss was hot.

Edward's restaurant was small but exquisitely appointed, with colorful encaustic tiles on the back wall and a striking gold chandelier in the center of the dining room. It was classy and inviting. It was all Jane.

"The legend in the flesh," Merit heard Cory say from behind her, in a voice that was so jovial he didn't sound like himself.

"What an ass kisser," Jane said over Merit's shoulder as she gave her a quick hug. "You look spectacular," she said in Merit's ear. "And your husband is dreamy; nice work." She stepped past Merit and kissed Cory on both cheeks. It was Jane being Jane—or, at least, the version of herself she brought to client meetings, when she came across as breezy and charming and everyone's friend—but Merit could see on her face that something was up.

"Merit," Edward said, rising from his bar seat to take her hand. He was much taller than Merit was expecting, and his teeth were very white. "I've heard a lot about you."

"Uh-oh," Merit joked. It struck her suddenly that Edward might be older than her dad.

"I think you and I are the ones who ought to be worried," Cory said to Edward, reaching forward to shake his hand. "I suspect our wives do quite a bit of talking about us."

Jane made a sound in her throat. "Oh, Cory, don't flatter yourself. Merit and I have far more interesting things to discuss."

They each had a cocktail at the bar, then Edward led the way to a table in the front. There was a bottle of Malbec already open, a cutting board with bread and olives, a pitcher of sparkling water, and a dish of cut limes. The limes were for Jane's water; the bread, Merit knew, her boss wouldn't touch.

"Have you two been to Argentina?" Edward asked as they sat.

"We have," Merit said. "For our honeymoon, actually."

"So you don't need me to tell you anything about the food, then," Edward replied, pouring the wine.

"I could use the education," Cory said affably. "I don't know much, even after having been."

Merit looked at him. "We took a four-hour food tour."

"We did?"

Jane reached for Merit's glass. "LB, you need a lot of wine. Let them talk about chimichurri and we'll discuss important work stuff." She gave them both heavy pours then touched Edward's shoulder. "But before you get too deep into the virtues of Argentine grilling techniques, could you order us another bottle? People find me funnier when they're drunk."

Cory laughed, louder than Merit thought was necessary. He was probably trying to seem agreeable; he did that sometimes with Merit's friends, an overcorrection sparked by a game of Celebrity several years before during which someone put Cory's name in the bowl and the person who pulled it used the words "standoffish" and "particular" to describe him. He smiled more now in group settings, and apparently he also guffawed on double dates? It was mildly embarrassing, but also endearing. Merit wondered what Jane thought.

Edward did order another bottle of wine, which they finished before the second course arrived. Merit lost count of how much she'd had; Jane kept refilling her glass as they made small talk about nothing either of them cared anything about. Jane nibbled on olives and Sardo. Merit ate six pieces of bread.

Edward and Cory were hitting it off, Merit noticed, half-listening to them as they talked about the restaurant business and the cattle industry and the Internet of Things.

"They're getting along well," she said to Jane at some point.

Jane smiled a little. "Like a house on fire." Her lips were tinged purple with wine. Beside her, Edward was using his cutlery to explain smart farming to Cory. Cory's hand was resting on Merit's knee.

"This is fun," she said, turning her body toward Jane. Cory's hand slipped from her knee.

"It is," Jane said, but she didn't mean it, Merit could tell.

"What?"

Jane pushed her hands through her hair. "Nothing."

"You're not having fun."

"I am!"

"Liar."

"Who's lying?" Cory asked. "And about what?"

"Merit doesn't like the wine," Jane said.

"Yeah, it's awful," Merit said, and took a long sip. At this point, there was no way to avoid the headache she'd have the next day. She slid her glass toward Jane for another pour.

"Edward is very proud of his wine list," Jane said as she refilled their glasses.

"Oh yeah?" Cory looked at Edward. "Are you a big wine guy?"

Merit grimaced at her plate.

"My wife thinks I have expensive taste," Edward said with an easy laugh. "She acts like that's a bad thing!" Merit glanced over at Jane. Her expression did not match his.

"Honey, it's not your taste I question," Jane said. She gave her husband a highly manufactured smile. "It's your decision to sit on a wine inventory that's double your monthly revenue. Then again, what do I know? I've never owned a business."

There was a pointedness in her voice that was hard to miss.

Edward looked at Cory. "She fails to mention that our wine program was written up in the *Chronicle*. Front page of the Food section last fall."

"I don't need to," Jane said mildly. "You always do."

Merit saw Cory shift uncomfortably in his seat.

She turned to Jane. "Remind me, when did the *Chronicle* do that big designer profile on you?"

A look passed between them. Merit wondered if their husbands saw it.

"It's been a few years," Jane said. Merit could tell she was trying not to smile.

"They called her the queen of the Queen Anne," Merit told Cory. "They compared her to Norman Shaw! It was a very complimentary piece." She did not look at Edward.

"So historic properties have always been your thing?" Cory asked. He seemed relieved to be off the topic of Edward's poor business judgment and eager for Merit to stop complimenting Jane.

"Actually, no," Jane replied. "I started out doing high-design affordable housing, which I loved. But then I bought a hundred-year-old house and didn't want to pay anyone else to draw the plans." She smiled in her way. "So I figured before I fucked up an actual historic treasure, I should get some experience in preservation design. Fifteen years later, my house still isn't renovated, but it appears I have a career."

"The house is beautiful," Merit chimed in. "It's an Edwardian in Sausalito."

"No relation," Edward joked.

Jane and Merit looked at each other. Cory laughed.

"How'd you end up working for Lars and Erik?" he asked when no one said anything else.

Jane made a face. "Wow, Merit, your husband really wants to kill my buzz."

"Are they really that bad?" Cory asked. He sounded amused. Merit felt a flash of embarrassment for him that she couldn't quite place.

"My wife has difficulty with men in positions of authority," Edward said.

"Is this true?" Cory asked, his eyes pinging from Edward to Jane.

"Edward really enjoys this narrative, so I would hate to dispel it," Jane said dryly, and picked up her glass.

"She gave Lars his first job," Edward said.

Merit looked at Jane in surprise. "You did?"

"To be fair, it was before he was pretending to be an architect," Jane said. "But yes. I hired him as a conceptual designer on a buzzy reno in San Rafael a few years ago."

"The Robert Dollar Estate?" Merit asked. It was one of Jane's more well-known projects. It'd been at least three years since then.

Jane nodded.

"Why didn't you tell me this before?" Merit asked.

"You never asked, birdie."

"Have you ever thought about starting your own firm?" Cory asked.

Jane looked pointedly at Edward. "It's a good question. I should."

"I'd come with you," Merit said.

Jane smiled at her. "I know you would, LB."

"WHY LB?" CORY asked on the ride home. Merit was slumped down in her seat, trying to ballpark how much wine she'd had. Between the four of them, they'd finished five bottles.

"It's short for 'little bird.'" Her tongue felt thick and dry. "It's what she calls me at work."

"Women are bizarre."

"What's that supposed to mean?"

"The way you guys interact with each other. My male boss would never give me a pet name."

"The man calls you 'chief' almost exclusively."

"That's not a pet name. That's, like, B-school douche jargon."

"It's exactly the same thing."

"It feels different."

"It's not. Is there any water in here?" Her temples were already starting to pound.

"Here." Merit felt Cory reaching across her to the seat back pocket, then a cool plastic bottle on her legs. "Careful, it's open."

"Thanks." She took a long swig. Seriously, how much wine had she had? Cory didn't even seem drunk.

"You feel okay?" Cory asked.

"Yep." She guzzled the rest of the water. She felt some dribbling down her chin, no doubt spotting her silk. The romper needed to be dry-cleaned anyway. Midway through the meal she'd dropped an olive on her lap.

"I thought dinner went well," Cory said. "After that awkward exchange about the wine."

Merit nodded. She didn't want to post-game with Cory. She wanted to post-game with Jane.

"I didn't think the food was all that great, though. Did you?"

Merit couldn't remember a single thing she ate.

"Jane told me the chef is new," she said, to say something. "Maybe he's still working out the kinks."

"She."

"Huh?"

"The chef," Cory said, reaching for the empty bottle in Merit's hands. He would take it with him when they got out and immediately recycle it. Merit had the urge to snatch it back and toss it out the window, just to see what he'd do.

"Edward told me she's a woman, from Buenos Aires. I was a little surprised she didn't come out to the table, weren't you?" Cory looked over at her. "Isn't that what you do when the owner comes in?"

Merit hadn't given a single thought to the chef. She shrugged and then yawned.

"Edward invited us out on his boat when the weather warms up," Cory said then. "He said to bring the kids."

"Fun," Merit said. "I'll talk to Jane about it."

She knew she never would.

AT MIDNIGHT THAT night, Merit woke up with a horrible taste in her mouth and a pulsing headache from the wine. Cory was snoring beside her. She shook him and told him to roll over, then went downstairs for Advil and water.

As she was filling a glass at the kitchen sink, she wondered if it would be weird to text Jane. It wasn't that late, and she knew her boss barely slept. She wanted to talk to her about dinner. She didn't have anything particular to say.

She gulped the water and went over to her phone. She could thank Jane for the meal, at least. Not to would be impolite.

we had a lovely time tonight, she wrote, then deleted it and started over.

thx so much for dinner! next time, our treat! She hit send before she could overanalyze it. Two seconds later, Jane was typing a response.

Merit pictured her doing it. Sitting in bed with her readers on, probably in silk pajamas, most certainly on luxury sheets. She had to remind herself that Jane would be in her condo in the Marina, likely in a bed with her husband, not alone in her Sausalito house where Merit had always thought of her before. Was her bedroom uncluttered and organized, the way her office was? Did Edward snore after he'd been drinking like Cory did?

Jane's text popped up.

JANE: ur welcome lb

Before Merit could decide which emoji was the proper response, Jane was typing again. Merit waited.

JANE: next time lets leave the boys at home?

Merit smiled at her screen.

MERIT: yes lets

five

"I NEED YOUR HELP on a new project," Jane said one Friday at lunch. It was mid-summer, and the sun was out, so they were sitting on the patio at their new favorite seafood place enjoying the unexpected warm weather. Merit wondered if the sun was the source of Jane's good mood. She'd ordered two dozen oysters and a half bottle of Chablis as soon as they'd sat down, which was a bit bacchanalian for a work lunch, even for Jane.

Friday day-drinking was their new thing, implemented a few weeks earlier after a very serious discussion about the impact of Jane's shampoo schedule on their working relationship. After much analysis, they'd decided that the cleaner Jane's hair, the better their designs turned out, which was problematic because she only washed it on weekends. They experimented with a dry shampoo on Wednesdays, but it just made Jane crabby (the spray allegedly itched her scalp). White wine seemed to help, though, so they'd taken to splitting a glass every Friday at lunch. They did really stellar work on Friday afternoons.

"Who are you, stockbrokers in the eighties?" Cory had asked her the week before.

"It's half a glass of wine!"

"During a workday. I work at an overfunded start-up, and we don't even do that."

"Jane's European."

"Whatever you need to tell yourself, babe."

They'd dropped it after that, but it still irritated Merit every time she thought about it. She was a thirty-eight-year-old woman. She didn't need to be interrogated by the propriety police.

Even so, she would not be mentioning that they'd tripled their intake today.

"I need more food," Merit told Jane now. "If you're going to get me drunk in the middle of a workday and force me to do high-quality architectural work afterward, you have to at least feed me properly." She'd skipped breakfast and was already buzzed from the Chablis.

"Fair," Jane said. "But in my defense I didn't think one glass of white wine would put you under the table."

"A glass and a half."

"I will stipulate to your glass and a half if you'll say yes to the perfectly reasonable request I'm about to make."

"Hm. Why do I sense that this doesn't end well for me?"

"You're drunk, who cares." Jane smiled indulgently. "Okay, so, here's the deal. Lars and Erik somehow managed to land a Painted Lady renovation."

"An actual Painted Lady? On Postcard Row?" The brightly colored Victorians on Alamo Square were a San Francisco icon.

Jane nodded. "Seven twenty Steiner. One of the Seven Sisters."

"Wow. That's huge."

"It is." Jane refilled Merit's glass with the rest of the wine. "I want you to draw the plans by yourself."

"Like, as a test?"

"No, weirdo. Because you're a very talented architect, and I know you'll do an excellent job."

"What's the real reason?"

"That is the real reason."

"What's the other reason?"

Jane tried not to smile. "I don't want to cancel my birthday vacation."

"Now it makes sense." Merit picked up her glass. "But, sure. Of course I'll do it."

"Here's the thing, though," Jane said, so nonchalantly it was almost comical. "If you're doing the drawings by yourself, then you should be the architect of record."

Merit blinked. She'd done the first round of drawings on plenty of their designs, but she'd never been lead, and she'd certainly never had her name on the plans. "Wait. Really?"

Jane nodded. She seemed pleased by Merit's obvious shock.

"I mean, if you're up for it."

"I *so* am," Merit said emphatically. This was a career-making project, and they both knew it.

"Good," Jane said, and reached for another oyster. "Because the master plans have to be filed with the city September eighth, and I'll be gone that whole week."

Merit took this in. She wouldn't be able to go to Minnesota with Cory and the boys for Labor Day. They'd already bought the tickets. But Cory could go anyway, with the kids. With a surge of delight Merit realized she didn't actually *want* to spend four days with Cory's sister and her two kids in his dad's cramped three-bedroom house in Saint Paul. And now she didn't have to! She took a triumphant swig of her wine.

"What?" Jane asked.

"Nothing. I'm excited. Do Lars and Erik know?"

"Yep. We're meeting with them this afternoon to discuss."

Merit set her glass down in horror. "I'm half drunk!"

"Five minutes ago you claimed to be all-the-way drunk," Jane pointed out. "And, anyway, it's irrelevant because we already decided we're getting you more food. Why aren't you eating your oysters?"

"You know how I feel about mollusks," Merit said, being salty on purpose. She was annoyed about the wine.

"It was supposed to be celebratory," Jane said. "But now I realize that maybe I should've saved the alcohol until after our very important meeting with our CEOs." She sounded legitimately apologetic, which freaked Merit out even more.

Merit buried her face in her hands.

"You'll be fine," Jane promised. "It's not like the client will be there. It'll just be the four of us. Completely low-key."

WHEN THEY WALKED into the conference room two hours later, it was the opposite of low-key. Seated around the table were the very stylish lesbian couple that owned the house, their interior designer, the general contractor, his project manager, a structural engineer, and two preservation consultants. Merit shot Jane a look.

"They didn't tell me, I swear," Jane whispered.

Lars and Erik were, predictably, ten minutes late.

Lars ran the meeting. Erik sat at the opposite end and smiled sanguinely at no one in particular while pointedly avoiding eye contact with Lars. Merit wondered, not for the first time, what was up between the two men. They'd recently started bickering at staff meetings in a way that made her very uncomfortable but seemed to thrill Jane to no end. But whatever was going on between their CEOs personally, it didn't seem to be affecting the firm. They were busier than ever. And now they'd landed a Painted Lady. That was no small feat.

It took all of five minutes for Merit to understand how they'd pulled it off.

Lars was sleeping with one of the owners.

He was his regular *is-he-charming-or-is-he-a-condescending-asshole* self, but it was obvious from the way one of the women kept looking at him that they'd had sex. Merit was so focused on trying to figure out how the two of them ended up in bed together that she almost missed the moment everyone at that meeting would come back to again and again.

"We want to get rid of the fireplace in the front room," the woman Lars wasn't sleeping with said.

One of the preservationists audibly gasped.

"You can't," he said vehemently. "The mantel is hand-carved, the tiles are hand-painted and hand-glazed, and the Inglenook design is classic Queen Anne. It'd be a tragedy to destroy it."

The woman pulled a face. "The 'tragedy' is my spending three million dollars on a house with a dining room that won't seat twelve."

"Merit can look at opening up the entryway," Jane offered. "But they're right. The fireplace has to stay."

"Who's Merit?" the woman asked.

"Your architect," said Jane.

Merit was already looking at the as-builts on her screen. "I think we can probably widen the entryway to give you more room," she said, zooming in. "But maybe instead we re-envision the dining room as the master bedroom, keep the fireplace, and open up the wall between the kitchen and the living room to give you a really epic entertaining space?" She looked up.

"That's interesting," the woman said, glancing at her wife, who was preoccupied with staring at Lars.

Lars, meanwhile, was looking at Merit.

"It's smart," he said, in that particular tone men use when they're pleasantly surprised by the competence of a person who isn't a man.

The preservationists bobbed their heads enthusiastically.

Merit glanced over at Jane, feeling weird about the fact that she'd made such a bold suggestion without running it past her and annoyed with herself for feeling like she needed to. But Jane's eyes were on her phone.

Merit's phone buzzed on the table.

JANE: dont let them think u need my approval lb

"We have a plan, then," Merit announced, confidence clicking in. "Let's talk closets now, because I'm sensing one walk-in won't be enough for you two." She smiled conspiratorially at the owners, who laughed.

Lars pulled Merit aside when the meeting was over.

"Nice work," he said, giving her a double thumbs-up. His pupils were huge. Merit wondered if he was on something. "You killed it. She's trained you well."

Instinctively, they both looked over at Jane. She was on the other side of the conference room talking to Rob, the general contractor, who was perfectly nice but looked like he belonged in construction-themed soft porn. They'd seen a lot of Rob lately, and his shirts seemed to get tighter with every meeting. He was doing the Nob Hill renovation, and they'd recently hired him on Chloe's Sausalito project, which was six months behind schedule because of a probate issue that had just gotten resolved the previous week. Jane insisted that he was the best in the city, but Merit had difficulty taking him seriously. (Did his muscles need to be that big? Also, it was July in San Francisco. Why was he so tan?)

Merit watched as Jane touched Rob's robust arm. "She's such a tease," Lars said with a gravelly laugh, and then he walked off.

The owners cornered Merit on their way out. She was distracted by Lars's comment about Jane and desperately had to pee.

"We were dreading this meeting," the one who wasn't sleeping with Lars said. "We thought it was going to be a bunch of old white dudes telling us what we couldn't do." She rolled her eyes dramatically. "But if we can pull off the things you suggested and not ruin their precious relic, then we're totally on board. I'm Regina, by the way. And this is Allie, my wife."

Merit wanted to like these women but realized at this moment that she unequivocally did not. She wasn't some ardent preservationist, but the house they were talking about was an actual historical treasure and one of the most iconic homes in the city. What size ego did it take to feel entitled to destroy it?

"I think you'll be happy with it," Merit said. She suspected these two were very rarely happy with anything.

"How long have you worked for Lars?" Allie asked. Merit looked at her and realized she thought Merit was a threat. It was gratifying, but felt anti-feminist to enjoy it.

"It'll be a year in September," Merit replied. "Though technically I work for Jane." She shifted her weight and started doing Kegels to avoid peeing in her pants.

"She's gorgeous," Regina said. "Is she gay?"

Merit laughed out loud, peed herself a little, then immediately brought her hand to her mouth. "Sorry," she said quickly, horrified at herself. "I don't know why I laughed. No, she's not gay. She's married. To a man."

The women both smiled. "So were we," Regina said.

"THEY ASKED ME if you were gay," Merit told Jane later, as they were leaving the office that night. The sun had just set, streaking the summer sky in magenta and tangerine. Wistfully, Merit thought of her drawer of oil paints in the laundry room. Would she ever paint again? Did she care?

"How flattering," Jane said. "What'd you tell them?"

"That you aren't, obviously."

"Obviously. Does Regina realize her hot young wife isn't, either?"

"I think she's sleeping with Lars," Merit said.

"She is one-hundred-percent sleeping with Lars," Jane replied. "Everyone in that room other than her sugar mama knew it. Which, regrettably, doesn't bode well for this project."

"Did *you* ever have a thing with Lars?" Merit asked casually.

"I hope you're joking." Merit wanted to read her face but Jane was looking away. "Why is my Uber still four minutes away? It's been four minutes away for four minutes."

"It's trying to drive you insane."

"It's working." She made a face at her phone.

"He called me your minion," Merit blurted out. Jane looked up.

"What?"

"A few months after I started. He said you liked minions of a certain age."

"What the fuck does that mean?"

"Great question."

"What an asshole. I hope you told him to go fuck himself."

"Yeah, that's exactly what I did. I told the CEO of our company to go fuck himself."

"Well, you should have," replied Jane. "I would've protected you. He can't talk to my people like that."

"You mean, your minions?"

"Exactly." Jane frowned at the blue sedan idling at the curb. "Is that my Uber?"

Merit reached for Jane's phone and checked the license plate.

"Yes," she said, and handed the phone back. "Truly, how did you function before me?"

Jane started toward the car then stopped and turned back. "Just so we're clear, you're not my minion. You never were. Lars was just being a dick."

Merit smiled a little. "Noted."

Jane blew Merit a kiss and got into the car.

"Is this a good time to ask for a raise?" Merit called after her.

"Don't push your luck," Jane called back, and pulled the car door shut.

THE NEXT FIVE weeks were brutal. The actual architectural work wasn't so bad; the wall between the kitchen and the master wasn't load-bearing, and the plumbing upstairs would be easy to re-pipe. But the rest of her job, which consisted of managing the contractor and the engineers and the preservationists and the god-awful twenty-four-year-old interior designer—who felt compelled to chime in on every structural decision with an incoherent reply-all email even though no one was ever asking for her opinion—made Merit want to pluck her hair out strand by strand. This wasn't meaningful design work; it was overseeing a fucking kindergarten playdate. Though to be fair this was pure conjecture since Merit had neither the time nor the inclination to oversee an actual kindergarten play-date, despite the fact that Jude had been invited to no less than thirteen of them in the two months leading up to his first day of elementary school.

Merit told herself it wasn't a big deal that he hadn't been to any because he would soon get off the waiting list for their first-choice kindergarten, and there was no point in getting to know kids he'd never see again. In reality, she had no confidence whatsoever that he'd get off the waiting list but was in deep denial about it, because if he didn't, then someone was going to have to figure out the logistics of getting a five-year-old to his assigned school in the Outer Richmond by eight-twenty every morning. If their pre-school experience was any indication, that someone wasn't going to be his dad.

Jane, meanwhile, was staying pointedly removed from the whole pro-cess. She didn't want to be copied on emails. She didn't want to weigh in. Which Merit understood, and on some level appreciated, but it was really quite annoying to ask your boss for advice and instead be given some infu-riating quip about the necessity of "spreading your little bird wings to fly."

It wasn't even that she needed Jane's input. She just wanted to feel as if there was one area of her life where she wasn't completely on her own, and it had become increasingly apparent that it wasn't going to be at home. She'd hoped that someone—her husband? the nanny she was paying eight hundred dollars a week?—might step in to pick up the slack when she started working sixteen-hour days. But the groceries remained un-shopped for and the laundry stayed unwashed and Merit didn't have the bandwidth (had she really become a person who used the word "bandwidth"?) to look for extra help. If she'd had the bandwidth to consider it, she would've found the whole thing deeply demoralizing. Instead, she'd developed a patch of hives on her chest that wouldn't go away, and started eating red licorice for lunch.

"You look tired," Jane said the day before she left for her vacation. She and Edward were going trekking in Cambodia for ten days for Jane's birth-day. Jane seemed genuinely excited about it, which Merit found baffling. She couldn't imagine Jane roughing it in a tent.

"You need to take care of yourself," Jane added when Merit didn't respond.

"Awesome," Merit replied sourly. "I'll get right on that."

Jane frowned. "Hey. Are you okay?"

Merit sighed. "I'm fine."

"I feel bad that I'm leaving you."

"No, you don't."

"Only because I know you're doing a kick-ass job. And Lars agrees. He brought it up yesterday, unprovoked."

Merit looked away. She didn't want a pep talk about her competence. She wanted someone to understand that it wasn't about competence; it was about being trapped in the double bind of being a working mom. But who could she call to commiserate? Her college friends were either childless lesbians or so rich they had teams of nannies, and the women she hung out with now all worked from home.

Any of them would've been better than Cory.

"The boys miss you," he said when she climbed into bed that night.

"Yeah, well. I miss them, too." She was dreading their upcoming trip to Minnesota. The best part of her days lately had been kissing their sleeping foreheads every night after work. She hadn't been home early enough to put them to bed in weeks.

"It wasn't a criticism," Cory said. "It was supposed to be a compliment."

"Telling me that I'm an absent mother is a *compliment*?" She hated how bitchy she sounded. She wasn't even mad at him. The only person she was mad at was the pain-in-the-ass interior designer who kept wanting to talk about light fixtures for 720 Steiner when they hadn't even submitted the construction plans yet.

"You're not absent," Cory said. "You're just busy at work."

Merit felt tears spring to her eyes. She didn't know why.

"The pendulum will swing the other direction," Cory added, going back to his laptop. "Work will slow down and you'll have more time with the boys."

The tears evaporated. She sat up in bed.

"Why isn't it a pendulum for you?"

"It is," Cory said, not looking up from his screen. "Work gets busy, and then it calms down. Ebb and flow."

"That's not a pendulum."

"It gets busy, and then it recedes." He did a pendulum motion with his hand. "How is that not a pendulum?"

"Because it isn't. It's a wave!" Was she shouting? Her throat was hot. "You're describing a wave," she said as calmly as she could. "A pendulum doesn't recede. It swings between two extremes."

Cory looked at her. "I don't understand the point you're trying to make."

"I'm not *trying* to make a point," Merit snapped. "I'm *making* one. I'm pointing out that you only have one extreme. I have two. There is no ebb for me. It's all flow. Except it's not flow, it's a total fucking avalanche, and it never lets up."

Cory bristled at the f-word. Again.

"I'm sorry if my use of the word 'fuck' bothers you, Cory," she said evenly. "You know what bothers me? That we've been out of paper towels for three days and it hasn't occurred to you to go pick some up."

Cory closed his laptop, his passive-aggressive way of communicating that this conversation had interrupted his never-ebbing flow. A lightning bolt of rage zipped through her.

"Mer. You *wanted* to be a working mom." His voice was pointedly, laughably, infuriatingly calm.

Merit wanted to hurl his laptop across the room and scream *FUCK YOU!!!* at the top of her lungs. Instead, she got up and went into the bathroom and slammed the door. It rattled in the frame.

She sat on the edge of the tub, elbows digging into her knees. She waited for the static in her head to settle, for a single thought to push through.

She hated that she'd been so dramatic. Storming out, slamming the door. This was the kind of shit she used to pull in her twenties, before kids, when Cory's unassailable calm sometimes felt like a pillow over her face she couldn't remove.

She stared at the bath mat. The red polish on her toenails was badly chipped.

I didn't eat dinner, was the thought that finally surfaced.

All the nights over the past ten years that Cory had come home late from work, all the turkey sandwiches she'd made him, the leftovers she'd heated up without his having to ask. When she'd walked in at nine-thirty, he hadn't even gotten up from the couch.

Tears dripped on her bare feet.

She'd been here before. Rowing upstream, alone in her boat. It was the metaphor she'd used the one and only time she and Cory went to marriage counseling. The therapist had asked her to elaborate. "My arms are tired," was all she'd finally said. The night after that session, while Cory slept beside her, she'd prayed for the first time in years. She'd asked for inner strength.

She wished she felt like praying now. She wished she had the energy to get on her knees and ask God to take the ache in her chest away. But tonight she didn't want a burst of supernatural resilience; she just wanted someone beside her in the boat. She longed, suddenly, for her mother. Her mom sucked on so many levels, but at least she'd care that Merit hadn't eaten, which seemed at this moment like the truest definition of love. When was the last time they'd spoken? It'd been weeks. Maybe a month. She'd never felt farther away.

(Was it too late at night to call Jane?)

There was a quiet tap on the door.

She stood up wearily and pulled it open.

"I'm sorry," she said immediately. "I overreacted."

It wasn't everything she was feeling as she looked at him, but at the same time it felt honest and uncomplicated, and in the moment that seemed like enough. Also, she was very tired. She didn't want to talk about emotional labor or her never-ending second shift. She wanted to go to sleep.

"I know I don't get it," Cory said. "But I appreciate all that you do."

It wasn't the perfect thing to say. It wasn't even an original thought. In fact, it struck Merit that it was probably, verbatim, what every working father said to his working wife to smooth things over when it became clear that she was at the end of her rope. But it was kind, and it sounded sincere, and Cory looked very handsome in his reading glasses and the penguin pajama pants she'd given him for Christmas.

"Thank you," she said, standing on her tiptoes to peck his cheek.

"We good?" Cory asked as they climbed back into bed.

Merit nodded with her eyes closed. "We're good."

She fell asleep wondering what this meant.

JANE HAD BEEN in Cambodia for twenty-four hours when their Painted Lady went careening off a cliff.

It was the Thursday before Labor Day, five days before the master plans were supposed to be submitted to the planning commission. Merit had emailed the final package to Regina and Allie at four that afternoon for their final approval. They'd obviously forwarded it to their insufferable interior designer because thirty-four minutes after Merit pressed send—just as she was walking out of her office to meet Cory and the boys for pizza before they left for Saint Paul the next morning—her cell rang and it was Chanel. Because, of course, her name was Chanel.

"I'm concerned about the front window," she said with excessive vocal fry. "The angle makes me nervous."

"The angle," Merit repeated. "Of the window."

"Cars turning left onto Steiner," replied Chanel. "The headlights will shine into their bedroom."

"So hang some drapes," Merit said. She wasn't using her most diplomatic tone.

"Reg and Al want natural light in their bedroom," Chanel said.

I want a lot of things, Merit thought. She waited for Chanel to get to the point.

"We need to go over there tonight and take a look after dark. Can you be there at nine?"

"Okay," Merit said, and swallowed a sigh. At least she could put the boys to bed first.

After three slices of pizza, two glasses of wine, four bedtime stories, and a maddening interaction with an iPad that refused to download the movie Jude wanted for the flight, Merit took an Uber to 720 Steiner. The other women were gathered in the front room. Regina was standing in front of the window with her eyes closed, waiting for a car to pass.

"See what I mean?" Chanel pressed. "It couldn't be in a more worse place."

Merit didn't react. This was a pointless exercise. They couldn't move the window. The Historic Preservation Commission would never allow it. Also, "more worse" wasn't a phrase.

Merit waited. Regina was still standing there with her eyes closed. She seemed to be pretending to sleep. Allie was on her phone. Merit wondered if she was sexting Lars.

"Why don't you just turn the bed?" Merit suggested. "Face it away from the street."

Chanel looked at her like she was an idiot. "Um, hello? Feng shui?"

Merit swallowed. Parenting a five-year-old had equipped her for this. The key was not to react.

A car made a left turn onto Steiner. Merit watched its headlights slide across Regina's face.

"I can't sleep in here," Regina said abruptly, and opened her eyes. "It's not even the lights. There's too much street noise." She looked at Merit. "Let's go back to the original plan. We'll tear out the fireplace and make this the dining room and keep the master on the back where it is now."

Merit stared at her. "The plans are due on Tuesday. It's Thursday night."

"Yeah, but this can't be that big of a thing, right?" Regina looked at Chanel as though Chanel were an authority on architectural design.

"It's a huge thing," Merit said, trying to channel Jane's icy resolve. She had to shut this down, fast. "We've spent over a month perfecting these designs. We can't start over three days before they have to be filed with the city. Not to mention the fact that, as we've discussed many times, that fireplace is a historic treasure."

"So move it, then," Chanel said. "Put it in the master on the back of the house."

Merit tried to keep her breathing even. "It's a fireplace. You can't move it. It's connected to a chimney that goes all the way up."

"Then we're taking it out," Regina declared. "I didn't want it to begin with."

Merit went outside to call Lars. He picked up on the first ring.

"They're going back on everything," she said in a low voice. "They're saying they want to get rid of the fireplace."

Lars didn't hesitate. "Then do it. It's their house."

"The *fireplace*, Lars. The mantel. It's a work of art. The craftsmanship alone is—"

Lars interrupted again. "I get it, it's a shame. But it's their call. How quickly can you revise the plans?"

She hadn't considered that he wouldn't back her up. But apparently, a one-of-a-kind historically significant fireplace wasn't worth rocking the boat with his girlfriend's rich wife.

"We agreed it would stay," Merit said pointlessly.

"Merit." Lars sounded annoyed. "How long will it take?"

"I don't know. Two days, maybe."

"We don't have two days," Lars said. "If we're going to submit the plans on Tuesday, then we need revised drawings by end of business tomorrow."

"Shouldn't we run this by Jane?" Merit asked, knowing it was impossible. Jane was deep in a rice paddy somewhere. All of a sudden Merit hated her immensely for going away.

"Hey, Merit? You're the architect of record on this project. Can you do the work or not?"

"Yep," Merit said flatly. She despised him. "I'll get started on the revisions."

"Great," Lars said, and he hung up.

"YOU DID WHAT?"

Jane's eyes were the coldest Merit had ever seen them. Merit felt stupid and small.

Jane had sauntered into Merit's office a week after Labor Day looking tan and pretty and just a little bit smug, the vibe of a person who'd had a really satisfying vacation and now wanted to brag about it. Merit could tell immediately that she didn't know what had gone down with 720 Steiner. Of course Lars hadn't told her. Maybe Merit didn't have to, either.

Merit debated the possibility of never telling her for approximately four seconds before interrupting Jane's description of the rice paddy where Edward had gotten diarrhea two days into their trek with, "We took out the fireplace at the Painted Lady, I had no choice!"

That's when Jane's blue eyes went gray. Instantly, like a cloud passing over the sun.

"You did what?"

"They decided they couldn't sleep in the front room because of lights and street noise," Merit said as calmly as she could. "Allie had already gotten to Lars. I had no support." She was trying to sound reasoned and strong. Her armpits were sweating profusely.

"I don't understand." Jane hadn't blinked. Her pupils were tiny black pricks.

Merit hated when Jane did this—feigned confusion to communicate how idiotic she thought you were. Mostly she hated it because there was no good way to respond. Jane didn't actually want you to explain anything, because she already understood everything perfectly. Including why you'd done whatever misguided thing you'd been dumb enough to do.

"I know it's not ideal but—"

"Not ideal?" Jane's eyes flashed.

Merit kept her voice level. "It was what the clients wanted, Jane. And our CEO signed off. What did you expect me to do?"

"Uh, I don't know, your job maybe?"

Merit's throat stung. "I did do my job."

"No. Your job was to protect a historic icon from the idiots who bought it. Instead, you let yourself get completely steamrolled. Did you agree to put a hot tub in the living room, too?"

Merit felt her composure snap. One moment she was the measured, laid-back person she'd been in every workplace situation up until this one. The next moment, she was someone else.

(She would ask herself later if the someone she became in that moment was Jane.)

"You know what? Fuck you, Jane. *Fuck. You.* Not only did you put me in charge and then refuse to fucking engage, you then left the fucking country and were totally unreachable." Her voice was low and wobbled with rage. "I pushed back with the client. Then I pushed back with our boss who is fucking the client. What was I supposed to do? Chain myself to the fucking fireplace?" She had never used the word "fucking" so many times without taking a breath. She had also never in her life actually uttered the words "fuck you" to anyone. And now she'd just done it twice, to her boss.

"You got lazy," Jane said flatly. "You got tired and overwhelmed and that made you lazy."

"Lazy!" Merit stared at her incredulously. "I put everything into that stupid house! I busted my ass for six weeks while you couldn't be bothered to read a single fucking email!" Her voice was raised now. She wondered if there was anyone listening in the hall.

Jane's eyes flashed. "It wasn't my project, Merit. It was *yours*. That's what it means to be in charge of something. It's called accountability. You don't blame Mommy when you fuck up."

"Please leave my office," Merit said as steadily as she could. She hated how much her voice shook.

Jane turned and walked out.

The tears practically shot from Merit's eye sockets, hot and indignant. She swatted at them, hating herself for fucking crying in her office. It was anger that she felt most of all, at herself for not having more of a backbone, at Jane for being such an unmitigated bitch.

She fumbled for her phone and texted Cory.

MERIT: im quitting my job.

She felt better as soon as she'd sent it. She wouldn't quit on the spot—that would be self-sabotaging and stupid, plus it would make Jane think she had all the power. She would find a good job—a better job even—and she'd give notice unemotionally and enjoy the look of utter shock on Jane's face when she did.

Her phone buzzed with Cory's reply. Predictably, a series of question marks. Unpredictably, she didn't engage. Instead, she googled "architecture recruiting firm bay area" and called the first number that came up. She didn't need Cory's permission. She hadn't asked for it the last time she quit. This was her career. She could do what she wanted with it.

The recruiter was nice, and assured her that there were a number of "exciting opportunities" for someone at Merit's level. Merit spent the rest of the morning updating her résumé, then ducked out early for lunch so she wouldn't run into Jane.

Cory had texted her nine times and called twice, but she didn't feel like talking to him yet. He'd ask her what happened, and she'd be forced to admit that she wanted to quit her job because her boss had hurt her feelings. But Jane was more than just her boss, which Cory knew but didn't really understand. How could he, when Merit didn't fully understand it herself. She didn't have words to put around her relationship with the woman she worked for, who was technically old enough to be her mother and unlike anyone she'd ever known. It wasn't entirely normal, she knew that. She couldn't explain why Jane's opinion of her mattered as much as it did, or why she sometimes dreamed about her, or why their fight that morning had felt more like a high school breakup than a professional disagreement at work.

She was finishing the last bite of a limp kale salad when her phone rang.

Jane—cell

She stared at her screen for several seconds before finally taking the call.

"Where are you?" Jane demanded before Merit could even say hello.

"Lunch," Merit said.

"I have two speeches," Jane said. "One's an apology, the other is supposed to make you feel like shit. Which one do you want?"

"The apology," Merit said.

"Then tell me where you are. It requires hand gestures I can only do in person."

"This isn't funny," Merit said quietly.

"It's a little bit funny," Jane replied. "We fight like a bunch of girls."

"Disagree. You acted like a dick. That was distinctly male."

"Do you forgive me?"

"No."

"C'mon, LB. You can't stay mad at me forever."

"You haven't apologized yet," Merit pointed out, though she realized it no longer mattered. She'd forgiven her already.

"Such attention to detail," Jane said. "But I was actually right, you know."

"You really excel at apologies."

"I have to be able to get upset with you." Jane's voice was serious now. "I can't be a total pushover just because I like you so much."

"I don't need you to be a pushover. But is 'exacting bitch' my only other option?"

"Maybe?"

"I'm serious, Jane. It really sucks to be second-guessed." How many times had she said the same thing to Cory?

"I said I was sorry."

"You didn't, actually."

"Well, I'm sorry. I'm sorry I was awful. I'm sorry I second-guessed you. I'm sorry I left you alone to deal with two raging cunts and Lars. He should've backed you up."

"I'm sorry I didn't fight harder," Merit said.

"I am, too."

"Jane!"

"What? I wouldn't be me without the impossibly high standards I apply to everyone other than myself."

"I wouldn't want you not to be you," Merit said, tossing her empty salad bowl into the trash. She needed to get back to the office. She had work to do.

"I wouldn't want you not to be you, either, little bird." The sincerity in her voice was hard to miss.

"Sometimes it's hard to separate myself from you," Merit heard herself say. "I mean professionally," she added quickly, which wasn't really what she meant.

"I get that," Jane said. "But it hasn't even been a year yet, birdie. You'll find your way."

Merit felt silly now for having said anything. Maybe it wasn't weird that they sat with their chairs touching in the conference room and drank from the same wineglass at lunch. She'd never worked for a woman before. Maybe this was what it was like?

"Okay, but I won't always do things the way you'd do them," she said, more for herself than Jane.

She heard Jane smile. "I'm counting on that."

s i x

MERIT WAS GULPING her third coffee of the morning and staring at an Edwardian loft she didn't know what to do with when Jane came into the conference room with news.

Merit knew it right away: the way she was holding her mouth, the very specific bounce in her step. Jane was practically bursting with it, whatever juicy bit of gossip she was dying to share.

"Tell me," Merit said, putting her mug down, taking the bait. By the afternoon they would be arguing about a floor plan, and by Thursday, they would both be snippy and terse, but right now it was a Monday morning, the time of the week when they liked each other best.

It occurred to Merit in this moment that she could teach a course on the intricacies of Jane. Her moods as evidenced by the subtle tilt of her head; her reactions before she had them; the way her eyes divulged her unspoken opinions on things. Merit was an expert on all of it now, having spent more time with Jane over the course of the past year than she'd ever spent with anyone other than her kids—and even that was arguable because the boys had always taken really long naps. Jane was always in Merit's office, or she was in Jane's, or they were side by side in a conference room arguing over a design. Lars had started calling them "Jarit" in staff meetings. They finished each other's sentences. They had countless inside jokes. Twice they'd screamed at each other in the hallway. Both times they'd made up. Merit imagined they would get sick of each other eventually, which was terrifying, considering Jane was the only person Merit actively liked most days. All she and Cory had been doing lately was bickering endlessly about pointless things, and Jude had entered a cranky and argumentative phase, which Merit was tempted to blame on Cory's DNA but probably had more to do with his new best friend in kindergarten, a little shit named Wesley, whose favorite phrases were "suck it" and "shut up." Nash was still lovely, but he was too young to speak in whole sentences, so he didn't count.

Jane chewed on her bottom lip. This was different. Merit frowned.

"What happened?" Merit asked.

"I think I'm going to book out of my marriage."

Merit blinked. "Wait. What?"

"I'm leaving Edward," Jane said. She sounded so definitive. So clear. So completely not upset.

Merit, meanwhile, felt like someone had just picked up the room and slammed it down.

"What happened?"

Jane hesitated. "Come down to my office?"

"Am I going to need to reheat my coffee for this?"

"Probably," Jane said. "Or maybe we should just take a walk, and I'll buy you another one."

Merit put her mug down and followed Jane out.

"Have I ever told you how Edward and I met?" Jane asked when they were on the sidewalk. It was chilly for November. Merit should've grabbed her jacket. She shook her head.

"We were at a party," Jane said. "A soft launch of a restaurant in North Beach that I helped renovate. It was this beautiful turn-of-the-century Italianate house, and the owner wanted to preserve the outside and gut the inside, which is nearly impossible structurally with a building that old, but we used diagonal crossbeams and—it doesn't matter. The point is, I was really proud of how it turned out."

"Was Edward the owner?"

Jane shook her head. "He was just there for the party, and I guess he saw me moving some wineglasses off this mid-century Venetian credenza I'd found for the entryway—the owners wanted it to have a 'homey' vibe—and anyway, he assumed I was a waitress."

Merit smiled. "Ha. You as a waitress."

"I'd make an excellent waitress!"

"I'm sure you would. But the point is that you were not and—I'm going to take a wild, uninformed guess here—never have been a waitress."

They'd reached the coffee shop on the corner. Merit thought about suggesting that they skip the coffee to avoid dealing with the crowd, but Jane was already pulling open the door.

"Let's get a table," she said. "And get our drinks in proper mugs. With a very fattening pastry to go with."

"Like ladies of leisure," Merit said.

"Exactly."

Merit went for a table while Jane got their drinks. She watched Jane as she stood in line, phone out, flying through emails the way she always did. Was this what was on the other side of a failed marriage: multitasking, espresso and a pastry, and Monday-morning hair?

Merit asked herself why she felt so rattled by the prospect of Jane and Edward getting divorced. What did she even know about their relationship? She'd only met Edward once. And it wasn't as if Jane had ever given her any reason to think they had a great marriage, especially after the awkwardness that night at dinner. Since then, she'd talked about her husband as much as Merit had talked about hers. Rarely, and only when pressed.

Did that mean Merit's marriage was just as bad?

Stop, Merit told herself. *This has nothing to do with you and Cory.*

Today was their wedding anniversary, which was probably part of it. Merit always got a little antsy on their anniversaries, as she tried to come up with something romantic but honest to write in whatever overpriced card she'd picked out. She penned these missives more for herself than for Cory; she was pretty sure her yearly state-of-the-union barely registered with him, even the one from three years ago, when she wrote that she finally understood what her college psych professor meant when he said marriage wasn't for everyone.

She'd been in a weird place that year. Nine months pregnant with Nash and scrambling to finish her gallery pieces in their living room while trying to potty train Jude. By then, the glorious euphoria of getting to make art all day long had passed. It had gotten to the point where she struggled to find enough time on any given day to wash her face, much less paint. And she knew Cory not-so-secretly resented her for it, because he wasn't around enough to understand that it was actually impossible to create something beautiful and transcendent while parenting a toddler without any help.

But they were on the other side of all that now. In a different phase. The boys were older. She had a job she loved. Cory had finally stopped making passive-aggressive comments about their retirement accounts. The card she'd bought him this year read, "Happy Anniversary! Things could be worse!" It was supposed to be funny. It was exactly how she felt.

Jane was making her way to their table with two mugs and a plate stacked with pastries.

"I might have gone a little overboard," she announced, and Merit laughed out loud. She'd literally never seen Jane eat a single bite of bread.

"As long as I'm allowed to have the croissant," Merit said, reaching for it.

"Not just the croissant!" Jane said. "We are eating our weight in refined sugar and carbs this morning. It's the least you can do in my delicate emotional state."

"I'm at your service, boss," Merit said. She tore off a piece of croissant and popped it into her mouth. Nothing about Jane seemed delicate, but she would happily binge on pastries if that's what Jane asked.

"So, that night at the party," Jane said. "The only reason Edward hit on me was because he thought I was a waitress." She broke apart a blueberry scone. "That should've been my first clue."

"Clue that . . . ?"

"He'd eventually fuck a waitress."

Merit's stomach sank. "No."

Jane looked her in the eyes. There was defiance there, and resolve, but also sadness and pain. Merit wanted to hug her, but couldn't, not with the crowd and a table full of pastries between them, which she now understood was the reason Jane had brought her there.

"Who is she?" Merit asked quietly.

"I don't know her name," Jane said. "All I know is that she's a size small in excessively whorish lingerie." She unzipped her wallet and pulled out a crumpled Victoria's Secret receipt. "I found it in his jacket last night. Because my husband is both that much of an idiot and that much of a cliché. I mean, honestly. He could've gotten her something from La Perla, at least."

"Oh gosh. Jane."

"Yep." Jane put the receipt back into her wallet.

"So did he admit it?"

"Haven't asked him yet."

Jane scraped at the scone with her fingernail. Merit noticed dark circles under her eyes that she hadn't before. A fan of fine lines Jane usually did a better job of covering up. "I've actually suspected for a while," she said finally. "It's not like he tries that hard to hide it."

"How long is 'a while'?"

"A couple months."

Merit reached out and touched Jane's wrist. "Why haven't you told me?"

"My husband's flagrant infidelity is not something I generally lead with," Jane said dryly. She turned her hand over so they were palm to palm for a second before she pulled her arm back. "But you're my friend, and I trust you," she said. "That's why I'm telling you now."

"So have you called an attorney?"

Jane shook her head. "Not yet. I want to talk to Edward first. I don't think he'll fight me on anything, as long as I let him keep the boat. The money's all mine, anyway."

Merit nodded. This wasn't a surprise, exactly, but Jane had never said it out loud before this.

"The restaurant's mine, too, technically." Jane pressed her finger into a blueberry, flattening it on her plate. "Fifty-one percent of it, anyway. Not that my equity is worth anything at this point. It's completely underwater." She smiled ruefully. "But hey, I could have my choice of some really stellar pinot."

"Oh," Merit said, when what she meant was *wow*. Cheating on your wife was bad enough; cheating on your wife with a twenty-something waitress at a failing restaurant your wife was bankrolling rose to a whole new level of dick.

Jane saw Merit's expression. "Don't be so serious, little bird. We're ladies of leisure, remember? Drink your latte and tell me some gossip."

Merit tore off more croissant. At some point Jane would check her phone and see the hundreds of new emails in her inbox and they'd have to hurry back to the office to deal with whatever crisis had cropped up. But for now they were here, in this moment, complicated and shitty but somehow kind of lovely, and Merit didn't want to disappoint.

"Rob is in love with you," she announced.

"Rob our contractor?"

"Yes. Every time you're around him, there's this . . . *vibe*."

Jane smiled a little. "That's just Rob being Rob. He flirts with everyone."

"He doesn't flirt with me!"

"Well, to be fair, you can be quite earnest when you're talking about architectural plans."

"I am not earnest!"

"A little bit? And, anyway, you should be glad. Having Rob flirt with you is very stressful."

"Why?"

"Because he's very good at flirting, and for the first few seconds each time you forget that he's actually skeevy and you flirt back, but then you remember and have to be aggressively bitchy so he doesn't get the wrong idea."

"You think he's skeevy?"

"Merit, honey, he's the definition of skeevy." Jane finished the scone and moved on to a giant muffin with a crumble top. "But he's really quite hot."

Merit made a face. "Not my type."

Jane chewed on her lip. There was something she wasn't saying.

"What?" Merit demanded.

Jane hesitated. "I might have kissed him once."

"You kissed Rob!"

"Ssh, LB, you're shrieking. In my defense I was mildly drunk."

"Um. Why were you drunk with Rob!"

Jane sighed. "It's a good question. It wasn't my best idea. But I had my suspicions about Edward, and I was loosely contemplating having an affair of my own."

"With Rob."

"It crossed my mind."

"Wow. Why didn't you tell me?"

"Because I knew you'd talk me out of it."

"Are you still considering it?"

"Not really. Infidelity seems very stressful and complicated, particularly if all you get out of it is sex." She sipped her coffee. "I'm too old for him anyway."

"You mean, too attractive and interesting and intelligent?"

"Yes. That's what I meant."

Merit wanted to ask her more questions but didn't want to pry. She stared at her latte and tried to think of something helpful to say.

"He started taking showers as soon as he got home at night," Jane said after a minute. "And the sex was less consistent. I should've put it together sooner, but, honestly, I was too relieved not to be pawed at every night."

Merit tried to keep her face neutral but failed. "You were having sex every night?"

"Not *every* night," Jane said, but Merit could tell that she was hedging because of the shock on Merit's face. "Why? How often are you doing it with Cory?"

"Uh, it's been a little spotty lately. Maybe once a week?" This was a gross exaggeration. There was no way they'd done it more than six times in the past six months.

"Why spotty?"

"My boss is very demanding and I'm less horny when I'm stressed?"

"Really?"

"Which part of that sentence are you questioning?"

"That your job has had a negative effect on your sex life."

"Okay, fair," Merit allowed. "We had sex even less before."

"You do have two young kids," Jane pointed out. "That has to take a toll."

"It was more my foray into unemployment. Turns out my husband isn't all that attracted to un-showered women in sweatpants covered in paint."

Jane frowned. "He said that?"

"He didn't have to." Merit played with the handle of her mug. "Things weren't great when I stayed home. We barely had sex at all."

"Why have you never told me this?"

"It's not like we're in the habit of discussing our sex lives," Merit reminded her. "You are my boss, remember."

"Yes. We wouldn't want to be unprofessional."

"Office decorum, and all that."

"Exactly." Jane reached for the rest of Merit's croissant. "Maybe I'll get divorced and gain two hundred pounds."

"Maybe I'll join you," Merit said.

Jane looked at her closely. "But you and Cory are happy, right?"

"Sure," Merit said, and shrugged. She meant it sincerely, but it didn't sound very convincing, even to her. She shouldn't have shrugged.

"But?" Jane prodded.

"There's no but," Merit said.

"There's always a but. Is it the spottiness of the sex?"

Merit shook her head. "Like you said, we have two young kids."

"Then what?"

She shrugged again.

"Merit."

"Our conversations are boring," Merit said finally. She'd never articulated this thought before, but there it was. Their conversations were excruciatingly dull. Even their fights were tedious. They'd argued the night before about whether it mattered that Jude wore mismatched socks every day. Merit was bored even now, remembering.

"In content or style?" Jane asked.

"See?" Merit said. "That's an interesting question. Cory would never ask that."

"He doesn't know your conversations are boring," Jane pointed out.

"'Boring' is the wrong word," Merit said. "It's more that we never talk about anything deep. It's either work or the kids. Or recycling. He's always up for talking about that." It was more than this, and Merit knew it. It was the fact that trying to have a meaningful moment with her husband made her feel like she was standing on the far side of a roaring river, straining to be heard, while he gestured at her not to shout.

"Okay, the recycling's a bit weird," Jane conceded. "I'll give you that. But the rest of it's probably normal, right? Phase of life, and all that."

Merit nodded. There was a weird lump in her throat. Had she and Cory ever had a conversation that wasn't about exactly what it seemed?

"But?" Jane prompted.

"But nothing." She shrugged again and hated herself for it.

"Merit."

"Fine. What if our conversations were always like that?" The thing she wanted to add but didn't was: *And what if I never noticed because I didn't have anything to compare it to before I met you?* It was actually quite odd, she realized, this inclination she had to hold her relationship with Cory up beside her relationship with Jane. One was a thirteen-year marriage to the man who had once been her college boyfriend, and the other was a peculiar sort of female friendship with a woman she'd only known for a little over a year and who was still very much her boss. She suspected her impulse to compare them was an important bit of data, but today did not seem like the appropriate moment to interrogate it.

"I'm sure they weren't," Jane assured her. Merit didn't want to be assured. She wanted Jane to acknowledge that thirteen years of surface conversations were the opposite of joy.

"So when will you tell Edward you know?" Merit asked, steering the conversation back to Jane.

"I don't know," Jane said, and sighed. "Honestly, the whole thing feels like a lot of effort."

"What whole thing?"

"Confronting him, listening to whatever excuse he'll make. He'll get defensive and somehow make it about me."

"It's not about you," Merit said firmly. "And you'll feel better once it's out in the open."

"Will I?" Jane smiled a little, then dug her phone from her jacket pocket. The signal that this conversation—and, by extension, this moment they were having that Merit distinctly did not want to end—was over. "Ugh," she said, grimacing as she scrolled through dozens of new emails. "Why are clients so annoying?"

Merit reluctantly fished for her own phone.

Jane was already on her feet. "Hey, want to come to Sausalito with me tonight? If I'm divorcing my husband, then I need to finally renovate my second house so it can become my first house again. You can make sure I don't kiss skeevy Rob again, and then you and I can grab dinner at this great little Indian place I love."

Merit did want to come to Sausalito and eat Indian food. She wanted to do whatever Jane asked.

"I can't," she said. "It's my anniversary." Not that they were doing anything to celebrate. Sierra had plans with her new boyfriend and couldn't stay late.

Jane gave her a funny look. "Your wedding anniversary?"

Merit nodded.

"Today?"

"Yep."

"How many years?"

"Thirteen."

"Same as Edward and me. Why didn't you mention it before?"

Merit shrugged. "It didn't seem important."

Jane cocked her head to the side. Her hair fell away from her face. Merit couldn't remember having ever noticed her ears before. There were tiny freckles on the top of her right one.

"You're a funny bird," Jane said.

"My boss was having a crisis," Merit said in protest.

"Priorities," Jane said, and smiled.

Merit smiled back. "Exactly."

Jane hooked her elbow through Merit's, and they walked back to the office like that, arm in arm.

THAT AFTERNOON, MERIT pulled out the anniversary card she'd bought and wondered what it said about her marriage that for the first time in thirteen years, there was nothing particular she wanted to write. *I'm glad we're not getting divorced?* Eventually, she added the word "much" before "worse" on the front of the card and signed her name inside.

She spent the rest of the afternoon thinking about sex.

Why weren't she and Cory having more of it?

She acknowledged that Jane and Edward weren't the best baseline because they didn't have young kids. But she had plenty of mom friends who talked about how insatiable their husbands were, how every night was a negotiation, how they wouldn't mind if they were doing it less. Merit would sit there and nod along, but the truth was she couldn't relate. Most nights Cory barely looked at her when he came to bed.

When had he stopped grabbing her ass when he walked by her in their bathroom? When had he stopped kissing that particular spot on her neck?

Better question: When had she stopped wanting him to?

She'd been sexier in her twenties, before she'd discovered that bras didn't *have* to have underwire, back when the only underwear she owned were skimpy lace thongs. She couldn't remember if she enjoyed sex more back then. She was definitely a better sport. She suspected that had something to do with the only advice she'd ever gotten from her mother on the matter, the night before her wedding, when she told Merit that it was important for Cory to believe she was always up for it, unless she wanted him to get it from someone else.

But then she got pregnant with Jude and started painting again, and something shifted. She found herself paying attention to what she actually *wanted* for the first time in her life, and sometimes what she wanted was to wear unflattering cotton briefs that didn't ride up her butt and sweatpants covered in paint. She was thirty-two years old that year and finally beginning to take shape as a person. She felt alive and powerful. She stopped taking Benadryl in order to sleep.

Meanwhile the twice-a-week sex became twice-a-month, and then every other, and then only when she and Cory were both in the mood and the baby was sleeping, which was like planning for an eclipse. Moments of emotional connection happened even less. And while it was tempting to blame the usual domestic clichés—pregnancy! a newborn! her busted vag!—she quietly suspected it was about something else. She'd taken an interest in herself, and her husband had quietly opted out. It made sense. He'd never cared for nebulous things.

The thing she never told anyone was how relieved she was when he stopped paying attention to her; how liberated she felt. Instead, she expressed concern over their lack of intimacy and suggested they see a marriage counselor. They went one time. Cory balked at the cost.

When they decided to start trying for another baby, the frequency picked up. She'd read online that doing it doggie-style increased your odds of getting pregnant, so that was the only position they used. The fact that they likely conceived Nash while her cheek was jammed against their headboard and he pounded into her like a battering ram from behind didn't strike her as odd. By then, they'd become people who communicated via Post-it notes stuck to the kitchen island. At least they didn't fight.

The sex basically stopped after that. At first it was the pregnancy, then a slow recovery after the birth, then sheer exhaustion, until neither of them felt the need to make excuses anymore. Cory took up cycling. Merit bought new bras and went back to work.

Had she gotten the job to save her marriage? Maybe she'd been trying to save herself. Maybe she could have a really deep philosophical think about it if she weren't so preoccupied with trying to figure out how concerned she was supposed to be that she and her husband weren't having more sex.

That night, after bribing the boys with chocolate chips for tomorrow's breakfast so they would go to sleep without a fuss, Merit went into her bedroom and put on her sexiest black bra and an ancient lace thong that almost matched. She put sweatpants on over the lingerie and told herself she felt sexy. In truth she felt the opposite of sexy. Her stomach still hurt from all the pastries she'd eaten with Jane.

It was only seven forty-five. Cory wouldn't be home until eight-thirty at least. She poured bourbon into a coffee mug, took the lacy bra and underwear back off, and ran a bubble bath.

It'd been so long since she'd lit the scented candles by the tub that a layer of dust had gathered on the wax. She fished a book of matches out of her bathroom drawer and lit the dusty wicks, then turned the overhead lights off.

As she waited for the tub to fill, she studied herself in the mirror in the flickering candlelight. God, she looked tired. She pulled at the skin under her eyelids. Should she be getting filler? Is that what aging women did? She made a mental note to discuss this with Jane.

Merit looked down at her naked chest. Her boobs reminded her of deflated balloons left over from a birthday party. She cupped them in her hands and they jiggled unappealingly. At least they were small.

She let her hands wander down her stomach to the space between her thighs. The only thing she hated more than her postpartum boobs was her postpartum labia. She'd made the mistake after Nash was born of putting a mirror between her legs to assess the damage. It completely ruined any chance Cory had of convincing her to let him go down on her after that. He insisted he didn't care what it looked like, but she didn't believe him, and it didn't matter anyway because his mouth down there never felt good enough to override the mental discomfort of it, even before her vagina got the shit beat out of it in childbirth. She loathed the way it felt against her fingertips, like two strips of soggy beef jerky, or poorly cut sashimi.

Ugh. She needed to shave.

She sighed and slipped into the bath. The water was hot and soapy. The candles smelled of bergamot and lavender and made her think of Jane.

She wished she'd gone to Sausalito with her. She wanted to be sitting across the table from a beautiful and brilliant woman talking about something unexpected and interesting, not psyching herself up for sex she didn't really want to have with a man she already knew everything about.

The ice in her drink shifted as it melted from the heat of the bath, clinking against the mug. She took a long sip. The bourbon was working, making her think less about everything that was wrong with her body and her marriage. On the whole, both were better than average, she knew. She and Cory loved each other. Her vagina still functioned properly, and her husband could still reliably get it up on the rare occasion that an erection was necessary. So what if their conversations were boring? Cory didn't have to be the most compelling person in her life. If she was honest with herself (and, really, what better time to be honest with yourself than when you were buzzed on bourbon in a bathtub at eight o'clock on a Monday night?), he never had been. And now she didn't have to be bitter about it. Now she had Jane.

It was probably a terrible idea to become this enmeshed with the person you worked for, but Merit was in too deep to care. Jane was the first person she texted every morning and the last one she texted every night, the person whose workout regimen she routinely troubleshooted and whose very strong opinion she sought before every online shopping purchase. So what if Jane was also her boss? At least she'd escaped the conversational loop she was stuck in with her other female friends, moms like Leena who worked from home and had Pinterest boards and were always making earnest endeavors to be more present and order less shit on Amazon Prime. Quite frankly, Merit wasn't sure *what* she and Jane talked about most days. Everything? Nothing? She just knew that when Jane came into her office, the room felt full.

Her relationship with her college roommate had been like that. Merit remembered how satisfying it had been to come back to her apartment after an exam or a bad date to find Cat on their green velvet couch with her chemistry textbook, ready to rehash all the details of whatever self-inflicted catastrophe Merit was facing with a jug of pink Carlos Rossi and a party-size bag of Sour Patch Kids. Maybe her relationship with Jane was simply another version of that. Maybe an office buddy was the grown-up equivalent of a college roommate, the person the universe put in your life to help you process your life without freaking the fuck out.

Merit leaned back and closed her eyes. She was overthinking it. It wasn't the worst thing in the world to have a girlfriend you liked better than the guy you married. Possibly, it was the secret to a happy marriage. A good and decent man with a working penis who was emotionally unavailable but would never physically leave, and a woman who made you feel like it didn't even matter that your husband didn't give two shits about your interior life because she already understood you better than he ever could. A woman who didn't need you to make sense, or fit into a box, or fill a category in her head. A woman who let you be creative and ambitious and practical and a little bit careless and wildly optimistic about unrealistic things without ever pointing out the contradiction in all of this, because she, too, was a messy combination of incongruent elements that didn't logically fit.

Merit slipped lower into the water and let her hands wander back between her thighs. She couldn't remember the last time she'd gotten herself off. Not since she was pregnant with Nash, when she was turned on all the time but not interested in having actual sex. Would she and Cory be doing it more if she were in the mood more often? Would masturbating more often get her in the mood? She touched herself a little, then sighed and pulled her hand out of the water. Maybe she should buy a vibrator. Maybe that would help.

She was rubbing lotion on her legs when Cory came into the bathroom looking for her. She'd put the lingerie back on, because her boobs looked better with something holding them up.

"Happy anniversary," he said, his eyebrows going up. "Are we going out?"

"Nope," she said. She could see herself in the mirror, her cheeks pink from the heat of the bath. "Wanna help me take this lingerie back off?"

"I do," he said, already unbuttoning his shirt.

It wasn't the best sex they'd ever had, but it was reassuringly hot. And they both came at the exact same time, which felt meaningful and lovely. It was also the reason neither of them noticed when the condom broke.

She found out she was pregnant three weeks later.

s e v e n

M ERIT WAS PRACTICING her speech in her head when
Jane appeared in the doorway of her office with a funny look on her
face.

Shit, Merit thought. *She knows.*

She hadn't been able to explain to Cory why she was so nervous about
telling Jane she was pregnant, or why she'd kept it from her for so long. She
was nine weeks already, with an official due date (August 22!) and a grainy
ultrasound pic taped to her fridge. When she first found out—after hyper-
ventilating for the better part of two days—she decided to wait until Jane
and Edward were officially separated to mention the baby, but then Christmas came and went and Jane still hadn't confronted her husband about his
affair. Now it was almost February, and Merit could barely button her
jeans.

"You think she's going to be mad at you," Cory said as they got into bed
the night before.

"No, it's not that."

"What then? Envious? Because she doesn't have kids?"

Merit didn't answer him. She regretted that she'd ever brought it up.

"It's not like you promised her you wouldn't have more kids," Cory added. Then he frowned. "Wait, did you?"

"No, of course not," Merit replied, rolling her eyes. "She just relies on me is all."

She knew Cory would assume she meant professionally. How could she explain to her husband that she and her boss had developed an unspoken but very clear arrangement that no other being would require more of Merit's energy than Jane did? Jude and Nash were cared for by other people for ten hours a day. A newborn would require full-time attention. Who would attend to Jane?

"It's not like you're quitting," Cory pointed out. "You'll only be gone a couple months."

BUT I AM HER PERSON! Merit felt like shouting at him. *If I'm gone, who is she going to talk to about the affair she's thinking about having with her skeevy contractor to get back at her husband who we suspect is fucking a twenty-two-year-old with fake boobs!*

"You're right," she said instead. "I'll just tell her."

And she was planning to, that morning, until Jane walked in with that funny look on her face.

"What is it?" Merit asked.

Jane just shook her head. Merit noticed now that her blue eyes were uncharacteristically watery and red around the edges, like she'd been crying.

"Oh, honey," Merit said, rising so quickly she knocked over her chair.

"Careful, LB," Jane said. Her lips turned up slightly at the corners.

Merit had planned to take her friend into her arms, but now that she was standing in front of her it seemed too awkward to attempt. So she caught Jane's hands in hers, which immediately felt more intimate than a hug.

"I had a mammogram this morning." Jane met Merit's gaze and held it. Her hands were cold. "They found a rather beefy lump."

Merit's mouth went dry.

"It could be nothing," she said immediately. She heard the desperation in her own voice. She felt desperate. *Please, God, don't let her have cancer. Please, God, don't let her die.*

"It could be nothing," Jane agreed. "But considering my mother died of breast cancer, the odds probably aren't fantastic?"

The last thing Jane needed right now was for Merit to start crying but the tears came anyway, even as Merit tried to blink them back. "Oh god, please stop," Jane said. "You look like you're having a seizure."

"I'm sorry!" Merit brought her hands to her face and pressed her fingertips to her eyelids. *Fucking hormones!*

"Wow, your tits look amazing," she heard Jane say. "Did you get a new bra?"

My tits look great because I'm fucking pregnant! But there was no way she could tell Jane now, not in the wake of this. "Stop trying to change the subject," Merit said, dropping her hands. "We're talking about *your* tits, not mine."

Jane smiled a little but it didn't reach her eyes. "Will you come with me to the biopsy?"

"Of course."

Jane nodded and hugged her. It was the most overtly affectionate she'd ever been, and it took every ounce of self-control that Merit possessed not to sob.

Jane pulled back first.

"Take my mind off it," she said lightly, sauntering over to the chair facing Merit's desk and dropping down into it. "How was your weekend? What's new with you?"

"Not much," Merit said as casually as she could. Her boobs felt like ripe cantaloupes on her chest. She crossed her arms in what she hoped was a casual fashion and returned to her desk. "How was yours? Did you see Rob?" Jane had hired him to manage the renovation of her Sausalito house.

Jane shook her head. "Edward and I drove to Napa." She pushed the sleeves of her T-shirt up over her shoulders and examined her biceps. "Are my upper arms looking crepey?"

"Stop." Merit rolled her eyes. "You know your arms don't look crepey. Whatever that even means. Why did you and Edward go to Napa?"

Jane shrugged. "He wanted to. A new restaurant opened that he wanted to check out."

"And you still haven't told him you know about the affair."

"You know I haven't. And stop judging me. If I'm dying of cancer the issue will resolve on its own."

"Jane," Merit said firmly. "You're not dying."

"Anyway, Lars asked me to go to New York with him next week," Jane went on. "So the biopsy will have to wait until after that."

"What's in New York? A pitch?"

"Don't think so," Jane said, re-examining her arms.

She was no doubt being cagey on purpose, so that Merit would ask questions, and Jane could act like she'd forced it out of her. But the news about the lump had shaken her, and Merit didn't feel like playing along. "What are you telling me? You've decided to fuck Lars?"

Jane whipped her head around. Her eyes were cold and intensely blue.

Merit felt her cheeks go warm. She dropped her eyes to her lap. "I'm sorry."

"Oh, don't be all pouty now," Jane said. "You're forgiven. But that was a shitty thing for you to say."

"So why mention the trip?" Merit asked. "You travel with Lars and Erik all the time."

"Exactly. It's always both of them. This time it's just Lars. And the trip's not on his calendar, and he told me not to put it on mine."

"Okay, but surely he gave you a reason, right? Like you're pitching a celebrity or something?"

Jane shook her head. "Nope."

"Okay, then that's weird."

Jane nodded. "Yep."

"So are you going?" It was a stupid question. Of course Jane would go. Because Lars had asked her to. Because she was curious. Because her husband was cheating on her. Because she might be sick.

Jane shrugged. "I guess I am."

"What hotel?"

"Some place downtown," Jane said vaguely, and Merit felt a flash of heat. It was the same hot, uncomfortable way she'd felt in fourth grade when her best friend Alice told her she was doing the talent show with Mary Beth Sutton instead.

Jane absolutely knew where she and Lars were staying. She'd no doubt clicked through the gallery photos on the hotel's website, critiquing the décor of the rooms. But Merit couldn't call her out for withholding. Not when she had a tiny human growing in her uterus that she still hadn't told Jane about. And *couldn't* tell her; not right now, anyway, because of the lump.

"Well," Merit said eventually when it was clear Jane wasn't going to give her anything else. "Let me know how it goes." It was a ridiculous thing to say. They'd talk a zillion times before she left.

"Of course." Jane stood back up. "You're definitely in for the biopsy?"

Merit nodded. "Just tell me when."

As soon as Jane had left her office, Merit called Cory.

"Jane might have cancer," she said as soon as he picked up.

"Really?"

No, I'm making it up. "Yes, really. They found a lump in her breast."

"Maybe it's benign."

Merit nearly hung up the phone. Why couldn't Cory just say *that's terrible / oh no / is she okay?* Why did every conversation with him feel like a battle, even when there weren't sides?

"I have to go," Merit said.

"Do you want to talk about it?"

That's why I called you, she thought. "Not really," she said.

"Okay. Well. I'm sorry, babe."

"Thanks," she said, and hung up.

LARS AND JANE left on Sunday for New York. Merit spent Monday morning pushing herself around in circles in the extra chair by Tony's desk. She hadn't gotten a single text from Jane.

"Have you heard from her at all?" she asked Tony casually.

"She called yesterday when they put her in a room by the elevator, natch. But, no, not today."

"Do you know who they're meeting with?"

Tony shook his head. "Lars wanted to keep the whole thing super hush-hush."

"Yeah, I know, but why?"

"Because the dude is bizarre?"

Merit spun around again in the chair. "I'm pregnant," she said abruptly. Tony's eyebrows shot up.

"Really? Congrats!"

"I haven't told Jane."

"She'll be happy for you."

"Will she?"

Tony grinned. "After she makes it all about her for a good thirty seconds, yes."

"Only thirty seconds? Have you met our boss?"

She was being uncharitable. It felt kind of good.

"What about you?" Tony asked. "How do you feel about it? Were you trying? Is that okay to ask?"

"Totally okay. No, we weren't trying. Apparently, sometimes condoms break?"

"No shit."

"Right?"

Merit spun in the chair again. Her preoccupation with Jane and Lars aside, she felt pretty great. She'd been nauseated for days, but she wasn't at all today. She'd be ten weeks on Friday. Maybe she was over the hump.

She heard Tony's phone *ding* with a new text. She knew it was from Jane before he checked it. She watched him read the message, then make a face.

"What?" she asked as nonchalantly as she could.

"Lars wants to change their dinner reservation," he said, turning back to his screen.

"Can't *his* assistant do that?"

Tony didn't respond. He was already immersed in the task.

Merit's good mood evaporated. She pushed herself out of the chair.

She didn't know why this New York trip was bothering her so much. Jane was a grown woman who could do whatever she wanted, including fly across the country for a mysterious three-night jaunt with her sex-addled boss. She didn't owe Merit an explanation, or details. But Merit couldn't help it; she wanted both. Mostly, she didn't want Jane to keep any secrets from her, especially not secrets that involved clandestine hotel sex.

(What kind of kinky shit was Lars into? Would Jane let him tie her up?)

Fuck. She had to think about something else.

Her mind fixated on Jane's lump.

She told herself that Jane's very capable doctors were being overly cautious because of her family history, that there was no need to panic, that people with cancer didn't glow like they were lit from within. She told herself these things so convincingly that by noon she'd concluded that it was actually impossible that Jane could be sick. The woman rode fifteen miles on a Peloton every morning! She subsisted on fish and celery and got infusion IVs! The lump had to be benign.

The effort it took not to obsess over Jane left no mental energy for work. Distracted and antsy, Merit texted Leena and asked if she wanted to meet for lunch.

"You're totally pregnant," Leena whispered as soon as she saw her. "You look amazing! How many weeks?"

"Nine and a half," Merit answered. "How could you tell?"

Leena grinned. "Well, it was either a baby or a boob job and I went with my gut. Are we excited about it yet or not?"

"Getting there, maybe?" She'd been so stunned by the pregnancy, then so nervous about telling Jane, she hadn't really let herself think about it much. She was having another baby! Maybe it would be a girl. She pictured Jane buying her little overpriced dresses and tiny frilly socks.

"We've talked about a third," Leena said when they sat. "According to Dev, the economics of it aren't great, but we'll see." Dev was Leena's husband, who worked in finance. Dev was always instructing Leena on the economics of things.

"At least you have three bedrooms," Merit said. "We'll have to move before this one comes."

"Oh, yeah? What neighborhood?"

"Hayes Valley, maybe? If we can afford it. I'd like to be close to work."

"So you think you'll go back?" Leena sounded surprised. "Even with three?"

Merit should have expected it. It was standard fare, this question, any time a working mom revealed that she was having another kid. Merit herself had been a part of this exact conversation with other women countless times before. She remembered how satisfying it'd been telling her friends she was having another baby when she was working from home. Everyone felt really good about the fact that Merit would be with her kids full-time. So what if her art was a financial and emotional drain on her marriage? At least she wouldn't have to abandon her children like the women who were selfish enough to want an actual career.

"I really love my work," she told Leena now, though she knew it wasn't the work itself she loved so much as the circumstances under which she got to do it—with Jane, in clothes that didn't smell like little-boy sweat, in a location that was not her home.

"Well, sure, I love mine, too," Leena said. She was a graphic designer who worked ten hours a week from home. "But I couldn't do it full-time with the girls as young as they are, and I definitely can't imagine going into an office every day."

"Yeah, it's hard," Merit said, to say something. She was regretting this lunch. She wished she were eating oysters and drinking white wine with Jane. Which, of course, she couldn't do again until August when the baby came. But she'd rather be stone-cold sober and starving with Jane than sitting here, doing this. "How're the girls?" she forced herself to ask.

"They're good," Leena said happily. "I can't believe they'll be *six* next month. Where does the time go, you know?"

"Totally," Merit said, bobbing her head. This was another familiar exchange—children getting older too fast, how fleeting it all was, how quickly the moments whizzed past. Merit was too busy to notice the speed at which time was moving. There was never enough of it, that much she felt.

(How long was this lunch going to last?)

As she walked back to the office afterward, she thought about all the times she'd met Leena for lunch when they were both home full-time with their kids. They'd drink rosé and bitch about how little sleep they were getting and laugh about how fucking demoralizing it all was. Back then, those lunches were a lifeboat that made her feel less like she was drowning.

She wasn't drowning anymore.

She texted Jane as she got on the elevator.

MERIT: bitch where u at?

The three dots appeared right away. Merit felt inordinate delight.

JANE: ughhhhhh. wish u were here.

Merit was smiling as she wrote back.

MERIT: me too

JANE'S BIOPSY WAS scheduled for Thursday, the day after she and Lars got back from New York. The plan was for Merit to pick her up at home to drive her to the appointment. It felt like an eternity had passed since they'd last seen each other, six days before, when Merit pretended to be doing the Whole30 to avoid having wine at their Friday lunch. Merit was giddy on the drive over, already anticipating Jane being Jane and regaling her with stories from New York, though she was determined not to be the one to bring it up. Having obsessed all week about what might have been happening in Jane's hotel room, Merit had resolved not to ask her anything about the trip.

Jane was standing on the sidewalk in black sweatpants, a T-shirt, and a puffy red vest Merit had never seen before.

"What are you doing?" Merit demanded when Jane pulled open the car door. "It's freezing."

"It's not freezing," Jane said, rolling her eyes. "It's fifty-seven degrees. I'd be in a tank top back home."

"Why were you outside?"

"Edward would've thought it was weird if I was still home at nine-fifteen."

Merit stared at her. "You haven't told him?"

"Little bird, can you just please drive your adorable Subaru to my appointment and not give me shit for not allowing my philandering husband to feel sorry for me?"

"My Subaru is not adorable," Merit said, putting the car into drive. She wanted to hold Jane's hand and tell her everything was going to be fine, but she couldn't because she didn't know if it was true. "How was New York?"

So much for not mentioning the trip.

"It was fine," Jane said vaguely.

"What was the point of it?"

"Just . . . meetings."

"Meetings," Merit repeated.

"Yes."

"About what?"

"Various business opportunities. Where are we on the Hunters Point project?"

"Why are you changing the subject?"

"Because we've exhausted the other one. You asked me what the trip was about, and I told you. Lars is exploring a few opportunities. There were meetings. That was it. Now tell me about Hunters Point."

"The soils report wasn't great," Merit said.

"Define 'not great.'"

"Highly liquefiable sands."

"Fuck."

"We'll figure it out. How are you feeling about today?"

"Fine."

"Liar."

"It is what it is, right?" Jane shrugged. "If it's cancer I'll deal with it."

"*We'll* deal with it," Merit said, and finally reached over and took Jane's hand. "But you don't have to feel fine. You can be freaked out."

"Okay, I'm freaked out."

Merit squeezed her hand. "I know."

"Mostly I'm freaked about the needle they're going to jam into my tit. A mammogram's bad enough, you know?" Jane glanced over at Merit then abruptly snatched her hand back. "Oh my god, you've never even had one, have you? You're not fucking old enough yet!"

Merit shrugged sheepishly. "Sorry?"

"When do you turn forty?" Jane demanded.

"A year from May sixth."

"Thirty-fucking-eight." Jane shook her head. "I'm not sure I can be friends with you anymore."

"You have to," Merit said. "I don't like any of my other friends."

"Since when?"

"Monday."

"What happened?"

"I had lunch with a friend who was shocked that I was planning to keep working afte—" Merit stopped abruptly. *Shit.*

Jane looked over at her. "After what?"

"After I turn forty," Merit said quickly.

"Why would you quit working at forty?"

"Exactly. It's dumb."

"It's absolutely absurd," Jane scoffed. "The average woman's earnings don't peak until age forty-four. Who are these misogynists you hang out with? Introduce me to them."

Merit almost told her right then. But blurting out *I'm pregnant* in the middle of rush hour traffic while driving her friend to a biopsy felt wrong. She'd do it right after the procedure. If the lump was malignant, there would never be a good time anyway.

Please, God, don't let the lump be malignant.

They'd reached the medical center. Merit pulled into the garage and parked. Jane sat motionless in the passenger seat, wringing her hands. She looked simultaneously years older and very young.

"Can we say a quick prayer before we go in?" Merit heard herself ask. She'd discarded so much of her upbringing, but she'd hung on to this. She expected Jane to make a joke about it, but Jane simply nodded. Merit covered Jane's hands with hers.

Jane took a small breath and closed her eyes.

"Hi, God," Merit began, keeping her eyes half-open to watch Jane's face. "Here we are. We know you hate cancer as much as we do. So we pray this lump is benign. We pray the biopsy will be as painless as possible and that Jane won't offend the doctors too much with her foul mouth." She saw Jane smile. "Amen."

Jane opened her eyes. "Thank you, LB."

Merit smiled. "You're welcome, boss."

"You never told me you were religious."

"I'm not really. Not anymore." It was so much more complicated than that.

"But you believe in God."

Merit nodded. It'd been such a long time since anyone had asked her what she believed. If they hadn't been sitting in a parking garage about to go for a biopsy, she might have told Jane that God was the reason she'd started painting, or that she felt most connected to the divine when she was standing at a blank canvas with a brush in her hand, or watching her sons sleep. She might have even attempted to explain the thing her parents had never understood, that it wasn't God she'd left at eighteen, but the version of faith that put divinity in a box that only a few people could access, on Sunday mornings, in a church.

"Yes," was all she said.

"And you think He gives a shit about the lump in my tit?" Jane asked.

Merit smiled. "Putting aside the fact that an all-powerful, divine spiritual being can't actually have a gender—which is an argument I've had with my mother nine hundred times—yes. I do."

"How very American of you."

Merit laughed.

"I hate this," Jane said quietly.

"I know." Merit squeezed her hand. "I'm glad I'm here."

They didn't speak as they walked inside the building, still holding hands. They both pretended not to see the sign by the elevator announcing that they were in a cancer center.

The receptionist called Jane's name a few minutes after they arrived. Jane stood, then turned back and looked at Merit.

"Will you come in with me?"

Merit nodded and stood up. She slid her hand back into Jane's. It was remarkable to her how easy this felt, being here with her, like this. She wondered what the nurses thought of them. She could've been Jane's daughter, but they looked nothing alike.

She held Jane's hand for the entirety of the procedure, despite the fact that the doctor performing the biopsy tried sincerely—multiple times—to kick her out. Jane was unequivocal that her friend stay. Merit had never felt so needed, or so uniquely equipped. She found herself thinking of her mother, and how she'd never let Merit hold her hand through something like this.

Her eyes never left Jane's face. She watched as Jane's blue eyes went vacant. She saw her hold her breath. She heard the only sound Jane made through the whole thing, a tiny whimper when the needle went in. Her mind stayed quiet except for the thought, *Please, God, let her be okay.*

After about forty-five minutes, the doctor said he had what he needed, and he and the nurse left so Jane could get dressed. Merit stepped outside to go to the bathroom. She had to pee so badly she was starting to cramp.

She was so distracted thinking about Jane and her results that she almost didn't see the blood.

But when she stood up to flush, it ran down her thighs.

She stared at it for what felt like an eternity, watching the blood drip from her body onto the toilet seat. It reminded her of red paint. The toilet seat was chipped.

"Please, God, no," she whispered finally, yanking the toilet paper roll with two hands. She told herself that spotting was normal. She'd seen a heartbeat two weeks ago. Yes, the baby's heart rate was a little slow, but her doctor said she wasn't worried about it. She'd given them an ultrasound photo! Everything was okay.

Except the amount of blood that was coming out of her body was more than anyone would call "spotting."

She fumbled in her purse for her phone and called Jane.

"Where'd you go?" Jane asked when she picked up.

"I'm—" Merit faltered, then immediately started to cry.

"Merit?"

Merit couldn't form words. She didn't know what to say.

"Where are you?" she heard Jane ask.

"Bathroom," she whispered, and hung up.

Jane knocked less than a minute later. Merit didn't bother pulling up her jeans before opening the door.

"Oh my god. Merit. What—"

"I'm pregnant," Merit managed through heaving tears. "Was. Pregnant."

"Can we get a doctor in here?" Jane yelled down the hall before stepping inside the bathroom and taking Merit into her arms. She lifted her back onto the toilet and wiped the blood off her legs with the wad of toilet paper in Merit's hands.

"It might not be what you think," she said.

Merit shook her head. She knew exactly what it was. This was why her morning sickness had stopped so suddenly on Monday. Her baby had died.

Jane knelt on the floor in front of Merit and took both of Merit's hands in hers. The women stared at each other, saying more with their eyes than either of them had words for.

"Hey, God?" Jane said softly, lifting her eyes toward the ceiling. "We don't understand why the fuck you'd let this happen, but if you're up there, please help."

Merit managed a tiny nod. Her belly was starting to cramp now. She had friends who'd had miscarriages. She'd pass the embryo soon.

She squeezed Jane's hands. "Amen."

e i g h t

THE ONLY SILVER lining that day was that she didn't have to have a D&C.

Jane insisted on coming with her to her OB's office on the other side of town even though Merit told her repeatedly that she was fine to go alone. It wasn't lost on Merit that she'd spent the morning holding Jane's hand but was having trouble letting Jane hold hers.

"You had a biopsy an hour ago," Merit pointed out as Jane ordered an Uber. They were still in the bathroom. One of the nurses had given her a pair of post-surgical disposable underwear to soak up the blood, which Merit was now wearing without any pants. "You need to take it easy," she told Jane. "You should go home and rest."

"Merit? I love you, but please shut the fuck up. I'll leave when Cory gets there." They hadn't been able to get hold of him yet. He wasn't picking up his phone and Merit didn't want to put *im having a miscarriage* in a text.

"I'll see if they have a wheelchair to bring you downstairs," Jane said then, pulling open the bathroom door.

"I can walk," Merit said hoarsely.

"Bitch, you're not walking," Jane said. "I'll be right back."

As soon as the door latched, Merit was crying again. She wondered how many bodily fluids she could expel before her insides dried up. The blood had slowed down a little after what she could only assume was the embryo had come out. Her body felt hollow, and numb. She knew, scientifically, that at nine-and-a-half weeks, that little mass of cells hadn't been a baby yet, and that most likely there'd been a problem with the chromosomes from the very beginning that would've prevented it from ever becoming one. But if that were true, what did she lose? Not an actual child but the illusion of one? It felt like a trick. She wasn't mad at God, but she did feel duped, like she'd been dumb enough to believe something she should've known wasn't true. She'd never been able to picture herself with a third kid. That should've been her first clue.

"You guys can try again," Jane had said to her earlier.

Merit had nodded, but she knew they wouldn't.

Her jeans were lying in a heap on the floor, badly stained with the blood in the crotch but you couldn't tell from the outside. Is that how she would be from now on, damaged in places no one could see? She held on to the wall bar as she reached for the jeans, feeling woozy from the blood. She'd expected her OB to tell her to go to the hospital, but the nurse had said it wasn't actually necessary. They could take care of everything in her office. Having a baby was a much bigger deal than losing one, it seemed.

Her phone rang. Cory.

She took a shaky breath and answered it. "Cory?" she said in a small voice.

"What's wrong?" he said immediately. "Is it Jane?"

Merit shook her head, then realized he couldn't see her.

"It's—" she began. Again, the words wouldn't come.

"Mer?"

"I lost the baby," she whispered finally. "I had a miscarriage." It was somehow easier to put in past tense even though technically it wasn't over yet. She could feel blood seeping into her padded plastic briefs. She should've asked for a second pair.

"Are you sure?" Cory asked. Unexpectedly, the question didn't infuriate her. She didn't want to scream *YES I AM FUCKING SURE!* and hang up the phone. Instead, she felt an intense wave of compassion for her highly rational, left-brained husband of thirteen years who had told her the night before that he was hoping for a little girl, and who'd just come out of his weekly staff meeting to news she knew he couldn't fathom simply because the odds of it happening had been so slim. Merit, too, had known that the chances of a miscarriage at nine weeks and six days when they'd already detected a heartbeat were less than one percent, but that hadn't stopped her from worrying about it. Not the way she had with Jude, maybe, but she'd been keenly aware of the possibility of her pregnancy ending ever since she'd peed on that stick. Cory, she knew, hadn't even considered that they might lose their baby. He probably didn't even know the mechanics of a miscarriage. He'd never seen YouTube videos about them or sat across the table from a close friend as she described what hers was like. He'd certainly never watched the remnants of the child he would never have come out of his body and plop unceremoniously into blood-tinged toilet water in a public bathroom like she just had.

"Yes," she said softly. "I'm sure."

He made a sound and Merit realized he was crying, too. The sound of his grief nearly put her over the edge.

"I'm so sorry," she said, choking back a sob.

"But you're okay?" he asked. His voice was so gentle he almost didn't sound like himself.

"Yeah."

"Tell me where you are. I'm on my way." She could hear the rustle of papers, the sound of his keys, his sneakers on the shiny concrete floor of his office in the South Bay. It would take him at least forty minutes to get into the city.

"It's okay," she said quickly. "You don't need to come. Jane is taking me to Dr. Ross now. I don't think I'll be there long."

"You're with Jane." She could hear his relief.

"We were at her biopsy when—when it happened. We're taking an Uber over to Dr. Ross's office then I guess home. We'll have to get my car at some point."

"We'll figure it out."

Merit nodded even though he couldn't see it. She didn't know what else to say.

"Babe?" Cory's voice sounded small.

"Yeah?"

"I love you. And I'm so sorry this happened."

Merit felt the tears rushing back. It wasn't about the baby so much this time, but the kindness in his voice. It made this awful thing better and, somehow, also worse.

Jane reappeared as they hung up.

"Cory?" she asked. Merit nodded. "How'd he take it?"

"Fine."

"Like, irritatingly fine?"

"No, he was good, actually. Sweet."

"Good," Jane said. "I couldn't find a wheelchair."

"I told you, I can walk." Merit stood, steadying herself on the wall. She felt a little light-headed, but mostly okay. She fumbled with the zipper on her jeans. They'd been hard to zip already, with the pregnancy. The bulky plastic underwear didn't help.

"Merit, just leave it," Jane said gently, touching Merit's right hand. She smoothed Merit's gray sweater down over her waistband and tucked her hair behind her ears. They both pretended not to note the bloodstain on her left sleeve.

"I'm glad you're here," Merit whispered.

"Me, too."

Arm in arm they made their way out of the bathroom and down the hall.

"How are you feeling?" Merit asked. "Does your boob hurt?"

"Who cares about my boob?"

"I do," Merit said. "I'm really sorry my miscarriage got in the way of your medical crisis."

It was her attempt at a joke but it didn't make Jane laugh.

"I don't understand it," Jane said as they got on the elevator.

"What?"

"Why God would let this happen to someone like you."

"It happens to a lot of people," Merit said.

"Yeah, well, a lot of people aren't as kind or as good as you."

Merit didn't feel all that kind, or particularly good, and she didn't want to get into a theology discussion with Jane. "Odds are it wasn't a viable pregnancy to begin with," she said.

"Does that make you feel better?" Jane asked.

"No."

She followed Jane out of the elevator and into the lobby. The fluorescent lights above them were nauseatingly bright. She could see their Uber idling outside. Now that she was up and walking it felt excessive that Jane was coming all the way across town with her. She put her hand on Jane's arm. "Hey, honestly, I am totally fine to go by myself to the doctor. You should go home and rest."

Jane stopped walking and looked at her. "Why are you trying to get rid of me?"

"I'm not!"

"You keep telling me to go home."

"I don't want to put you out."

"It's not putting me out. My best American friend just had a miscarriage and I'd like to be there for her."

"Um. 'Best *American* friend'?"

"I'm happy to let you vie for the global title, but I've known my friend Lise for half a century and she's twice your size and often drunk, so your odds aren't very good. Now can we just agree that I'm coming with you to the doctor and move on?"

Merit nodded.

"You're not used to people showing up for you," Jane said as she opened the car door for Merit and helped her inside.

"Maybe," Merit allowed. "But I also don't really need much from people. I never have." It was something her mother had always said about her. The nicest thing, in fact.

"*Or*," Jane said, "you've convinced yourself you don't have any needs so you won't be disappointed when people don't meet them. By 'people' I mostly mean Cory."

"Is this an intervention?"

"I'm serious. You can't keep everyone at arm's distance."

"I don't!"

"You kind of do." Jane looked over at her as the car pulled away from the curb. "Why didn't you tell me about the baby?"

Merit's shoulders rose and fell. She didn't know what she'd been so worried about. It seemed so silly now.

"Sure, our relationship is a little weird because we work together, and I'm old enough to be your teen mom," Jane said. Merit started to challenge the age thing but Jane waved her off. "But this friendship is super important to me, Merit. *You* are super important to me."

"It's bugging me out that you're using my real name. This is three times now."

"Little bird, I'm trying to have a sincere moment here."

"I know. You're super important to me, too." Merit smiled a little. "You might even be my best Danish friend."

Jane pulled a face. "You know, you were a lot less sassy when I hired you."

"You called me your best American friend!"

"I was hedging. I didn't want to be the only one with no other prospects."

Merit laughed at this and, for a few seconds, forgot she was having the second half of a miscarriage in a stranger's Ford Focus.

"It doesn't work, you know," Jane said then. "Pretending you don't have needs." She pulled Merit's hand into her lap. "This is pure speculation, of course, since I am unabashedly needy."

"The neediest," Merit agreed, laying her head on Jane's shoulder. Jane's puffy vest was cold beneath her cheek.

"I'm so sorry this happened," Jane said quietly. Merit only nodded.

"Did you ever want kids?" she heard herself ask.

"I always wanted kids," Jane replied. "Unfortunately, there was no one to have them with."

"Edward didn't want them?"

"Decidedly not."

"Well. You would've made a really excellent mother," Merit said softly. "For what it's worth."

Jane squeezed her arm. "Thank you, birdie. Maybe if I'd been younger or saner at the time, I would've pushed for it. But I was forty-three and in a dark place and not certain of much. Edward was certain of everything."

"Sounds like Cory."

"Except Cory would never cheat on you. Different breed in that respect."

Merit couldn't argue with this. She turned her head a little.

"Am I allowed to ask why you haven't told Edward you know about the affair?"

"Are you going to judge me for my answer?"

"Probably."

"I don't really blame him for it," Jane said. "So it feels disingenuous to play the jilted wife."

Merit straightened up. "You don't blame your husband for cheating on you?"

"I should never have invested in the restaurant," Jane said wearily. "He didn't ask me to. But I knew he thought I didn't believe in him, and I wanted to prove that I did."

"Did you actually?" Merit asked.

"Fuck no. The man has zero business sense. And now the restaurant is bleeding money and I'm bitter and resentful and he knows it."

"And that entitles him to have an affair."

"Not entitles, necessarily, but the male ego is a delicate thing."

"So you're not angry."

"Of course I'm angry. If I took an Ambien I'd probably kill him in my sleep."

Merit laid her head back on Jane's shoulder. "So are you happy?" she asked softly. "Aside from the murderous rage, I mean."

Jane turned her chin. "With Edward, or with life in general?"

"Either one."

"I'm not *unhappy* with Edward," Jane replied. "And life improved considerably when you showed up."

"Right back at you," Merit said, her voice buckling a little.

"Just promise me we'll be like this forever," Jane said, sounding very serious all of a sudden. "Even when we get other jobs."

Merit was so caught up in the tenderness of the moment she didn't notice that Jane said "when" instead of "if."

Merit smiled a little. "Now that you've seen my vag I think we're bonded for life."

CORY WAS HOME when Merit got back. He was the only one there, thankfully. Jude was still at school and Sierra had taken Nash to the park.

The visit to her OB hadn't been that bad, considering. The doctor who'd delivered both her babies confirmed that she'd already expelled the fetal tissue (the word "expelled" felt appropriately violent) and seemed confident that Merit's body would take care of the rest on its own. As long as she felt okay, she should be fine to go to work on Monday, though Jane was adamant that she take some time off. Merit said she'd think about it. She understood she needed to take it easy, but she wasn't sure sitting in her apartment with her empty womb would make her feel better. Maybe she would paint.

(She couldn't imagine that she would paint.)

Cory met her at the door when she walked in.

"How do you feel?" he asked.

She shrugged. "Sad, I guess. A little numb."

"That's normal," Cory said assuredly.

"Yep." She sank down on the couch and pushed off her boots.

There were several seconds of silence. She wanted a bath, but she was suddenly overcome by inertia. She hoped Cory wouldn't ask her any more questions because she wasn't sure she had the capacity to form more words.

Cory stood there looking at her. She'd never seen him so completely at a loss for what to do.

"I'm okay, Cory," she said finally. She wanted to give him more than that, but it was all she had.

"Okay." He seemed unsure. More silence. She wished he'd just go upstairs.

"Dr. Ross said we can't have sex for six weeks," she said then, inexplicably.

Cory blinked. "Are you thinking—"

"No," she said immediately. "I told Dr. Ross I want an IUD."

"There's no need to rush anything," he said.

She reached for the remote and turned on the TV.

"We could order pizza tonight," he suggested. "I could go pick up a good bottle of wine? If you feel like drinking. I don't know. Just tell me what you want."

"Pizza is fine," Merit said. "The boys'll like that."

"Okay," he said for the seventeenth time. She felt his eyes on her for a few more seconds, then he sighed and turned to go upstairs. She realized after he was gone that he hadn't even given her a hug.

"Hey, Cory?" she called.

"Yeah?"

She heard him coming back down the stairs.

"Are you sad?" she asked when he appeared at the side of the couch.

"Of course I'm sad," he said.

"But?"

"There's no but."

"There's always a but," she said, sounding like Jane.

"There's no but, Mer," he said. "We lost a baby today. I'm sad."

It wasn't satisfying. Was it because she didn't believe him? Had she expected him to confirm what she suspected, that he wasn't actually sad because his brain didn't dwell in what-ifs like hers did, because it was built for if/thens? Did she want him to say aloud what she assumed he was thinking, that if there was something wrong with their baby's chromosomes, then it wasn't actually a child they'd lost, but only a misconception based on limited information, which wasn't something to grieve? Or was it the opposite; had she been hoping this terrible thing would crack him open, that his reaction might be visceral instead of practical for once?

"Okay," she said, and went back to the TV. At some point, he left.

Her Netflix options felt overwhelming. She clicked on a Danish political drama that had good reviews. The lead reminded her of Jane. She was halfway through the third episode when Sierra brought Nash back from the park.

"Mommy!" he yelled when he saw her, scrambling onto the couch. He was bigger at two than Jude had been, and happier. She braced for the impact of his solid little body. He had mud on his nose from the park.

"Gentle, Nash, Mommy isn't feeling well," Sierra said, catching him right before he landed on Merit. She knew from the look on Sierra's face that Cory had told her.

"He's okay," Merit said quickly, pulling him to her. She suddenly wanted nothing more than her youngest son on her lap. She wanted to feel the weight of him and hear his breath and smell his little-boy scent. He bounced onto her stomach and slammed his head into her shoulder for a hug.

Sierra tugged at his arm. "Come on, little man. It's time to get Jude. Let your mommy rest."

Nash didn't move. He pressed his head harder into Merit's shoulder, tightened his finger grip on her arms. She felt his sticky cheek on her neck. It was hard to imagine that he'd been the size of a cherry once, that there was a time when his existence hadn't been guaranteed. He could've ended up in the San Francisco sewer system instead of here, in her arms, rubbing snot on her neck. She held him tighter.

"He can stay," Merit said. "We can watch something on TV."

Sierra seemed unsure of the wisdom of this. Merit couldn't tell if it was the thought of leaving a woman recovering from a miscarriage alone with a rambunctious toddler or the prospect of midday television.

"We'll be fine," Merit assured her. "It'll be nice, having him with me."

"I'm so sorry this happened," Sierra said awkwardly. Merit had never seen her so out of her depth. They clearly hadn't covered miscarriage etiquette in any of the child and family studies classes she was always talking about.

"Me, too," Merit said.

Nash, sensing that he was being allowed to stay, loosened his grip on Merit's arm and sat back on her lap. "Mommy," he said, putting his palm on her face.

"Nashy," she replied, kissing the inside of his elbow. He giggled with delight.

Sierra paused at the door. "Will you text me if you need anything?"

"Please don't worry," Merit said. "We'll be fine."

Sierra nodded, then left. Merit worried she'd been too curt.

"Mommy," Nash repeated when they were alone.

"Nashy," she said again, tickling his belly. As he laughed and laughed, her heart stung with longing. For the baby that would never be. For the baby Nash had once been.

Her eyes filled with tears as she held him. She loved being a mother, more than she'd ever expected to, but she couldn't pretend she'd been a great one in recent months. Mornings were a frantic fire drill, evenings were a grind, and weekends were a blur of activities she regretted paying for and birthday parties she didn't want to attend, all of which she did by herself while Cory worked. She tried to enjoy it. She told herself to stay present. She was the opposite of present. Most days, the only way she got through it was to think about something else.

"Mommy's sick," Nash said, frowning. His slick dark hair was falling in his eyes. She swept it off his face. He looked so much like Cory.

"Nah, Mommy's okay," Merit told him. She had no idea if this was true.

She heard Cory on the stairs.

"Hey, Nacho." Nash looked elated to see him, then confused. What was his dad doing home in the middle of the day? "Where's Sierra?" Cory asked.

"Went to get Jude," Merit said.

"Can I hang out with you guys?" The question was directed at Merit. She nodded and reached for the remote. She couldn't remember the last time she and Cory had watched TV together. She wasn't sure they'd ever done it in the middle of the afternoon.

She expected him to take the chair in the corner, but he sat next to her on the couch and lifted Nash into his lap. "What're we watching?" he whispered to Nash.

"Mickey Mouse," Nash whispered back.

Merit put the show on and leaned against Cory. All the ambivalence she'd felt earlier seeped away. He'd come home. He was there. He'd shown up.

"Would you be up for going to church on Sunday?" she heard herself ask. "I could find one that isn't awful, I think."

She felt his surprise. She also felt his effort not to show it. "Sure," was all he said.

Nash giggled as Mickey came on-screen. Merit saw Cory hold him a little bit tighter. She didn't let herself cry. They were lucky, all things considered. They hadn't lost this.

nine

S HE WAS DOING hip thrusts on the floor in their bedroom when Cory came out of the bathroom in a towel. He looked down at her with one eyebrow raised.

"You just got back from Pilates," he said.

"Yeah?" Merit didn't stop thrusting. "So?"

"You've worked out four times this week." It was Thursday morning.

"What's your point?"

"I'm just trying to understand what's going on with you. All the working out."

"'All the working out,'" Merit repeated. "You mean the single hour of low-impact exercise I do each day? This coming from the man who rides his bike at five A.M. and lifts weights during lunch?"

Cory sighed and sat down on the bed. "I don't want to be the guy who doesn't get it," he said wearily.

Merit dropped her butt to the floor. "Who doesn't get what?"

"You went through something really traumatic six months ago. And now you're exercising every day like a fiend."

She didn't point out that it hadn't even been five months. The miscarriage was in late January. It was early June.

"Okay," she said instead. "And? If Pilates and butt-lifts are the way I'm coping, is that really so bad?"

"It feels like you decided for both of us that we aren't having another baby," Cory said carefully. "And that you're trying to convince yourself that it's the right decision by doing all the stuff you couldn't do if you were pregnant right now."

She was shocked that he had gotten it so completely right.

"We never wanted a third kid, Cory." She hated how defensive she sounded. "Yes, we got on board with the idea, but neither of us wanted it when it happened."

"I know that, Mer. But that doesn't mean it wasn't the right thing."

"No, the fact that a bloody embryo came out of my vagina meant it wasn't the right thing." She regretted it as soon as she said it. "Sorry," she said, and sighed.

"I'm not saying I definitely want a third," Cory said. He was being careful again. "But I'd like to at least talk about it."

"Okay, so let's talk about it." Merit sat up and crossed her legs. "I don't want another baby."

"Why not?"

"Because I'm happy with two. Because I have a demanding career that I really enjoy and when I'm not working, I'm single parenting while you work. Because I don't want to buy a house right now. Because I'm turning forty next year and don't want to go back to sleepless nights and breastfeeding and flabby abs."

"Your abs were never flabby," Cory said.

"That only proves you weren't paying attention."

"Wouldn't it be fun to have a little girl?"

"Sure. But that's not a reason to have another child. Look at our lives, Cory. We're at capacity as it is."

Cory rubbed his forehead.

(Was she giving him a headache? She was kind of giving herself one.)

"Are you unhappy, Mer?" he asked then.

"No. Do I seem unhappy?"

"Sometimes," he admitted. "Lately. Maybe 'unhappy' is the wrong word. Distracted, I guess."

"I *am* distracted," she said tersely, and got to her feet. "I have six projects in the middle of construction, eight in the drawing stage, two in appeals with the planning commission, and three pitches next week. On top of that, I've got a two-year-old who refuses to potty train and a first grader who has four cavities that I have to figure out how to get filled because his fucking dentist requires that a parent bring him to the appointment and they close at six."

"Got it," Cory said flatly. "No third kid."

"Honestly?" She knew he hated when she started sentences that way. It was a habit she'd picked up from Jane. "It baffles me that you want another one. You spend so little time with the two we already have."

"That's not fair."

"How is it not fair? It's true."

"I don't bust your balls because *you* work."

"Okay, first of all, please don't use the phrase 'bust your balls' unless we've somehow been transported to a locker room in the late nineties."

Cory laughed out loud at this, which instantly lightened the mood the way his laughter always did. Merit smiled a little.

"Second," she went on, "I spend my entire weekend, *every weekend*, with our kids. You're with us maybe three hours on Sunday mornings. And I do bedtimes every night."

"You *like* doing bedtimes," Cory pointed out.

On their dresser, Merit's phone buzzed with a new text. It was almost eight. The text would definitely be from Jane, moaning about how poorly she'd slept. Ever since her breast cancer scare in January, Jane had been obsessed with high-quality sleep. Merit had been in Jane's office when she got the call from the doctor that the lump was benign, the Monday after the miscarriage. Jane had wept, unself-consciously, with relief.

"Nobody likes doing bedtimes," Merit said. "It's a lie moms tell themselves so they don't divorce their husbands for not helping." She was preoccupied now with checking the text.

From the kitchen, Jude yelled for more milk.

"Well, I think a third kid could be great," Cory said, and stood up. "For what it's worth."

"I'm sorry, did you not participate in the conversation we just had?"

He smiled and kissed her. He tasted like Listerine.

"You sure you don't want to try for that baby *right now*?" he asked, grinning as he unwrapped the towel from his waist.

He was kidding, but Merit felt a swift kick of guilt. She hadn't told him she'd already gotten the IUD. It hadn't felt like something she'd needed to discuss with him, which now seemed rather challenging to explain. She'd talked about it at length with Jane, whom she'd forced to watch videos of insertions to ascertain by the patients' reactions how badly it would hurt (not so badly, it turned out).

Jude yelled again for more milk. This time Nash chimed in with an indecipherable squeal.

Merit and Cory looked at each other.

"I need to get in the shower," Merit said.

"We could *both* get in the shower," Cory said. "They won't find us there. And I could make it *very* fast."

Merit hesitated. She had no desire for a quickie in the shower right then, not with their sons shouting like drunk frat boys from the kitchen. But she also didn't want to turn him down. They'd only had sex once since the miscarriage, on her thirty-ninth birthday in May, and it hadn't been great. So not great that Merit had called her doctor about it, who'd told her it was probably hormonal and recommended a lube that Merit hadn't bought.

"MOMMY!"

"To be continued," she said to Cory, kissing him quickly before stepping past him to go downstairs. She was at the door before she remembered her phone, the unanswered text. Cory was standing between the door and their dresser with his semi-erection and his semi-bruised ego. Jane would have to wait.

Merit refilled the boys' cereal bowls then dashed back up to her bedroom to shower. Cory was fully dressed by then. "Want me to take Jude?" he offered.

"Really?" It was wildly out of his way.

"Sure," he said. He bent over to lace up his sneakers. She wasn't even annoyed that he was wearing them upstairs.

"Thanks," she said, wishing now that she'd been up for that quickie before. "Love you," she added.

"Love you, too," he said, and walked out.

So elated was she by the prospect of showering for longer than five minutes that she almost forgot to check her phone.

Almost.

The text was, in fact, from Jane.

JANE: can u meet for coffee before work?

Merit frowned. This was unusual. Something was up.

THEY AGREED TO meet at their regular spot, around the corner from the office. When Merit came in, Jane was seated at their usual table, with a spread of pastries and two lattes in ceramic mugs. She looked especially chic in a white silk blazer with big gold buttons and bright feather earrings. Merit felt her shoulders relax. Whatever the news, it couldn't be terrible if Jane had blow-dried her hair.

"Sorry I'm late," Merit said, shrugging out of her jacket. "It's freezing out."

"It's sixty-two degrees."

"It's June."

"In San Francisco."

Merit gave her a look. "Yes. And it's fucking cold."

"You're feisty this morning." Jane sipped her latte with inscrutable calm. "Why does your hair look so good?"

"You say that every time I wash it."

"Maybe you should wash it more?"

"It's still adjusting to my new workout schedule," Merit protested. "You're the one who told me this would be a thing, and that I had to wait it out. You said I shouldn't wash it more than twice a week!"

"And now I'm saying maybe I underestimated the dedication of your oil glands, and perhaps we should reassess."

"I hate you," Merit muttered.

"You love me. Here, have some scone." Jane slid the plate across the table.

"I can't be distracted," Merit said, ignoring the scone. "Why are we here?"

"There have been some developments," Jane said cryptically. "One affects me, and the other affects both of us. Which do you want first?"

"Your thing," Merit said, now panicked that the lump in her breast hadn't actually been benign and she was about to receive some sort of morbid invitation to her wake.

"Edward is leaving me."

Merit blinked. The sentence literally did not compute. "Wait. What?"

"Turns out he wasn't having an affair with a slutty waitress. He's been fucking his chef."

"The one from Argentina?"

"Her name is Valentina. She's sixty-one and quite lovely. And apparently my husband wants to marry her."

"Jane."

"It's fine."

"It's not fine. It's awful."

"Because she's older than I am," Jane said.

"No."

"Because if it's not just sex, then it's actually about me."

"It's not about you," Merit said firmly.

"It kind of is," Jane said. "If she were younger, or dumber, or had bigger tits, I could blame it on his bruised male ego. But this isn't him acting out. This is my husband falling in love with a woman I actually respect." Jane sipped her coffee calmly. She could've been talking about the weather or work. "I misread it. It's just annoying that I can't be angry with him anymore."

"Um. Why can't you?"

"Because he's so obviously happy with her. How can I begrudge him that?"

"He's your *husband*, Jane. He's not supposed to be in love with another woman."

"I don't think he did it on purpose," Jane said. "You love who you love. And, anyway, I think it'll be good for me overall. The timing's good, and there won't be any of the unpleasantness of a nasty divorce." She popped a piece of scone into her mouth. "You ready for the second thing?"

"I don't know," Merit said uncertainly. Jane's positivity was freaking her out. "Am I?"

"Yes." Jane leaned across the table on her elbows and lowered her voice. "Lars is selling his half of the company. To a boutique in New York that wants to expand to the West Coast. It's been in the works for a while, but the deal finally closed last night."

It took a second for this to register. Lars and Erik were parting ways. Jager + Brandt would no longer exist. Was Jane telling her she was out of a job?

"I wanted to tell you months ago," Jane was saying, "but I knew it'd put you in a moral quandary because you'd feel obligated to tell Erik. And also Lars made me sign an NDA, which I would've broken for you, but I thought you might judge me for it."

"So this is what the super-secret New York trip was about."

Jane nodded. "Are you mad at me for not telling you?"

"No." She was. "So what happens now?"

"Up to you. I know Lars wants to bring you with him. Or you could go somewhere else."

Merit felt her stomach contract. "What about you?"

"Confidentially?"

It was an insulting question. Merit didn't answer it.

"You slept with him," she said instead. She realized when she said it that she'd wanted to say it for months.

Jane's smile faded. "I hope that's a joke."

Merit just looked at her. "Did you?"

"How can you even ask me that?"

"The two of you have history, and he's always been obsessed with you. Some women find him appealing."

"Not me," Jane said firmly.

"But he tried," Merit insisted. "In New York."

"I really hate to ruin this story in your head. But no, little bird, Lars did not proposition me on our work trip. Putting aside that he's my boss and would probably sleep with a cadaver, I'm flattered that you think he would."

"Of course the man wants to sleep with you," Merit said irritably. "You're beautiful and talented and occasionally funny."

"I am frequently funny. And you're very sweet to call me beautiful but you're approaching forty and maybe should get your eyes checked." Jane smiled. "Talented, I'll accept. But truly, what is your obsession with me and Lars?"

"I don't know," Merit admitted. "I always assumed there was something I didn't know."

"Why?"

"Because you keep things from me that have to do with him?"

"That's not fair," Jane said. "This was the only time and it was a very particular situation." She hesitated. "Though now I'm realizing this is a very unfortunate segue to my other piece of news."

"You're starting your own firm," Merit said flatly. It was the only thing that made sense.

Jane nodded. "With the cash I'll have after Edward uses his girlfriend's money to buy me out of their restaurant love nest. It's part of why I can't be too upset about the dissolution of my marriage. It's perfect timing, career-wise. Assuming Lars doesn't murder me in my sleep." She was trying to make light of it. It was falling kind of flat.

"That's great," Merit said. She wanted to cry.

"Obviously you'll be my first hire," Jane said quickly. "But there's a non-compete clause in my contract that Lars will absolutely enforce as soon as he finds out I'm not going with him. Plus, I can't afford you yet."

Merit nodded. There was no way she could speak without choking unattractively on a sob.

"You and I will see each other all the time," Jane said, reaching for Merit's hands. "And it'll be better, because now you can tell me to go fuck myself anytime you want."

Jane smiled her classic Jane smile, and Merit's tears spilled over her bottom lids.

"It's hormones," Merit said stupidly, her excuse for everything these days. For one irrational moment, she wished she were pregnant again, if only to have something that didn't depend on Jane.

Jane slid her chair over so it was touching Merit's and pulled her into a hug. It was surprising and intimate and it only made Merit cry harder. "You're not getting rid of me, bitch," Jane said hoarsely in Merit's ear. "I'm still your person. And we'll be working together again in no time, so enjoy the break while you can."

"I don't even know why I'm crying," Merit managed. She wanted to bury her face in the curve of Jane's neck and breathe her in.

"You're crying because I'm awesome and not seeing me every day sounds like a punishment you don't deserve," Jane said.

She wasn't wrong. Merit laughed against her shoulder. She could smell Jane's perfume.

"Are you getting snot on my chic silk blazer?" Jane demanded.

"Maybe."

"Good thing you're my favorite," Jane said, giving her a squeeze.

Merit squeezed back. "Good thing."

MERIT LEFT WORK early that afternoon, making an excuse to Jane about having to pick up Jude early from school. She'd been out of sorts all day. It wasn't the prospect of having to look for a new job that worried her; it was her suspicion that she wouldn't *want* whatever new job she ended up with if it wasn't working for Jane. The idea of going to an office every day and not seeing her literally made Merit's stomach cramp. And that was deeply unsettling, because it meant that embedded within the very convincing narrative she'd constructed in her head—the one that said she was in a really good place right now because of her very fulfilling career— was an unexamined assumption that her career would continue to revolve around Jane.

(She'd never had a therapist, but she suspected a therapist would have a fucking field day with this.)

Cory, predictably, took the practical view when she called him. "Why not go with Lars?" he asked. "If Jane's leaving, he'll need you even more. Tell him you want a promotion and a raise. That's better than being unemployed."

It wasn't like Merit hadn't thought of that. "He's not a good person," she said irritably.

"Don't miss out on a good career opportunity for emotional reasons, Mer."

Merit wanted to hurl her phone at the sidewalk.

"My thinking that he's a self-absorbed asshole is not *emotional*," she said calmly. "It's factual. And, by the way, it's not actually a good career opportunity. Without Jane, he'll fail."

"What does she think you should do?" Cory asked.

"Whatever I want," Merit said sourly.

"Well. It's not like you have to decide anything right this second," Cory said. But she already had. She'd made up her mind before she called him. She wouldn't work for Lars. She'd find a new job. And she'd hate that new job because it wouldn't involve Jane.

"Do you think I idolize her?" Merit heard herself ask.

Cory was quiet on the other end of the line. She wanted to take the question back.

"You can be honest," she added, even though Cory was never anything but.

"Nah," he said finally. "I think you think she's really good at what she does."

"She is."

"And I think you see parts of yourself in her."

This wasn't what Merit expected him to say. "What do you mean?"

"She's ambitious and talented, like you always were. And I think before you went back to work, you'd forgotten those parts of yourself."

She knew he meant it as a compliment. It didn't feel like one.

"Which is why I'm suggesting you at least consider asking for a bigger job at Lars's new firm," Cory went on. "You're up for the challenge, Mer. You always were."

"Am I? Maybe I should just retire and have a third kid," she said lightly.

Cory laughed a little. "For the record, if having a third requires you to stay home, then I'm happy with two."

Merit managed to match Cory's laugh. "Noted," she said.

The tears didn't come until after they'd hung up.

She cried all the way to St. Francis, the quirky little church she'd found after the miscarriage. The old redbrick Gothic in the Castro with its rainbow flag and its gender-neutral language was nothing like the church she'd grown up in and everything she'd been hoping to find. It had taken her until Easter to finally get there, but she hadn't missed a Sunday since. She didn't know what her lapsed-Catholic husband thought of his wife's newfound interest in progressive Protestantism. She hadn't asked.

The small sanctuary was empty when she walked in. It smelled like it always did, of cedar and old library books and grace. Merit sat in the back pew and let herself cry into her palms. She couldn't have said what she was so upset about. It had something to do with Cory. It had everything to do with Jane.

Her phone was next to her on the wooden pew. She felt it when the text came through.

> JANE: i know ur with Jude but if u have a sec
>
> i need ur tech support

Merit called her.

"Hey," she said when Jane picked up. "I'm not with Jude. I lied when I said I was getting him. What's up?"

"Wait—what?"

"He's still at school. I left because I was sad about you leaving. And then Cory made me even more sad. So now I'm sobbing in a church pew by myself."

"Seriously?"

Merit wiped her nose on her sleeve so Jane wouldn't hear her sniff. "Regrettably, yes."

"Little bird."

"It's fine. You caught me off guard is all. And my husband has a knack for making me feel like shit. But I'm available for tech support, just tell me what you need."

"Do they let heathens into this church of yours?"

She thought about telling Jane not to come. But pretending she was fine suddenly felt like too much work.

"They do," she said.

"Text me the address. I'm on my way."

Twenty minutes later, Merit heard the heavy door open behind her, and then Jane's presence filled the room. The sound of her heels on the stone floor. The snap of her gum. Then, the flurry of familiar smells. The musky sandalwood of her perfume. The lavender hand lotion she kept in her bag and had no doubt just reapplied. Her cinnamon gum. Merit could even smell her lipstick, the only makeup Jane consistently wore, Yves Saint Laurent Le Nu.

Merit closed her eyes and breathed her in. She remembered how the phone in her parents' house always smelled like drugstore lipstick and Chanel No. 5, and how as a child she would sometimes pick up the receiver just to breathe her mother in.

"I haven't been struck dead yet," Jane said as she slid into the pew next to her. "Maybe God likes me better than I thought." She turned her head and looked at Merit. "So what are we doing here?"

"We're not sure."

"Okay. What happened with Cory?"

"Nothing."

"Merit."

"It's too demoralizing to talk about."

"Does it involve his sleeping with a sixty-one-year-old chef?"

Merit, indelicately, laughed. "I'm sorry," she said immediately, bringing her hand to her mouth.

But Jane was laughing, too. Soon they were shaking with it, clutching their sides, unable to breathe. Merit couldn't remember the last time she'd laughed like this. It reminded her of helium, or a lantern, or warm rain.

"It's all going to be okay, you know," Jane said when they'd recovered. She took Merit's hand and held it in her lap. "We'll see each other all the time. And you and Cory will figure it out."

Merit studied their hands. Jane's French manicure. Her own bare nails. The gold watch Jane never took off. Merit's wedding ring.

"When did you become such an optimist?" she heard herself ask.

Jane laid her head on Merit's shoulder. "When I met you."

t e n

MERIT HANDED IN her notice on a Friday afternoon in late September. Erik thanked her for staying as long as she had; Jane had been gone since early August. By then, Lars and his "team"—if two junior architects and a mid-level designer could properly be called a "team"—had moved to their new offices in Oakland. Tony was staying on as Erik's assistant at what was left of J + B, newly branded as Brandt & Associates, though after Merit's departure there wouldn't be any "associates" left. Merit had been hired as a senior architect at a big firm downtown. The pay was decent. The offices were nice. Her new boss wasn't Jane.

Merit was looking forward to the change, if only because she figured it would be less weird not seeing Jane every day if she were in a new place. She missed her friend madly. There were moments when the absence physically pained her, like hunger, or homesickness, or a phantom limb. She found herself using Jane's phrases. She dreamed about her more nights than not.

It was withdrawal, she'd decided, and only natural, after nearly two years of spending five days a week together and then abruptly being cut off. They were still texting all the time, but they'd only seen each other twice since Jane's last day, both times for lunch, and both times their conversations were disturbingly organized and linear, about one thing and then the next, instead of nineteen separate threads all going at once. Both times when the waiter brought their check, they neatly wrapped everything up.

(Would they ever be normal again?)

Merit decided alcohol would help. Five minutes after she gave notice, she texted Jane and asked if she wanted to meet for a drink.

> JANE: even better, come see my house and i'll
> make u a gin fizz!!!!

Jane had recently become obsessed with making the perfect gin fizz, and with her new home office ten feet from the mid-century armoire she'd turned into a liquor cabinet, she had plenty of time to practice. She claimed that working by herself was both luxurious and lonely, and that she stayed in gym clothes most days. Merit tried not to hate her for her super rough life.

When Merit arrived at her front door that afternoon, Jane was in cashmere sweats and fuzzy slippers, her blond hair pulled up into a ponytail. She looked like a teenager ready for a sleepover, which Merit told her immediately.

"I am always ready for a sleepover," Jane said, leading the way through her newly renovated dining room to the kitchen. "And I have a very comfortable guest room if your husband will let you stay."

Merit followed slowly, taking everything in. She'd helped a little with the architectural plans, but this was the first time she'd been inside. The finishes were all so quintessentially Jane, from the vintage tufted chairs, to the art on the walls, to the blown-glass chandelier over the dining table. It was the opposite of a condo in the Marina. Or a loft in the Mission, for that matter. This was a grown-up's house. A wealthy, stylish grown-up, without a husband or kids.

"It's perfect," Merit said.

"It's getting there," Jane said.

"Happy birthday, by the way." Merit pulled a bottle of champagne from her bag. Jane had turned fifty-nine the previous week.

"Thank you for remembering, little bird," Jane said, taking the bottle. "The countdown to sixty begins." She made a face.

"If I hadn't seen your driver's license, I wouldn't believe you."

"You lie, but I love you for it."

Merit followed her into the kitchen. There were light pink dahlias on the island and a massive cutting board stacked with charcuterie next to an unopened bottle of gin.

"Wow," Merit said of the spread. "Look at this."

Jane popped a piece of prosciutto into her mouth. "I don't have a stove yet, so I'm living on olives and cured meats. It's pretty spectacular."

While Jane made the drinks, Merit stood in front of the massive kitchen windows, looking out at the sun-drenched bay. There was a deck off the kitchen, with a small stone firepit and two wooden Adirondack chairs with fuzzy blankets draped over the arms.

"Can we sit outside?" Merit asked.

"Sure. You'll be cold, though. I'll run upstairs to get you some sweats as soon as I'm done." She was hand-whipping an egg white with intense concentration. "I like to pre-beat the egg," she explained. "Makes it even more frothy."

"Don't be silly, I'm fine," Merit said. "There are blankets out there anyway."

"Please, put on sweats. Your stylishly shredded jeans are making me feel aged and inferior." She spooned the egg into a metal tumbler and gave the whole thing an aggressive shake.

"This drink seems very serious," Merit noted.

"The key is Lisbon lemons," Jane said, pouring the concoction into two highball glasses. No surprise she had exactly the right vessel for her perfect drink. "And good ice, obviously. I bought a special mold just for these."

"Of course you did," Merit said, smiling as she watched Jane expertly cut two curly twists from the leftover lemon rind on the counter, aware that there was nothing in the world she would rather be doing than exactly this.

Jane dropped a twist in each glass and handed one to Merit. "To us," she said.

"To us," Merit said, and took a long sip. As soon as the gin hit her tongue she remembered she hadn't eaten lunch.

"You know, technically with the egg white it's called a Silver Fizz," Jane said between sips. "I've done it with a whole egg, which is a Royal Fizz, but I don't like it as much."

"If architecture doesn't work out, might I suggest you open a cocktail bar?"

"Only if you'll do it with me," Jane said. "Lemme get you those sweats." She took her drink with her and headed down the hall. "Come on," she called. Merit followed her up the black-and-white-tiled stairs.

Jane disappeared into her walk-in closet as Merit stepped inside the bedroom. It was a cocoon of white. White sheets, white walls, white upholstered bed frame with gold studs on the ends. It wasn't particularly tidy—there was a lacy blue bra on the floor and an array of hair products on the vanity and the bed wasn't made—but it smelled of lavender and was invitingly calm. Merit set her glass on the nightstand and plopped down on the bed. She could smell Jane's perfume on the pillowcase.

"Don't pass out on me already," Jane said, emerging from the closet with a hooded sweatshirt and a pair of gray joggers. "I have a three-drink minimum."

"I envy your house," Merit moaned without moving. "I love my children deeply but if they didn't exist I could have upholstered dining chairs and a bedroom like this."

"Yes, but instead you have younger humans to take care of you when you're old and senile," Jane said. She tossed the sweats onto the bed.

"So do you," Merit said, and sat up. "Me."

The late afternoon sun coming through the window fell across Jane's right cheekbone as she tossed her hair and smiled. "I'm gonna hold you to that, bitch."

"Don't move," Merit said suddenly.

"Uh . . . what?"

"The light, on your face right now. It's incredible. Like butter almost. I want to paint it."

"Like, right now?"

Merit was already on her feet. "No, I'm much too interested in getting drunk and watching the sunset to do it now, but if I take a picture I can do it later. Hold on, lemme get my phone."

"You're not taking a picture of me!" Jane protested.

"Shut up. And don't move. I'll be right back."

Merit dashed down the stairs for her phone, surprised at how intense this urge felt. She hadn't picked up a brush in almost three years. Part of her had wondered if maybe she'd never make art again. But now suddenly she wanted nothing more than to capture Jane's sunlit profile with paint.

"Do I have to see this masterpiece when you're done with it?" Jane asked as Merit took photos of her from every angle. The images didn't capture how pretty she looked, or how young, or how the sun danced on the sharp curve of her cheekbones, lighting up her whole face. Merit wanted to reach over and pull her hair down from the ponytail, but she didn't need to. She'd spent enough time looking at it—and evaluating every new haircut to assess whether it was too short—to paint her blond strands from memory. Jane's eyes would be the tricky part. They were such a particular shade of blue.

"Not if you don't want to," Merit replied. "I mean, I'll be completely offended, but if you can live with that . . ."

"What if you're a horrible painter?" Jane demanded. "Or, worse, what if you're a fantastic painter and I still look like a hideous old beast?"

"But you've seen some of my paintings," Merit said. "Haven't you?"

Jane shook her head.

"How is that possible?" Merit was already typing in the address for the website she created back when she thought she was going to have an art career. It occurred to her now that she should probably stop paying for the domain name. "Here"—she held out her phone—"these are the pieces I did for my failed show."

"I can't," Jane said, putting her hands over her eyes. "It'll make me feel too awkward."

"Looking at my artwork will make you feel *awkward*?"

"Extraordinarily. It's like listening to someone's poetry. It's too much."

"Only if the poetry is bad!"

"No," Jane said. "Even good poetry is hard to listen to. Maybe even harder, actually."

"Honestly, you are a bizarre human being," Merit said. The light was fading now. The sun would set soon. "But I'm willing to pretend you haven't implied that I suck at painting if you make me another drink."

THEY SAT ON the deck in sweats and puffy coats and drank their way through the sunset. At some point Jane lit the firepit and they switched from gin to white wine. Merit felt like she was on vacation. She didn't want to go home.

"How are things with you and Cory?" Jane asked at some point.

"Fine," Merit said. "I think he's relieved I found another job."

Jane rolled her eyes. "Like you were ever *not* going to find another job."

"My husband might be less convinced of my awesomeness than you are?"

"Then he's dumber than he looks."

Merit laughed. "I love you."

"I love you, too. But seriously. The man has to know he hit the jackpot with you. You're kind, you're smart, you're beautiful . . . and I'm sure you're fucking fantastic in bed."

"Obvs. Anyway." Merit took a long sip of her wine. She was already buzzed from the gin. "How's life without a husband?"

"Honestly? A little lonely," Jane admitted.

"Well. Life *with* a husband is pretty lonely," Merit said, and emptied her glass. "Maybe we should've married women instead."

(Later she would wonder what prompted her to say it. She would never be sure.)

Jane reached for the bottle to refill Merit's glass. "Does that mean you've been with one?"

It was a totally natural question. Maybe even an obvious one. But something about the way Jane asked it made Merit's cheeks flush. "No," she said awkwardly, and nearly knocked over her glass. "Have you?"

Jane, uncharacteristically, looked away, and Merit knew.

"Really? When? Who?"

"I'm not telling you. You'll be weird about it."

"I won't. Tell me."

"It was a long time ago," Jane said.

"Tell me."

Jane hesitated.

"Jane."

"The first one was right after I broke up with my hunky American," she said finally. "When I was twenty-nine."

"The *first* one? How many were there?" It was suddenly difficult for Merit to take a full breath.

"You said you wouldn't be weird about it!"

"I'm not! I'm just—processing. You've slept with multiple women and I've only ever slept with two guys."

Now Jane looked shocked. "Really?"

"I met Cory in college!"

"Okay, fair. So who was the other one?"

Merit hesitated. She hadn't thought about Felix in years. Cory knew about him, but she usually left him out when talking about her past. It was easier to let people think she'd lost her virginity to the man who became her husband than to try to explain why a girl with a purity ring had sex for the first time with a guy she wasn't even dating and, honestly, didn't even like all that much. She'd slept with Felix simply because she'd drunkenly proclaimed to her roommate one night at a house party that she was going to, despite the fact that she'd only hooked up with him once, and awkwardly, in the storage closet of the crew team's boathouse, and in theory wanted to wait until she was married to go all the way. But for some reason that night, emboldened by vodka and boredom and on an indefinite hiatus from church, her twenty-one-year-old self looked across the room at Felix Durant and his floppy blond hair and declared that she would sleep with him, and in her mind, there was no walking that back. She didn't want to be the sort of person who didn't follow through.

"You whore," Jane said when Merit finished telling the story.

"Don't mock me! It felt very scandalous at the time."

"I'm sure it did, little bird. Was the sex good at least?"

"If awkward humping in a dorm bed is your thing, then, yes, it was incredible."

"Hm," Jane said.

"What?"

"Have you ever had incredible sex?"

"Of course," Merit said quickly. Did she sound defensive? She felt defensive. "With Cory."

"Once a month."

"Now you're being mean."

"I'm not! I'm sincerely asking."

"We have great sex," Merit said. "Obviously I don't have a lot to compare it to, but I enjoy it. A lot."

"And you get off."

"Yes."

"Good."

"Why are you so interested in my orgasms?"

"Because I just learned that you've only had sex with two men in your life, and I suddenly got very concerned that you've been deprived sexually."

"I haven't been deprived sexually. My husband is very attentive."

"If you say so."

"Is lesbian sex so much better?"

"I'm not a lesbian."

"And yet, between the two of us, you're the only one who's had a woman's tongue on her clit."

"Don't be crass."

"Are you honestly not going to give me any details?"

"What do you want to know?"

"Everything! How it happened, what it was like."

"You promise you won't be weird?"

"Why would I be weird?" Merit asked.

It was a great question. She had no reason to be. Her college roommate, Cat, was a lesbian. There was very little about having sex with women Merit hadn't dissected in extreme detail already, sometimes with Cat's very anatomically correct visual aids. And she lived in San Francisco for fuck's sake! She'd been to gay bars and marched in Pride parades and had once been propositioned in a bathroom by a very beautiful woman with a shaved head. So why did she feel so completely rattled by the idea of Jane hooking up with girls? The fact that she was so shocked made her feel silly and sheltered and, worst of all, like she didn't know Jane as well as she thought.

Jane seemed to be considering how much she wanted to say.

"Now you're the one being weird," Merit pointed out.

"I feel weird," Jane admitted.

"Why?"

"I don't know. Because it's you."

"Well, get over it," Merit said, and got to her feet. "Where can I find another bottle of wine?"

"Fridge," Jane said.

Merit definitely didn't need any more wine, but she suddenly felt compelled to get ridiculously drunk.

She returned to the porch with a bottle of sauvignon blanc and a block of Gouda she'd found in the cheese drawer. Jane had her knees pulled up to her chest and was looking out at the lights across the bay. "I miss you," Merit heard herself say.

Jane laid her cheek on one knee. "I'm right here, birdie."

"You know what I mean."

Jane nodded a little. "I do."

Merit refilled both their glasses.

"Just so you know, I'm not gay," Jane said.

"It wouldn't matter if you were," Merit told her.

"But I'm not," Jane insisted. "That was the whole thing. There were only two, and with both of them, I never . . . *reciprocated*."

"So, what, you just laid there and let them go down on you?"

Jane smirked. "They weren't complaining."

Merit felt herself flush again. "I'm sure they weren't." She sipped her wine and tried to seem nonchalant. "So what were they like?"

"The first one was ten years older than I was. An ancient thirty-nine." Jane laughed a little. "We met at a rave in SoMa, back when SoMa was a place where you could reliably find a good rave."

"I've never been to a rave," Merit said.

"Of course you haven't."

"You think I'm very unworldly, don't you?"

"You're from Florida," Jane said. "It's not your fault."

"I've done my share of partying!"

"I'm sure you have."

"Stop patronizing me and finish your story," Merit said. "I want to hear about this crone who hit on you."

"Heather," Jane said. "She came up to me while I was dancing and asked me if I was single. I told her I wasn't gay and she laughed."

"Because it didn't matter or because she didn't believe you?"

"Unclear. Probably both."

"Did you ever see her again?"

Jane hesitated. "We dated for a couple months, actually. I didn't want anyone to know, so we only ever went out with her friends."

Merit was expecting a drunken hookup or a one-time experiment. But this was an actual relationship, with a woman. She couldn't help but imagine it; some woman's hands on Jane's body, Jane's hands in some woman's hair.

"What are you thinking right now?" Jane demanded.

"I'm not thinking anything," Merit lied. "Were you in love with her?"

"God, no," Jane said. "But she was beautiful and smart and she seemed very certain that we should be together, and she wasn't the kind of person it was easy to argue with."

This made Merit laugh.

"What?"

"Just the idea of you agreeing to be in a relationship with someone because you didn't want to argue about it."

"I was very agreeable in my twenties," Jane said.

"Apparently," Merit said. "So who was the other one?"

"Pia," Jane said. "We met right after Fred died. So I must've been thirty-six? She'd inherited a ridiculous piece of property in Mexico and hired me to design the house. It's spectacular—probably my favorite thing I've ever done."

"How long were you together?"

"Six months, maybe? On and off. It wasn't great. We fought a lot."

"Why?"

Jane hesitated. "I was in a bad place," she said finally. "Fred was the only family I had left, and suddenly he was gone, and I had no idea how to deal with it." She took a long sip of her wine. "Turns out Valium doesn't mix so well with tequila and coke. Unless what you're going for is volatile bitch." She smiled a little. "Plus I wasn't a lesbian."

Merit gave her a weary look.

"I know how it sounds," Jane said. "But it was a real issue for me."

"Why?"

Jane considered it. "I don't know, honestly. Probably something to do with Fred. Like I'd be taking his thing." She shrugged a little and looked down at her glass. Merit couldn't see her eyes in the dark. "Anyway, it was twenty years ago. Water under the bridge now." Merit could tell she didn't want to talk about it anymore.

"So tell me about this spectacular house," Merit said.

Jane brightened. "You'd love it. I did the whole thing without any corners, which was harder to pull off than it sounds. And we put in an infinity pool that's literally perched on the side of a cliff. It's unreal."

Merit had so many questions. None of them were about the architecture.

"We should go down there sometime," Jane said then. "Pia's offered me the house a million times."

"You're still in touch?" Merit asked casually, as if the idea of Jane keeping up with a woman she used to have sex with didn't bother her in the least. In fact, it bothered her quite a bit, but that was something she couldn't begin to explain to herself, much less to Jane.

"Yeah, we've kept up. She came to my wedding, actually." Jane smiled. "She told me it wouldn't last."

"Really? How come?"

"She never believed I was straight."

"Ha!" Merit said, much too loud.

She gulped the rest of her wine. Her mind was spinning with thoughts she didn't let herself think.

Jane pressed Merit's knee with her toe. "Hey. You okay?"

Merit bobbed her head. "I'm great."

Jane giggled. "You're so drunk."

Merit slumped down in her Adirondack. It was nice, having Jane's foot on her leg. "It's your fault," she said. "You know I need bread when I drink."

"Gimme your phone." Jane held out her arm.

"Why?"

"Because I'm calling Cory. I'm not putting you in an Uber like this. You're sleeping over."

"I can't," Merit said. "Jude has soccer in the morning, and I'm supposed to bring snacks."

"So I'll wake you up early and we'll go get some snacks. I'll even pay for them."

"I don't need your charity snacks."

"Phone."

Merit fished her phone out of her coat pocket and handed it to Jane. Cory would probably be annoyed that she wasn't coming home. But by now the boys were in bed already anyway, so why should he even care? He'd be on the couch with his laptop, watching the Giants game. If she were to walk in their front door right now, they'd talk for five minutes in the living room, then she'd go to bed, hours before he did, like she did every Friday night.

"I'll bring her home first thing," Jane was saying. "After I make her feel extremely embarrassed for getting so drunk in front of her very respectable former boss."

Merit stuck her tongue out at Jane. Jane grinned.

Jane hung up and handed Merit's phone back. "Now we can have dessert."

"It doesn't count as dessert if it doesn't have sugar."

"You really think I'm no fun at all, don't you?" Jane stood up. "Wait till you try my cake pops."

"You have cake pops?"

"Only the best cake pops ever." Jane went inside.

"From where?" Merit called after her.

"I made them!"

"You made cake pops? For what purpose?"

"To eat them?"

"I don't understand. I have only ever seen you eat carbs in a crisis, and now you're telling me you keep homemade cake pops on hand? How? You don't even have an oven."

Jane returned with two cake pops and handed one to Merit. The icing was bubblegum pink.

"I didn't bake the cake. I just made the fondant. And added the weed." Jane bit into hers.

"You're joking." Merit surveyed her pop.

"I'm not. And it's not as easy as it sounds. I had to use a flour sifter to get it super fine."

"You're a real artisan," Merit said, and then popped the whole thing into her mouth. The cake tasted distinctly of pot.

"I do love a cake pop," Jane said, finishing hers in two bites.

"Is there anything else about you that I should know?" Merit asked, scraping cake off the stick with her teeth. "I'm not sure I can handle any more surprises."

"It's not my fault you assumed I was more boring than I am."

"Not boring," Merit replied. "Just calorie-conscious and straight."

"I am straight!"

"So you'd never do it again?"

"Sleep with a woman?" Jane considered it, then shook her head. "Probably not."

"So I'm not missing out," Merit said.

"I thought you were having incredible sex," Jane said.

"I am!"

Jane smiled indulgently. "Then no, little bird, you're not missing out."

MERIT LET JANE talk her into another cake pop and Jane let Merit talk her into ordering a pizza. By the time it arrived, Merit was ravenously hungry. And indisputably stoned.

When they finished, they lapsed into a comfortable silence. Merit felt her eyelids drooping. She was falling asleep.

"Let's go inside," Jane said, reaching for Merit's hands. "Before you pass out and I have to carry you to bed." They grabbed wrists and pulled, propelling each other up. Merit tottered on her feet, giggling uncontrollably. Jane caught her by the arms. "Careful, birdie."

This made Merit giggle even more. Her body felt fizzy. She told herself it was the weed.

She managed to get inside and onto one of Jane's bar stools without toppling over, which seemed to her an impressive feat.

Jane reached out and touched Merit's nose. "Your little beak is frozen."

She smiled against Jane's palm. "I'm cold!"

"You're gonna have to toughen up before I take you to Denmark."

"When are you taking me to Denmark?"

"Whenever you can go," Jane said. "But we should go to Pia's house in Mexico first. For your fortieth maybe. In May, right? That would be fun."

Merit couldn't tell if Jane was serious. She was too stoned to process anything. She was feeling a thousand things at once and all of them were confusing.

"Why'd you marry Edward?" she heard herself say.

"Because he asked," Jane said. She kicked off her slippers and put her bare foot on the rung of Merit's stool. Merit was suddenly intensely aware of their proximity, of her open legs, of Jane's shin between her knees. She felt Jane's nearness like static on her skin. She wanted to be even closer. She wanted Jane's hands on her—

"I should go home," Merit said abruptly.

"Stop. We already decided you're staying."

"It'll be better if I go." Merit swung her leg over Jane's and nearly fell trying to stand up without touching her.

"Are you upset about something?"

"Of course not." She couldn't make eye contact with Jane. "I'll just feel better tomorrow if I wake up in my own bed, you know?" She fumbled for her phone. "How long do you think it'll take to get an Uber out here? Oh, awesome, only four minutes. Great. I'll just grab my shoes." Her heart felt like a trapped bird in her chest.

"Are you okay, LB?"

"Totally! Tonight was so fun." She sounded ridiculous, even to herself.

"You're acting very strange."

"It's been a long day." Merit still couldn't make eye contact.

"Well. I guess I'll walk you out, then."

"No, that's okay, I got it." She was already halfway to the front door. "I'll text you when I get home!"

It wasn't until she was on the Golden Gate Bridge in the back of a Prius that smelled like bathroom cleaner that she let herself wonder what the fuck had just happened. She knew what it *felt* like. For one dizzying moment, it felt like she was attracted to Jane.

She did not immediately blame it on the cake pops or the existential boredom of middle age; that would come the next morning, when her rational brain would try to make sense of this thing that made perfect sense already and in fact explained everything she'd never understood. That night she was too stunned to do anything but revere the audacity of it, this sea swell of desire that did not care about boundaries or propriety or fucking up her very orderly life.

Her phone buzzed with a text.

JANE: u ok?

Merit wrote back immediately with an exuberant yes!!!! then promptly passed out in the car.

CORY WAS IN the living room with his laptop as she'd predicted. The Giants were up 5–2.

"I thought you weren't coming home," he said when she opened the front door.

"I changed my mind." She tottered a little in her boots. She still had Jane's sweatpants on. "How were the kids?"

"Fine. So what'd you guys do?"

"We just hung out at her house," Merit said casually, bending over to unzip her boots. She lost her balance and toppled onto the floor.

"Wow," Cory said. "You guys had a fun night."

"I might be a little stoned," Merit admitted, climbing onto the couch.

"So Jane's good?" Cory asked.

"Why wouldn't she be good?"

"I wasn't implying she wasn't."

Merit didn't want to talk about Jane. "So are you still working or can you be distracted?" she asked coyly, pulling Jane's sweatshirt over her head. It smelled like Jane's perfume.

Cory closed his laptop and set it on the coffee table. "Oh, I can be distracted."

"Good," Merit said, unhooking her bra.

"The people across the street can probably see us," Cory said as he pulled her onto his lap.

"Then we'd better give them a good show," she said, pressing against him. He slid his hands down her bare back and into Jane's sweatpants. She felt like someone else.

"Want to go down on me?" she whispered. She'd never uttered these words to anyone in her life.

"Absolutely," he said immediately.

When Merit orgasmed a few minutes later, she pretended she wasn't thinking of Jane.

e l e v e n

SHE AND JANE didn't see each other for nearly two months after that. Merit made all kinds of excuses; her new job, Jude's soccer schedule, Cory's fortieth birthday party, a flu she didn't actually have.

bitch why r u avoiding me? Jane texted at some point.

lol, Merit wrote back.

It wasn't particularly artful, but Merit hadn't thought any of this through. She'd never sort of/maybe/probably been attracted to her closest female friend, the person she talked to about everything but couldn't talk to about this.

"I can't stop thinking about it," she finally confessed to her college roommate over the phone one Wednesday night when the kids were in bed and Cory was working late. It was the first live conversation she'd had with Cat in years. *Hi, I'm good, yep, I had a second child, please tell me if I'm queer now, thanks.*

"And?"

"And I have to stop!"

"Because you want to act on it," Cat said. Her voice was very matter-of-fact.

"No!"

"You sure?"

"I'm married, Cat."

"I know this. I wore a hideous orange bridesmaid's dress at your wedding."

"Um, fuck you very much, it was candlelight peach. And I've never once thought about cheating on Cory. Not even remotely." She'd once had a disturbingly graphic sex dream about the boys' pediatrician, but she blamed that on the 103-degree fever she'd had at the time.

"Are you thinking about it now?" Cat asked.

Merit's stomach turned over. "No."

Cat laughed. "Liar."

"I've never been attracted to women, Cat. Literally, not ever. You know this about me."

"It doesn't sound to me like this is about 'women.' It sounds like it's about this particular woman."

Merit knew all the things—orientation is a spectrum, desire is fluid, most people are a little bit bi—but the calmness with which Cat, a very experienced lesbian, was accepting that she might actually want to have sex with Jane was stressing her out.

(But didn't she expect this reaction? Wasn't this exactly why Cat was the person she'd called?)

"We've always had an unconventional relationship," Merit allowed.

"Maybe that should've been your first clue?"

"This is not helpful," Merit said darkly.

Cat laughed. "What do you want me to say?"

"That it was nothing. That I'm overthinking it."

"It was nothing. You're overthinking it."

"Cat. I'm serious. She's my closest friend."

"Then maybe you should both acknowledge that you're attracted to each other instead of burdening busy lesbians with your angst."

"You're not that busy," Merit said. "And for the record, she is *not* attracted to me."

"Uh-huh."

"She's not."

"Merit. Between the gin and the cheese platter—

"It was meat, not cheese."

"—whatevs. She got you drunk, fed you hookup food, made you take your pants off—"

"To put on sweats! She's Danish. Hygge is a real thing!"

"—then told you she'd slept with women, then gave you drugs? Bitch was coming on to you. Full stop."

"I'm telling you, she wasn't," Merit insisted. "She's not like that. She didn't even want to talk about the women she'd slept with. I brought it up."

"Okay. But if she were a man, you wouldn't be debating it. You just can't see it because you're straight."

"So you think I am, then," Merit said. "Straight."

Merit could hear her friend—who had talked her through every bad hookup in college and had once come with her to the health center for a pregnancy test Merit was convinced she needed even though she hadn't had sex yet—smile.

"I think you're as straight as your friend Jane is," Cat replied.

TWO DAYS LATER, she met Cory for dinner after work. They hadn't been out without the kids since Cory's fortieth in October, which was also the last time they'd had sex—if what they'd done that night even counted as sex. Cory had been so drunk that they'd essentially given up halfway through.

She didn't want to evaluate the strength of their marriage on the quality of their sex life, but what other measure did she have? Their day-to-day interactions were an exchange of facts and logistics, Nash says his belly hurts / Jude has soccer tomorrow / Can you be home by seven tonight? / There are leftovers in the fridge. Whole weeks passed without them touching. She couldn't remember the last time they'd kissed.

As she waited for Cory that night at the bar, Merit took a long sip of her drink—a gin fizz, she hadn't been able to resist—and asked herself what she wanted.

In theory, she wanted a good marriage. In theory, she wanted better communication and more quality time and emotionally connected sex that could convincingly pass as "lovemaking." In theory, she didn't want to consider cheating on her husband with her closest female friend.

"Wow, this place is packed," she heard Cory say, and jerked her head up. She felt her cheeks flush. What would her husband of fourteen years (their anniversary was next week, *shit*, she still hadn't bought him a gift) say if he knew that she'd been sitting at a bar, drinking a cocktail, and envisioning herself—or, at least, some alternate version of herself—with her tongue all over Jane?

"Do we have a reservation?" Cory asked.

Of course they had a reservation. Merit had made one the moment they decided to go to dinner, because that's what you did if you expected to eat at seven o'clock on a Friday night in San Francisco. She'd also arranged for Sierra to stay late, and ordered the pizza delivery that their sons would have eaten by now, and bought the new tube of bubblegum-flavored toothpaste to replace the empty one sitting on their bathroom sink.

Merit was tempted to look at her husband blankly and say she thought *he* made the reservation. And, oh shit, who was watching the kids? But they'd long ago passed the phase where they could joke about stuff like that. If she said anything, he'd assume she was picking a fight.

(But maybe she wanted to pick a fight?)

"Yep," she said instead, sucking down the last of her drink. Jane's gin fizz was better. Merit ignored the sharp pang of longing in her chest.

She saw Cory's jaw muscle flex. "Should I order a drink here, or do you want to sit?"

"They won't hold our table much longer," Merit replied. She hadn't intended this to be a jab at his lateness, but she could tell from Cory's face that he took it as one.

"I got here as fast as I could, babe."

"I wasn't being critical," Merit said wearily. "Just tell the hostess we're both here, okay? I'll close out."

"Great," Cory said in a tone that would have been more appropriate for "go fuck yourself." Merit tried to summon the energy to care.

She decided to get him a drink as a peace offering. As she read through the options, she held her face in an amiable expression and refused to allow herself to become aggravated by the fact that although she could easily pick from this list of nine trendy craft cocktails which one Cory would like best, he'd never be able to do the same for her. If the roles were reversed, he'd be absolutely stymied by the choices, and then he'd end up ordering her some puzzling vodka concoction even though she'd stopped drinking vodka literally a decade before.

She was determined not to let this realization irritate her, but it was, in fact, very irritating. Her husband was an engineer with a photographic memory. It was not beyond his capabilities to keep track of what his wife liked and disliked. Instead, he'd made one mental note, a dozen years before, and hadn't updated it since.

Jane, meanwhile, had kept up with her milk migration from whole to soy to almond to oat back to whole again without getting her latte wrong once.

Stop. Comparing him. To Jane.

As she made her way toward their table with Cory's lemon basil mojito and the second gin fizz she'd gotten herself, Merit told herself she was being unfair. Her husband was the same handsome and hardworking and maddeningly left-brained man she'd married, the practical thinker with a sense of humor who loved surprises and hated pickles. So what if he never got her drink order right? At least he wasn't addicted to porn like her friend Amanda's husband was.

"I'm starving," she said as she sat.

Cory handed her a menu.

"What looks good?"

"Haven't looked yet." Cory took a long swig of his drink. Merit put her menu down and arranged her mouth in a genial smile.

"So how was your day?" she asked brightly.

"Fine."

"Fine good?" she pressed.

"Fine *fine*," Cory said pointedly. "How was yours?"

I don't feel like talking about my day, either! she wanted to scream at him. *BUT THIS IS WHAT PEOPLE IN A FUNCTIONAL RELATIONSHIP DO!*

"Busy," she said as pleasantly as she could, which was actually quite pleasant because after fourteen fucking years, she was a pro at this. "We landed this huge mixed-use project along the Embarcadero on Monday, and the developer wants initial plans by the end of the month, which is totally insane but for whatever reason Joel isn't telling him that." Joel was her new boss, one of eight lead architects at the giant firm that now employed her. He was good at his job but not great. He was no Jane.

(No one but Jane was Jane.)

"Cool," Cory said.

Cool?

She picked up her menu.

"What are you in the mood for?" she asked mildly. She would not succumb to the irritation. She would not let his mood ruin hers.

"Could we share something?" Cory asked. "I ate lunch at three, so I'm not that hungry."

Cool.

"You know," she heard herself say. "I've been thinking. Maybe we shouldn't celebrate our anniversary this year." She hadn't been thinking this at all, not until the words came out of her mouth, but there was no going back now. She kept her eyes on her menu. "I mean, we don't have to pretend it's not happening or anything, but I probably can't commit to plans, and I definitely can't go away with the way things are at work. So maybe we just agree not to do anything now, so it doesn't become a thing? Ooh, the halibut looks good." She was aware of how transparent it was, her making this ridiculous suggestion at this particular moment, and for that reason alone she regretted saying it because it wasn't like they'd actually do this silly thing, and now Cory would know he'd hurt her feelings.

Had he actually hurt her feelings? And if he had, was it because he clearly didn't care at all about her workday, or because he'd shown up for dinner at the restaurant she'd been wanting to try for months with a full stomach? She couldn't tell anymore what she was reacting to when she reacted to him.

She kept her eyes on her menu and waited for Cory to tell her she was being dumb.

"Fine by me," she heard him say instead. "If you're sure you won't be upset when I actually do it and don't get you anything."

As long as you won't be upset when I have sex with a woman.

"Deal," she said.

SHE WASN'T ACTUALLY going to have sex with a woman, obviously.

She wasn't a cheater. Or gay. Or, quite frankly, dying to have more sex.

What she was, she decided, was a thirty-nine-year-old woman with a husband and two kids who was having a completely predictable mid-life crisis brought on by a looming landmark birthday, some existential boredom, and too much medical-grade weed. It wasn't about Jane at all, she told herself, it was about her, and the fact that she was turning forty in a few months, which was causing her subconscious to freak the fuck out because maybe she wasn't as happy at this point in her life as she thought she'd be. Part of it was her marriage, surely, but it was also her career, and the kids, and the fact that most days she felt like she was on a hamster wheel she couldn't stop. And the person who would understand exactly what she was going through—and would help her troubleshoot her way out of it without judging her for the fact that she was far more of a cliché than she'd ever imagined—was Jane.

So the Saturday morning after her dinner with Cory—which ended as poorly as it started, with Merit going to bed alone and Cory staying up to finish something for work—Merit texted Jane to ask her if she wanted to hang out with her and the boys in the Presidio that afternoon. She knew Jane would wonder where this invitation was coming from—in two years of friendship, Merit had never once invited her to get together with her kids—but she also knew that unless Jane had other plans, she'd say yes, because unlike Merit, Jane had never tried to compartmentalize their friendship.

If it bothered Jane that Merit kept her separate from the rest of her life, she never let on. But she had to be aware of it. She knew more about the complexities of Merit's marriage than anyone, but other than that one couples' dinner they'd had at Edward's restaurant, Jane hadn't had a single in-person interaction with Cory. She'd never been inside Merit's apartment. She hadn't been invited to any of their Christmas parties, or to the kids' birthday celebrations, or even to Cory's fortieth, despite the fact that they'd inexplicably invited a girl Merit lived with her first year at Berkeley and literally hadn't spoken to since. Jane was the person Merit had spent the most time with over the past two years, more time than she spent with her children even, the person she confided in about everything, the person who'd held her hand through a freaking miscarriage, yet when Cory put her name on the guest list for his party, Merit immediately took her off.

"She won't know anyone," she'd explained when he asked about it. And that was true, because Merit had never made any effort to introduce Jane to any of her other friends. Not because she had any doubt that Jane would win them all over within five seconds (ten if her first joke ran long); it was that she knew they would be different with each other in a setting like that. It happened automatically any time they were in a group. They'd never discussed it, but they'd been doing it from the beginning, both of them in equal measure, modifying their behavior whenever other people were around. They were less comfortable, less casual, less crass, less . . . *them*. Jane would become insufferably polite and Merit would talk too much and say awkward things and it would be difficult for them to make eye contact with each other. The more Merit thought about it, the odder it was, so she avoided thinking about it at all. She just took Jane off every guest list for every party and told herself it was totally normal to have one friend you kept separate from everything else.

Today, though, they would integrate. Today, she would bring her mom self to the Presidio in workout pants and sneakers and no makeup (okay, she'd wear some makeup, but not a lot) and she and Jane would hang out with her kids. And yes, maybe they'd behavior-modify a little because her kids didn't need to hear every iteration of the word "fuck," but she wouldn't let Jane be weird.

Her own weirdness was a different story.

The kids were a ploy, she knew that as she crafted her nonchalant hey what's up wanna come to the presidio with the boys and me this afternoon?! text to Jane. If they hung out with Jude and Nash, she wouldn't feel what she'd felt in Jane's kitchen. Not in workout pants, in broad daylight, at a family-friendly park. She'd probably run into someone she knew, another mom whom she would then be forced to introduce to Jane, and their worlds would converge even more.

It was a solid plan, and Merit was confident this playground outing would set her straight. And that was good, because she wanted to go back to the way things were before, when Merit had never fantasized about anyone other than Cory, and Jane was a brilliant and talented architect who only slept with men.

Except, of course, that was never who Jane was. From the very first moment they met that morning in the J + B lobby—Merit in her stretchy T-shirt, Jane in that borrowed designer dress—she was a brilliant and talented architect who'd also slept with women. Which was fine, and so completely not a big deal . . . except that for the duration of their relationship, Merit had been operating under the premise that whatever she and Jane were to each other, there was no chance whatsoever that they could end up having sex.

No chance whatsoever, Merit told herself as she loaded Jude and Nash into the car that afternoon. She believed it as much as she believed her other new mantra: *I am not attracted to my friend.*

The question of whether she would ever cheat on Cory was nowhere in her head.

"Where are we going?" Nash asked from his car seat.

"To see Mommy's boss," Jude told him.

"She's not my boss anymore," Merit said. She glanced at Jude in the rearview mirror. "She used to be. Now she's just my friend."

"What's her name again?"

"Jane."

"Isn't she old?"

"No, she's not old. Older than me, but not old."

"Does she have any kids?"

"Nope."

"That's weird," Jude said.

"No, it's not," Merit said. "Plenty of women don't have kids."

"Mommy has two kids," Nash piped up.

"Why are we having a playdate without any other kids?" Jude demanded.

"Because the playdate's for me," Merit said. "And I'm being nice enough to bring you two along because I know you love this playground." In reality, it was Merit who loved it. It was scenic and secluded, with a dramatic ridge of trees on one side and a deep slope on the other that looked out over the bay. The view of the Golden Gate Bridge was glorious on a clear day, but Merit liked it best on foggy mornings, when she could fill her lungs with dense, damp air and pull her hands up into the sleeves of her sweatshirt and imagine that she was on a cliff in Wales living a wild and artistic life. When Nash was a newborn and she was home full-time painting, it was her favorite place to take the boys when she needed to clear her head.

Today there was no fog. The sun was bright and warm and the playground was as crowded as she'd ever seen it. She was glad she'd told Jane three-thirty. It gave her twenty minutes to get the boys set up and find the right spot to sit. She felt the need to have this afternoon go smoothly, with exactly the right park bench and an appropriate amount of shade. She was already regretting her outfit. It was hotter out than she expected; her butt was starting to sweat in her leggings, which were decidedly less moisture-wicking than the label claimed. Her mouth was dry. She was nervous about seeing Jane.

There was an empty bench on the far side of the playground. Merit sat down and stared at Pacific Avenue, where she'd told Jane to park. The boys were already immersed in the playground. She watched Nash on the kiddie slide. She couldn't believe he was turning three in a month. *Shit.* She'd promised him a party. At least she didn't have her anniversary to think about anymore. After how blasé Cory had been about skipping it, she'd resolved to not even get him a card.

A dark blue Tesla with excessively tinted windows came crawling down Pacific.

There she is.

Her nervousness evaporated as Merit watched Jane attempt, badly, to parallel park. She was laughing when Jane finally gave up and got out of the car, the Tesla cockeyed and two feet from the curb. She had on baggy boyfriend jeans, a black muscle tee, and red Nike trainers. It wasn't an outfit Merit would ever have imagined her in—the jeans were too loose, the sneakers too bright—but then again, she'd never hung out with Jane on a Saturday afternoon.

"Nice parking job," Merit called out.

Jane pushed her aviators off her face and smirked. "Their fault for not having valet."

As Merit watched her friend cross the street, it was her walk that did it. The particular way Jane moved, with her characteristic bounce, springing off the balls of her feet the way she always did. Her Tigger step, Merit called it. It was familiar and a little kooky and, suddenly, the sexiest thing Merit had ever observed. Desire welled up inside her like floodwater.

There would be no nipping this in the bud. Never in her life had Merit been as certain of anything, as suddenly or as unequivocally, as she was of this. For several extraordinary seconds, she felt the ground moving beneath her feet as the planet that would never look the same to her again careened forward through space. In the time it took for Jane to cross Pacific Avenue, Merit's entire existence changed. It wasn't the intensity of the desire that undid her. It was that she finally unearthed where the desire had sprung from.

"Fuck," Merit heard herself whisper.

She was in love with Jane.

SHE WOULD SIT with it for weeks. Through the wedding anniversary she and Cory wouldn't celebrate, through Nash's third birthday, through the busy blur of Thanksgiving and Christmas, as she baked cookies and bought presents and fantasized incessantly about Jane. She would carry her feelings with her to St. Patrick's cathedral in SoMa one Saturday morning in January, where she would find herself kneeling at the marble altar in her workout clothes instead of doing hot yoga at the studio next door. Through all of it, Merit would nurse this truth inside her the way a gardener might tend to a garden, or a bird might sit on an egg, waiting patiently for the inevitable moment when it would burst through the surface into life.

twelve

MERIT DIDN'T KNOW what to do with her eyes. If she were with any other girlfriend on a beach weekend, she'd check out the other woman's body and compliment her swimsuit, no big deal. But here Jane was, draped in Merit's doorway in a skimpy black string bikini, all curvy and toned and perfectly proportioned, and Merit didn't know where to look. She wanted to stare.

Technically, this trip had been Jane's idea, but it was Merit who'd made it happen. She'd casually mentioned Pia's house in Mexico at their Presidio playdate in November and suggested that maybe they could go sooner than her fortieth birthday in May. How did January sound? They had plane tickets by Monday afternoon, before Merit had even discussed it with Cory. But it wasn't like she needed his permission to go on a girls' weekend, which was the attitude she took with him when she finally mentioned it on the anniversary they weren't celebrating, daring him to tell her she couldn't go away. But to her surprise, he was all for it. It helped that the house they were going to was free.

"How does Jane know this woman?" Cory had asked.

"She was a client," Merit had told him, leaving the rest of it out.

And here they were, at Jane's former lover's breathtaking private enclave on the Pacific coast of Mexico for three nights, alone except for José Luis, the house manager who'd met them in the driveway with fresh margaritas, and the very discreet staff. Jane had insisted that Merit take the master bedroom, which is where she'd been the past ten minutes, sitting cross-legged on the king-size bed in a sort of fugue state, gulping her margarita and staring at the wall. Until Jane knocked on her door in her black bikini and asked what was taking her so long.

"Sorry, let me just—"

Merit fumbled in her bag for her own swimsuit, a navy two-piece with tiny gold stars that she'd bought the previous week. She'd put it on twice at home, studying her butt in the full-length mirror, feeling ridiculous for caring so much about how she looked in it. What did she expect, that Jane would notice how incredible her ass looked (so. many. squats.) and suddenly want to get naked with her? It was silly. Yes, Merit had been fantasizing about this vacation in exquisite detail since the day they booked it, imagining what it would be like to do all sorts of things to Jane, but her friend wasn't in the same headspace. So if Merit really wanted to cross that line, she would have to initiate it, which, yes, was a thrilling prospect she'd played out in her mind nine thousand times since that moment at Presidio Park, but was also the most terrifying risk she would ever take.

And then there was the fact that she was married. There was Cory, the man she was married to. There were the vows she'd taken before God, at an altar, in a church.

She thought back to the previous Saturday, to that moment at that beautiful cathedral when she'd finally let the thing inside of her breathe.

For months she'd been alone in her feelings for Jane; their intensity, the complexity, that sense that she was being propelled forward by a tremendous wave. She'd needed to admit to someone what she'd come to want so badly it had eclipsed everything else, to confess it before she did something she could never undo. She'd thought about telling Cat, but blurting it out over the phone to a friend who would turn it into a thing to be analyzed and discussed was the opposite of what she wanted. What she wanted was to stand in silent awe of it, this thing that had changed her from a person who would never even consider cheating on her husband into a person who could no longer imagine doing anything else. With God, she didn't have to explain it, at least. She'd gotten on her knees to pray, but she'd just cried for an hour instead. "You know how much I love her," was all she finally said. She hadn't expected divine permission to have an affair, but the silence that followed was deafening. *You're on your own,* the silence said.

"Cute suit," Jane told her now, nodding at Merit's bikini. "You gonna put it on?"

"Yes! Sorry, I was just—"

Imagining us naked.

"Just give me one sec," Merit said, darting into the bathroom.

As she stepped out of her underwear, the skin underneath still pink from having every strand of her pubic hair yanked out, she wondered if her traveling companion had also gotten waxed before their trip. Had it also crossed Jane's mind that they might end up naked together in a beautiful oceanfront bedroom thousands of miles away from their regular lives?

Stop.

Merit tied the straps behind her neck and wadded her clothes into a ball. It wasn't a particularly tiny bikini—she'd worn much tinier in her life, without a second thought—but as she stepped out of the bathroom, Merit felt completely exposed.

"Look at you," Jane said, her eyebrows going up. "Who knew you had such a hot little body?"

Merit didn't know it was possible to blush on your thighs but she felt heat rising from her knees as she stuffed her clothes into her suitcase. Should she grab a pair of shorts?

But Jane had already turned and was headed out the door.

"To the pool!" she called over her shoulder.

Merit dropped the shorts and followed her out.

THEY DRANK EXPENSIVE tequila with fresh squeezed limes and ate truckloads of chips and guac. At some point, Jane asked Merit to rub sunscreen on her back. Merit had a spray bottle in her bag but she didn't dare point that out. Her eyes fluttered shut as she moved her hands over Jane's shoulders. *God her skin is so soft.* She slid a thumb under Jane's bikini strap and felt like she might pass out. It was not lost on her that touching Cory's body had never affected her like this.

She stood up from the edge of Jane's chair and tottered in bare feet.

"Careful, little bird." Jane gave her an amused look. She was lying on her stomach, knees bent with her feet in the air, flipping through a Scandinavian design magazine. Her blond hair was tucked into a giant straw hat that would've looked ridiculous on anyone else. Merit couldn't stop staring at the curve of her neck.

"The ground is uneven right here!" Merit bent over to pick up her glass.

(Was it her or did Jane just look at her butt?)

"Whatever you need to tell yourself," Jane said.

"Listen, bitch, I just gave you a very even application of sunscreen. That takes a sober eye."

"Mm-hmm."

Merit slurped down the rest of her drink. What was left was cold and tangy and sweet. The skin on her arms prickled with sun and expectation.

"You really do have a fantastic body," Jane said lightly.

Merit let herself smile. "You sound so surprised."

"Honestly? I am. I mean, I knew you worked out, but you've got an actual ass."

"Thank you for noticing."

Jane laughed. The sound reverberated between Merit's thighs. "So what should we do for dinner tonight?" she asked, going back to her magazine.

"Whatever you want," Merit said. "I'm easy." She was still standing. She was too antsy to sit back down.

"They'll cook for us here," Jane said. "But maybe we should go out." She was twirling a strand of hair that had slipped from her hat.

"Sure," Merit said. She saw Jane's eyes drift down her torso.

(Or was she imagining that?)

Merit raked her hands through her hair and looked out at the ocean. There were storm clouds in the distance. It would rain soon. But not yet.

She inhaled, filling her tight lungs with salty sea air. She felt like the clouds over the ocean, filled with something she couldn't contain much longer, on the brink of finally spilling out.

For more than two months, she'd managed to corral it. Through intimate dinners and cozy coffee dates, she'd exercised commendable restraint. She didn't want to hold it in anymore. She wanted to fling open the gate. She was not under any illusion that pursuing this was a good idea. It was wrong. It was risky. It would turn her into a person she once thought she could never become.

"I have to pee," she announced. "Do you want anything from inside?"

Jane shook her head. "All good, thanks."

In the bathroom, Merit stared at herself in the macrame mirror. The mascara she'd put on that morning at home was migrating down her face, and there was a bug bite on her left cheek, which was splotchy from the heat. She looked at her reflection, pushed off the balls of her feet to get closer to herself. The tequila had made her wobbly. How many had she had? She put her hands on the stone vanity to steady herself, her fingertips pressing into the cool porcelain of the sink, and stared herself down.

She was asking herself for permission. That's what she'd say later, anyway. She looked herself in the eyes and asked if it was okay to do what she'd already decided to do. She'd never be able to pinpoint exactly when she made the decision to tell Jane how she felt, only that there came a moment when it was no longer conceivable to keep it to herself.

"I have to," she said to her reflection. She wouldn't remember if she said it out loud or just in her head.

José Luis was in the kitchen coring avocados.

"*Hola*," Merit said, hanging in the arched doorway. "*Más aqua, por favor?*"

(Why was she speaking broken Spanish to a man whose English was impeccable?)

"Absolutely, *señorita*," José Luis said, setting his knife down. "Would you like some fresh lime in your glass?"

"Yes, please," Merit said, smiling like a lunatic because now even limes made her giddy with possibility, because limes made her think of Jane, and in particular the shape of her lips and how her mouth might taste. "For my friend, too. And maybe two more margaritas?"

"Of course."

She stood in the archway, gathering her nerve, while José Luis cut the fruit. There was no coming back from what she was about to do. She would always wonder if she would've been brave enough to actually do it had it not been for the tequila. She'd never know.

When the drinks were ready, she followed José Luis back out to the pool. Jane was sitting on the ledge overlooking the cliff, hat off, legs dangling. The storm was closer now. The sky over the water was the color of a bruise.

"It looks like you will eat inside tonight," José Luis said, and Jane turned her head. It was an exquisite portrait, and Merit wanted desperately to paint it. Jane's face in profile, the line of her jaw, the strength in her shoulders, the white stone ledge and the darkening sky. "Do you know what you would like to have?"

"I think we're going to hit the town for dinner, José Luis," Jane said, swinging her body all the way around. "We're two girls on vacation! We need to see and be seen, don't you think?"

José Luis laughed. "Of course. Have you been to Punto Como? The view will be nice in the rain."

"Perfect," Jane said. She hooked her hands over the ledge and arched her back in a stretch.

The desire was dizzying. Merit lifted the two cocktails off José Luis's tray and handed one to Jane.

"You look like a teenager," Jane said, taking the glass. "Are you old enough for that drink?"

"Barely," Merit said, tossing her hair. Her margarita sloshed against her wrist.

Jane laughed. "You're so cute."

"Right back at you," Merit said, her heart fluttering wildly in her chest. She sipped her drink until José Luis was back inside the house, then she swung one leg over the ledge and slid toward Jane. Her desire was a living, breathing, physical thing; she could feel it inside her, pushing on her rib cage, throbbing between her legs. For one strange, woozy moment, she felt as if she were giving birth to it, to this force she could no longer contain. It was coming out whether she wanted it to or not.

Jane brought her knees up to her chest. "This is nice, right?"

Merit nodded. Jane turned to look at her, resting her cheek on the top of her knee.

"What are you thinking about in that pretty head of yours, little bird?"

Merit didn't let herself hesitate. "You."

Jane picked up her head. "What about me?"

"How pretty you are."

"You're very sweet."

"I'm serious," Merit said quietly. Could Jane hear the tremble in her voice? "You're beautiful. I want to paint you."

"Haven't I already agreed to that? You can entitle it, *Aging Woman on a Ledge*."

Merit took a long, shaky breath.

"I prefer, *Beautiful Woman to Whom I'm Wildly Attracted and Whose Naked Body I Want Desperately to Ravage Tonight*."

Jane stared at her. All the air had left Merit's chest.

"It's a provocative choice," Jane said finally. Her voice was hoarse in her throat.

"I'm serious," Merit whispered. "I want you. So badly."

Jane kept staring at her. Merit didn't blink.

"Say something," she said finally.

Jane opened her mouth. Seconds passed before words came out. "I'm flattered," she finally said.

Merit felt a surge of gratitude she'd had so much tequila. Instead of hurling herself over a cliff, she managed a laugh.

"Ouch," she said, and picked up her drink.

"I didn't mean it that way." Jane touched Merit's knee. "I adore you. You know that."

"It's fine," Merit said lightly. Did her face look normal? She felt like a paper doll version of herself.

"This friendship is everything to me," Jane said. Her voice sounded funny. Merit wanted to cry.

"I get it."

"I don't want to do something we'll regret."

"No, totally. You're right." Merit sucked on her drink. She could feel Jane studying her. She saw Jane frown.

"Will it be weird between us now?"

Merit shook her head. There was gravel in her throat. "Nope."

"You sure?"

"Positive." Merit sounded convincing, even to herself. "As long as I'm allowed to touch you a little." She had no idea where this had come from. Or how her hand had gotten from her lap to Jane's shin. "Platonically," she added. "Of course."

"Of course," Jane echoed, pushing her bare foot closer.

Merit slid her fingers around Jane's ankle.

"Is this okay?" Merit asked. Jane nodded.

She slid her hand up Jane's calf and felt the muscle go taut.

"Merit."

"Jane."

"It's you and me."

"I know."

"You're married with two kids," Jane said.

These words bounced off Merit like the raindrops that had started to fall, beading up on her sunscreened skin. She didn't know what Jane wanted her to say.

Jane looked up at the sky. Merit watched rain slip down her friend's neck.

"*Señoritas?*"

They both jerked in the direction of José Luis's voice. He was standing under the pool umbrella, a tray with their empty dishes in his hands.

"The storm will be heavy soon."

The women looked at each other. Jane smiled a little. Then she swung her legs around and stood up. "I think this calls for more tequila," she announced.

JOSÉ LUIS MADE two more margaritas, which he brought to Jane's bedroom. Merit was sitting on a wooden chaise on the enclosed patio when he arrived, staring out at the Pacific, mesmerized by the intensity of the rain. Jane had disappeared into her bathroom to take a bath. The drinks sat untouched on the table when he left.

As she watched the rain on the ocean, Merit thought again of that moment in St. Patrick's, when her entire body shook with the awareness of where she was headed: into a terrifying and exhilarating and inevitable future where she would confess her feelings and she and Jane would have a delicious, torrid affair. It seemed impossible to her then that nothing would come of it, that they would remain the people they'd always been.

"Hey," came Jane's voice behind her, and Merit turned.

Jane was wrapped in a towel, a patch of sudsy bubbles on her left shoulder. Seeing her there, like that, Merit's mind went blank.

"You okay?" Jane asked.

Merit nodded. She kept her eyes on Jane's face.

"This friendship is everything to me," Jane began. "I don't—"

Merit cut her off. "Truly, it's fine."

"I really don't want it to be weird."

"It won't be," Merit said, desire humming inside her like a tuning fork, or an electric fence. Nothing was weird in this moment, nothing could ever be weird, when the want was this intense. "We're good. I swear."

"Good."

Merit reached out and grazed the back of Jane's thigh with her finger-tips. Her skin was still damp from the bath.

"Little bird."

"We agreed that I could touch you."

"You can touch me all you want," Jane said. "But maybe not while I'm naked?"

"Of course not," Merit said, looking up at her friend through lowered lashes. Her hand on the back of Jane's leg made it difficult to breathe. "Oh, wait. Does this count as naked?"

"I'm pretty sure it does, yes," Jane said. She was standing very still.

"You should go get dressed, then."

"I should." Jane didn't move.

"Is this making it weird?" Merit asked.

"Nope."

"'Kay, good," Merit said. "I want to follow the rules."

"You're drunk."

Merit shook her head. "I'm not." (She absolutely was.)

Jane stepped back and readjusted her towel. "Rules are good," she said.

"Totally," Merit said, bobbing her head. "Yay, rules!"

Jane laughed. "You're ridiculous." She watched Merit for another several seconds, then turned to go back inside.

"But you love me."

Jane turned back, a look on her face Merit couldn't read. "You know I do."

"INSIDE OR OUTSIDE?"

Merit pointed at a table in the corner, tucked behind a divider, away from the others. Not that it mattered; the outdoor tables were all empty.

Rain pelted the restaurant's tin roof. "How about there," she told the hostess.

The hostess nodded and reached for two menus.

Merit slid into the booth. The rain was coming down with such intensity that she could feel the spray on her back. Rain had never seemed so erotic. She wanted to be standing in it with her hands all over Jane.

"How about I sit beside you," she heard Jane say behind her.

Merit bit back a smile. "Great."

The hostess laid down the menus but neither woman picked them up. They hadn't eaten in hours but Merit wasn't hungry. She wanted another drink.

"So today's been fun," Jane said.

"It has."

Jane crossed her legs and slid her knees toward Merit. There it was again, that dizzying ripple that made Merit's eyelids throb. Jane was looking at her without blinking, the way she had when they'd worked together and Merit had fucked something up. It used to make her so nervous, this look. Now she gave it right back.

She'd never felt more powerful in her life.

"It took a turn I wasn't expecting," Jane said.

"Oh yeah?" Merit tilted her head, let her fingers graze Jane's thigh. "How so?"

Her chest expanded with Jane's inhale. It felt like a rope, pulling her in. Jane let out a low laugh. "You bitch."

"So mean!" Merit said, sliding her thumb up Jane's thigh. She heard her friend's breath catch. "I'm sorry if I made you uncomfortable earlier," she said, never breaking Jane's gaze.

"No, you're not."

"You're right." Merit smiled. "I'm not."

(Who was this person and what had she done with Merit?)

Jane's eyes searched hers. "Can I ask where all of this is coming from?"

Merit tilted her head. "You mean, where on my body?"

"I'm being serious."

"I don't know," Merit admitted. "I think it's possible it was there all along. But something happened that night you told me you'd been with women. It's like a light came on."

"That was ages ago. Why didn't you tell me sooner?"

"It was a lot to process. Plus I wasn't sure how you'd react."

"And now?"

"Now I'm ready to take my chances." Her thumb had reached the frayed edge of Jane's shorts.

Jane looked down at her hand. "Merit."

"Jane."

"We discussed this."

"We did. You said you were flattered."

"I *am* flattered," Jane said. "You're gorgeous and kind and exceptionally sexy. That's always been true. But this is a line we can't uncross."

Merit tugged at a piece of the fray, her eyes never leaving Jane's. She had never been more aware of the sensation of having skin.

"You really think I'm sexy?" she asked.

"I believe I said 'exceptionally sexy.' But that isn't the point."

"I want you," Merit whispered. "More than I've ever wanted anything in my life. And I think you want me back."

"Fuck," Jane breathed.

"I mean . . . yes?" Merit let her hand slip under Jane's shorts. Jane sucked in a breath.

"We are at a restaurant."

Merit nodded. "We are."

"You're being very naughty."

"I am."

"Merit." It was firmer than before. A command but also, Merit understood, a plea.

Merit nodded a little and pulled her hand back. The waiter approached.

"Drinks?" he asked in a heavy accent, smiling eagerly at them. Merit wondered if he'd seen her hand on Jane's thigh. It didn't bother her in the slightest if he had.

"*Dos margaritas*," Jane told him, her eyes not leaving Merit's.

Merit reached for her water glass with two hands. There were no thoughts in her head. Her mind was eerily quiet, perceptibly dark, like a boat in dark water with its navigation lights switched off. She gripped the glass to steady herself, her eyes never leaving Jane's. Rain pounded the side of the building, spraying mist on her bare back.

"I'll stop," she heard herself say when the waiter was gone. "I'll keep my hands to myself." She wondered if she meant it.

They were staring at each other. Merit let her gaze drift down to Jane's lips.

"I don't want you to stop," those lips said.

Merit lifted her eyes back to Jane's, and for a second, the person she'd known for two and a half years was a total stranger, a woman she'd never seen before this. She'd try to describe it later, how Jane's face changed at that moment. Her blue eyes dilating, becoming inky black. She'd never be able to get the metaphor right.

"You're so in," Merit said. She didn't dare smile. She bit her bottom lip. She wanted to scream with relief. The air between them popped and crackled, like oil on a hot pan.

"It seems I am." Jane sucked in a breath. "Oh. My. God."

Merit slid closer. She put her hand back on Jane's thigh.

"Literally every cell in my body wants you right now," Jane breathed. "Every fucking cell."

"Right back at you," she said. Her fingertips pulsed with desire. She kept her other hand in her lap.

The waiter arrived with their drinks, and somehow, they both formed sentences to order food.

"Well, this is a development," Jane said when the waiter was gone. She ran her hands through her hair, damp and wavy from the rain. Her cheeks were flushed; her nose was dusted with new freckles from their day in the sun. Her blond eyelashes were bare. Merit had looked at her friend so many times, in so many different lights. She had never been more stunning than this.

Jane caught Merit staring and pursed her lips.

Merit let herself grin. "You want me back," she said.

"Don't gloat."

Merit laughed. "So what happens now?"

"We eat and we have several more drinks and we go dancing at the seediest dive bar we can find," Jane replied.

"And then?"

"And then we see what happens."

Merit smiled. "That sounds like an excellent plan."

"Are you worried?" Jane asked. "About what this could do to our friendship?"

Merit didn't hesitate. "No."

She took a long sip of her margarita. She could taste the tequila. She ran her tongue along the rim of the glass, licking the salt.

"Be careful, little bird." Jane's voice was hoarse again, rough in her throat.

Merit knocked back the rest of her drink.

"Don't tell me what to do."

JOSÉ LUIS WAS on the pool deck, straightening chairs and picking up leaves from the storm, when they got back to the house. He waved to them as they passed through.

"Más margaritas?" he called.

"Not unless you want to find us floating facedown in the pool!" Jane called back. José Luis laughed and went back to his chairs. He was still there when they returned a few minutes later in their swimsuits. This time he barely glanced up.

The lights in the pool were on, but the hot tub was dark. The jets were going, the water lapping over the infinity edge. The ocean roared against the rocks below.

Jane slid into the water and sat in the corner facing the ocean. With her hair clipped up and no makeup on, she looked decades younger than she was. Merit wanted to wrap her hands around her neck.

Merit dropped her towel and slipped in beside her. Under the bubbles, their thighs touched. Above the water, neither acknowledged it. Jane pressed her leg into Merit's, the water bubbling between her breasts. It took every ounce of Merit's willpower not to pull her friend's bikini straps off.

Merit looked over her shoulder at José Luis. He had a rag now, wiping down the tables. She willed him to finish and leave.

As a distraction, Merit looked up at the sky. For several seconds, the entire universe seemed to pulse with the desire she felt. The twinkle of the stars, her own heartbeat, the steady churn of the Jacuzzi jets. A symphony of energy reverberating in her chest.

"You're too far away," Jane said in a low voice.

Merit glanced toward the house. The lights were out now. José Luis was gone.

She slid off the tile bench and stood up. Jane was waiting beside her, but Merit moved away from her, to the infinity edge instead, her palms sliding over the rounded lip. She closed her eyes and drank in a breath. She felt Jane's eyes on her back, on her neck. She wanted Jane's hands on her skin. *How had it come to this?* She knew she'd led them to this moment, but she couldn't retrace her steps. It seemed as if everything that had ever happened between them had always been leading to exactly this.

Her mind drifted back to the first time they met. Sitting across from Jane in her office, electrified by her presence. It's how she'd felt ever since.

"Hey," Jane said quietly. Merit turned. Her eyes met Jane's. "You okay?"

Merit nodded. "Are you?"

Jane nodded back, her gaze steady as Merit lowered herself back into the water and moved toward her. As she got closer, Merit's mind got quieter and quieter until there was no noise at all in her head. It was as if essence of herself, trapped in her head until that exact moment, pinging around frenetically like a ping-pong ball on crack for thirty-nine years, had finally broken out of her skull and slipped down into the expanse of her body. All at once she could feel herself in her arms and in her legs and in the arch of her lower back. She wasn't thoughts or beliefs or fantasies or fears. She was bones, she was blood, she was muscles, she was skin.

Never before had she felt so intensely present in a moment, or as aware of the privilege of being alive. When her fingers brushed Jane's knee, there wasn't a single thought in her head.

Jane's skin was soft and slick in the water. She slid her hands up Jane's thighs, afraid Jane would stop her, more afraid that she wouldn't. She knew she couldn't stop herself.

The wind picked up. It was warm and damp on Merit's shoulders. She could see the heat coming off the water. Little blond baby hairs were curling on the back of Jane's neck.

"God, you're so beautiful," Merit murmured, and her hands reached for Jane's hips under the water. If she'd been capable of processing it, she might have marveled at how natural it was for her to be like this. Direct. Unflinching. Unafraid. Afterward, she wouldn't remember whether she pulled Jane off the bench or Jane pushed herself off, but all of a sudden her friend's legs were wrapped around her waist and Jane's lips were on her neck. Merit closed her eyes and inhaled. Her lungs expanded, her chest pressing against Jane's. She drank in the scent of salt and skin and rain and coconut shampoo.

I wonder if José Luis can see us?

Merit noticed that she didn't care.

Her hands had found their way up Jane's back to the strings of her bikini. She pulled them one by one and felt Jane's top float to the surface between them. Her breath caught as she slid her hands around her friend's body and up over her chest.

"Let's go inside," Jane whispered. Merit felt herself nod.

Merit's mind stayed quiet as they wrapped themselves in towels and picked up their stuff. The clouds were moving now, the clear night sky pushing through.

Neither of them spoke when they got to Merit's room. They didn't turn on any lights. They didn't look at each other as they peeled off their bathing suits and got into bed. The room smelled faintly of lemongrass. The air was humid, but not hot. The tile floor was cold. The sheets were soft. Merit noticed all of it. She inhaled slowly, drinking the details in.

After, she wouldn't be sure who reached for the other first. It felt like it happened at the same time, Jane's hand touching her waist at the exact moment Merit's hand found the back of Jane's thigh. What Merit would remember was the utter lack of hesitation. Hers. Jane's. She would remember how fiercely she wanted. How wanted she felt.

They were both still awake when the sun came up hours later. Or maybe they'd both slept and woken back up. Merit's memory of the night would be of reaching for Jane, over and over again. And, of being reached for, over and over again, by Jane.

"Morning," Jane said softly, rolling onto her side.

"Morning," Merit whispered. Her eyes drifted over Jane's cheekbones, along her jaw, down her neck. The light was bright through the curtains. Merit wanted to run over to them and fling them open, to let all of the brightness in.

"How do you feel?" Jane asked.

"I feel amazing," Merit said.

"Really?"

"Really."

"Not guilty?"

Merit hesitated. She wanted to be honest, particularly about this. She shook her head.

"What about Cory?" Jane asked.

"I don't want to talk about Cory," Merit said quietly. "I mean, I will. But right now, I just want to be here, with you."

Jane nodded. She looked tired, but still so pretty. "Whatever you want."

Merit laid her palm on Jane's cheek. "What about you? How do you feel?"

Jane turned her face to kiss the inside of Merit's wrist. "Hungry," she said against Merit's skin.

"Like . . . metaphorically?"

Jane laughed. "No, you weirdo. Like I want a pound of bacon and massive amounts of carbs." She sat up in bed.

Merit arched her back and stretched. She felt Jane's hand on her stomach, then around her waist.

"My little, tiny bird," Jane murmured, pulling Merit against her.

Merit's stomach fluttered. She arched her back more, pushed her torso into Jane's. Jane slid on top of her and scissored their legs.

"What happened to breakfast?" Merit whispered, lifting her hips.

"We should go have some," Jane said against her ear.

"Mm-hmm," Merit said back, then pushed Jane over so she was on top, pulling her legs up to sit on her knees. She'd straddled Cory a thousand times, knew that particular feeling of him being hard beneath her, arranging her body so she was at the right angle for him. This, being on top of Jane, was nothing like that. There was nothing pressing against her, the space between Merit's thighs hovering above the concave dip in Jane's stomach. Except for Jane's hands on her waist, their bodies weren't touching. There was delicious torture in this.

She leaned back and let Jane look at her.

"My god, you're perfect," Jane said, her fingertips climbing up Merit's rib cage until she had a palm under each breast.

"So are you," Merit breathed. Her insides ached with desire.

They were staring at each other, neither of them blinking. Jane slid her thumbs over Merit's nipples and Merit nearly cried out.

"Come here," Jane whispered, and Merit rocked her body forward to bring her lips to Jane's. They'd spent the entire night exploring each other's bodies, but they hadn't yet kissed. *What would it be like to kiss a woman?* Merit wondered briefly, and then she knew. It was like everything else with Jane. Different but uncomplicated, new but familiar, impossible and true.

They kissed for an amount of time Merit would not have been able to name. *Five minutes? Two hours?* It was too much and not nearly enough.

Eventually, they put on clothes and went to the kitchen for breakfast. The staff was waiting for them. Was it Merit, or did the two housekeepers exchange a knowing look? Her cheeks went hot as she remembered the Jacuzzi, Jane's legs wrapped around her waist. She was glad she wasn't wearing her wedding ring. She felt weird about having taken it off.

These thoughts didn't keep her from reaching for Jane's wrist as they followed José Luis to the table, or from twirling a strand of Jane's hair when they sat. She didn't mind that the staff was staring, or talking about them. Something had been unlocked inside her; some hidden part of her, uncaged. She couldn't keep her hands to herself.

They ate huevos rancheros and drank dark coffee with heavy cream as the surf pounded against the cliff, the roar magnified by the narrow cove. The sky over the ocean was extravagant with clouds. It would rain again, maybe soon, but for now the seascape was a glorious tableau. It reminded Merit of peacock feathers. Suddenly, she wanted a tattoo.

"What now?" Merit asked when they were finished eating. She didn't know if she meant right then or in general. The truth was, she didn't care either way and wondered why she asked.

"I'm thinking we hang out poolside," Jane said. "Preferably with tequila. Or maybe champagne?"

They opted for mimosas, and Merit finished hers in three sips. She stretched out on her chaise and fell deeply asleep.

She dreamed of the jungle. It was sprinkling when Jane woke her up.

"Come on. Let's go inside."

Merit followed Jane back to her bedroom and didn't speak as Jane led her to the bed.

"I want to look at you," Jane said, and Merit lifted her hips and let Jane pull her swimsuit off.

"I thought you weren't really into girls," Merit whispered as Jane parted her legs.

"I'm into you," Jane whispered back.

As Jane traced the line of her collarbone with a fingertip, then drew circles down her torso with her tongue, Merit felt her awareness of her body give way to a sensation that was the absence of self and the opposite of shame. There was no performance in how she responded to Jane's touch;

when she replayed it later, it would make her think about how much pretending she'd always done with Cory, the act of it all. There was none of that with Jane. Merit would remember how her hips moved when Jane's touch got hungrier and more urgent, the way she opened herself up, and she'd blush with disbelief after the fact. But as it was happening that afternoon, she wasn't thinking about herself or her appearance or of Cory. She thought of nothing but the pleasure in her body and the sound of the rain. She was aware in the moment of how whole she felt.

When the rain stopped, they were a tangle of arms and legs and sheets.

"This was one of your better ideas," Jane said, pulling Merit on top of her again. Merit leaned over to nuzzle the side of her neck. It was a gesture Cory hated, her breath by his ear. Jane swept her hair away to give Merit more room.

"You smell so good," Merit murmured, breathing her in. "Did you always smell like this?"

"Honey, I smell like you."

Merit kissed her neck, her jaw, her chin.

"Mm. Do you taste like me, too?" she whispered, running her tongue over Jane's lips.

"You naughty little bird," Jane breathed.

And then they were at it again.

thirteen

"MERIT?"

The new guy whose name she couldn't remember was in her office doorway holding an accordion file so thick with papers it made Merit's head hurt. She didn't know if it was the papers or just the idea of being forced to do work that pained her. Either way, she couldn't imagine having to interact with this person in her doorway, having to form sentences about anything other than Jane.

Her computer screen had gone dark an hour ago. She had so much shit to get done but she couldn't focus on any of it. She could think of nothing but Jane.

They'd parted at the airport on Sunday evening, awkwardly. Jane had gone home to her empty house in Sausalito. Merit had gone home to Cory. She'd been nervous coming in the front door; would he be able to see it on her, did she have a tell? She'd always been a terrible liar.

(Though she was questioning that now. Maybe she'd always been a truly excellent liar, especially to herself.)

The worry was unnecessary. When Merit came through the door, Cory was standing in the kitchen, waiting for the takeout he'd ordered. The boys were on their iPads on the couch.

"How was your trip?" he'd asked, glancing at his phone. "Sorry. This guy was supposedly 'arriving' four minutes ago. I'm gonna go outside and see if I can see him."

Jude and Nash, at least, seemed happy to see her. They both looked up from their screens for a good twenty seconds when she sat between them. She stayed there for several minutes, waiting for the guilt of what she'd done to hit. When it didn't, she got up and went into the kitchen, where she stood and stared at the countertop and wondered what would become of her life.

When the food finally arrived and Cory seemed to remember that she'd been gone for four days, he came around the kitchen island for a hug. "So did you have fun?" he asked, rubbing her arms up and down, the way he did sometimes when she was cold.

"So much," she said.

"I'm really glad," Cory told her, and she felt grateful, and so deeply misunderstood.

She'd gone to bed when the boys did, and she'd dreamed of Jane. At four in the morning she'd woken up and hadn't been able to go back to sleep. She spent the next two hours sketching in an old notebook, trying to capture her memory of Jane sitting on that stone ledge overlooking the ocean, wishing she could go back to that moment and do all the things that followed all over again.

Now it was Monday afternoon and Merit felt untethered and shaky. Why hadn't she heard from her? They'd promised each other to be careful with their communication, but they hadn't said they wouldn't talk.

The new guy whose name she didn't know was looking at her expectantly, holding his ridiculous accordion file with two hands. "Can we go over the soil report for the house in Nob Hill?" he asked. "I have some questions about it."

"Soils report."

The new guy looked at her.

"Soils with an *s*. It's called a soils report, not a soil report."

"Oh, okay," the new guy said. "Is that important?"

"Only if you care about not sounding like an idiot." It was something Jane would say. Merit felt like a bitch as soon as the words were out of her mouth. "Sorry. Come on in. What's your question?"

"The first one is about soil-bearing capacity. Can I sit?"

She tried not to sigh loudly as he plopped his giant file on her table and pulled out a chair.

There were sixteen questions in total, and somehow Merit answered all of them without throwing his accordion file on the floor.

When he finally left she checked her phone for the fiftieth time since lunch. Seventy-nine unread emails. Nothing from Jane.

She hated this feeling. It was the opposite of how she'd felt in Mexico. So confident about all of it. So sure.

She wasn't sure of anything now.

Except, she supposed, that she didn't regret any of it. She'd expected to, if not right afterward, then certainly at four-thirty in the morning as she sat at her kitchen table sketching the woman with whom she'd spent the past three nights having sex (though what she and Jane had done all weekend barely resembled the thing she'd been calling "sex" since Felix Durant laid on top of her grunting awkwardly in his dorm bed nineteen years before). But the regret hadn't come. Even more unsettling was the utter absence of shame. She'd cheated on her husband. With a woman. Her mother would call an exorcist if she knew.

The only person Merit wanted to call was Jane.

But what would she say when Jane picked up?

She'd fantasized about their weekend away for months, but she'd never once thought about what would come after, when they returned to their regular lives. What did she want to happen now? She wanted Jane, even more now than before, so much so that she could feel it physically, gnawing at her, like a sharp, hungry ache. But beyond that, she didn't know. It wasn't like she was going to declare herself a lesbian and leave Cory.

(Was she a lesbian? Did she want to leave Cory?)

Her phone buzzed in her hands. Her heart leapt, then fell. It was Cory, not Jane.

"Hey," she said. "What's up?" He rarely called her at work. "Is everything okay?"

"Everything's fine," he said, and she could hear him smiling. "I'm calling with a proposition."

"Sure, I'll take both boys to school in the morning so you can ride your bike before work."

Cory laughed. "I'll take you up on that. But that wasn't it. I was going to propose a family vacation."

Merit blinked. "To where?"

"I was thinking Hawaii. For spring break. One of those big hotels with waterslides and kid pools."

The suggestion was so unlike Cory it literally did not compute. It wasn't the idea of a family trip, but the last-minute spontaneity of it, and the expense. Cory's idea of extravagance was renting a camper van and driving up the coast. They'd never taken a vacation that involved plane tickets and fancy resorts.

"As in, three weeks from now?" Merit asked.

"Well, I wasn't sure of the dates. But yeah. Maybe Oahu? What do you think?"

"Uh . . ." What *did* she think?

"If it's too much because you just took two days off last week, I get it," he said quickly. "But the boys would love it. I could teach Jude to surf. And I think it'd be good for us, too."

Guilt slammed into her like a tidal wave.

"Let's do it," she heard herself say. Her voice was shaky. *Could Cory tell?*

"Great. I'll book the hotel. Which card should I—"

"AmEx. I'll text it to you." She needed to get off the phone with him. Her lungs were underwater. She couldn't take a full breath.

"And the exact dates? I was thinking Saturday to Sat—"

"The first week of March. Hey, I gotta go. Talk tonight?"

"Yep," Cory said. "I—"

She guessed he was going to say *I love you*. She'd already hung up.

It was the happiness in his voice that did it. For months, she'd been telling herself a story of mutual dissatisfaction within their marriage that neither of them was motivated enough to do anything about. Cory because he was fine with average—"average is average for a reason," he'd say, and *had* said, unironically, the one and only time they'd gone to therapy. Merit because she'd wanted permission to do exactly what she'd done with Jane. But the way his voice had sounded on the phone just now, so cheerful and upbeat . . . it reminded her of the *old* Cory, the one who used to plan elaborate date nights with carefully mapped-out stops all over the city at places she'd never heard of just because he knew she liked to try new things. She couldn't remember the last time he'd organized an activity for them, and here he was designing an entire vacation on his own.

She felt claustrophobic. She pulled off her sweater and stood up from her desk.

Did her husband finally grasp how bad things were, or was it the opposite: Did he think a spontaneous family trip was a good idea because things were so good? She didn't know, because for the past several months, she'd paid basically no attention to him. Ever since their un-celebrated anniversary in November, she'd been staying at the office later and going out to dinner at least once a week with Jane. Cory had definitely noticed the change, because he'd commented on how many nights she wasn't there to put Nash and Jude to bed, which he knew not because he was doing it, but because Sierra was still there when he got home, after both boys were asleep. But if it actually bothered him that she was gone so much, he never said. Of course he had no idea his wife was coming home giddy and un-characteristically horny at eleven P.M. at least once a week not because she was drunk (though she was, always, quite drunk), but because she'd just spent the evening sitting across a table from someone who turned her on in a way she'd never been turned on before.

She hadn't felt bad about it then. Partly because her attraction to Jane had significantly improved their sex life. But mostly because before Mexico, her preoccupation with Jane had seemed more like a thought experiment than a grenade in the center of her life. *Am I really in love with her? Could I really kiss a woman? Would something happen between us if I told her how I felt?* She could intuit the answers to these questions, but she hadn't lived them yet. It was still her husband she was coming home to, her husband she was having sex with, her husband she was waking up next to, hungover and thirsty and vaguely disoriented, the morning after her dinners with Jane.

She felt bad about it now.

On the upside, it was a relief to know she wasn't completely heartless; though, to be fair, it was her soul she'd been most concerned about, not her heart. Her heart she'd felt all along, palpably; a sensation half like a flutter, half like a throb, in her chest. It was her head that was hollow, like someone had vacuumed her skull out. She'd welcomed the quiet. According to her father, that was how people got lost.

But standing in her office that afternoon, staring at the photo on her home screen—a selfie she'd taken with Cory and the boys at church on Christmas Eve, which she'd posted on social media that night with some vapid caption about gratitude and faith, because even as she was fantasizing about sleeping with a woman, she was keeping her Instagram image up—it all seemed so fucking disingenuous. The guilt, the suffocating sensation, the nauseating *what-have-I-done*. She'd done exactly what she had set out to do, the very thing she'd thought about constantly for months, including the night she'd taken that selfie, standing with her husband and their two sons in matching red sweaters in a church pew, singing "Silent Night." To let herself indulge in a shame spiral now would make her even more of a cliché than she already was.

She sat down and called Jane.

"Thank god," Jane said when she answered.

"The phone works both ways, you know," Merit said. There was no way the grin that had taken over her face was attractive. At least the guilt was gone. The weight of it had lifted the moment she heard Jane's voice on the other end of the line. Whatever she was in right now, she wasn't in it by herself.

"I resolved not to call you," Jane said.

"Why?"

"I wanted to give you space," Jane said. "In case you were spiraling."

"And if I *were* spiraling, you decided the best course of action was to abandon me?" She was teasing. She wasn't teasing. She couldn't fathom not hearing from Jane.

"God, I miss you," Jane said.

There it was: the sensation half like a flutter, half like a throb, in her chest.

"I miss you, too," Merit said quietly. "So much."

"How were things with Cory last night?"

"Fine," Merit said. "Normal." She didn't want to tell Jane about Hawaii yet. She didn't know why.

"Good."

"I'm not spiraling."

"I know."

"Did you really think I would?"

"I thought it was a possibility," Jane said. "But I'm acknowledging that I might not know you as well as I thought."

"You know me," Merit said.

"I'm starting to."

"When can I see you?" Merit asked. *Did she sound as desperate as she felt?*

"Anytime you want."

"Tomorrow night?"

"Little bird. You've just been away from your family for four days. How about Friday night? You'll come over, and I'll cook."

"Since when do you cook?"

She could hear Jane smile. "Maybe you don't know *me* as well as you thought."

"MOMMY! ARE YOU even listening to me? Mommy!"

Merit was aware that her sons were both scream-crying. She could see them in the living room, the big fat tears dripping down their splotchy red cheeks. Nash was hysterical about a broken Lego spaceship. Jude was sobbing about some picture he'd drawn at school that he, in a fit of rage that was somehow related to his younger brother's Legos, had ripped in half and was now trying in vain to staple back together with an empty stapler.

To answer his question, no, she wasn't listening. She heard him. Everyone in their building could hear him. But she'd retreated so far inside her mind, to a hidden place where the memories of her weekend with Jane were playing on a loop, that it would take more than a seven-year-old's tyrannical shouts to pull her out.

Cory was still at work, which she couldn't even resent because it was only six forty-five. She'd left her own office at five and texted Sierra that she was coming home early and would feed and bathe the boys herself. She'd stopped at Trader Joe's on the way and had filled her cart with the types of things a responsible mother who wasn't having an illicit affair would buy for her children. Her plan was to make pasta primavera, the boys' favorite, but she'd burned the garlic, and the zucchini she'd bought was completely overripe, and at some point she'd said screw it and opened a jar of store-bought marinara instead. The evening had disintegrated from there. More than once she'd contemplated texting Sierra to please come back.

It wasn't the boys' fault. Somewhere between the charred garlic and the pasta water that bubbled up over the pot and onto her stove in a starchy hiss, she'd left the room. Not physically; she was still standing in the kitchen, stirring sauce, taking periodic sips of the water she was making herself drink instead of wine. But in her mind she was back in Mexico, hiking down to the beach on Saturday afternoon in a bikini top and frayed jean shorts she hadn't worn since college, with a woman who made her feel both like the girl she'd been at nineteen and someone else entirely; a version of herself she hadn't yet been.

She sighed and forced herself back to the present, to the pasta on the stove, to her crying children, to the chaos of a regular Wednesday night; except it wasn't regular, nothing was regular anymore. Five days ago, she'd shoved regular off a Mexican cliff.

"There's no need to shout, Jude," she heard herself say. "I'm right here."

"But you're not listening to me," he whined as Nash picked up the bin of Legos and turned it upside down on the couch. Jude shrieked as Legos went everywhere, then immediately bodychecked his three-year-old brother, sending Nash flying onto the floor in a fit of fresh tears.

"Jude! Apologize to your brother." She was on autopilot now.

"But those are mine!"

"No! They're! Not!" Nash shrieked from the rug.

"You guys. Please. Dinner's almost ready. If you can calm down and eat all your pasta, I'll let you have ice cream for dessert." She hated herself for the laziness of this. Her sons were being absolute assholes, and she was going to reward them for it.

"Do you promise?" Jude asked, eyeing her with suspiciously dry eyes for a child who had been wailing ten seconds before.

"I don't have to promise. My yes is my yes." It was something her mother always said, a reference to a passage in the Bible about not swearing oaths. Merit had never used it before with her own kids, and here she was, today of all days, invoking her trustworthiness with a straight face. A laugh—unhinged, maybe maniacal?—gurgled in her chest at the irony of this.

The bribe worked at least. Both boys immediately stopped crying and got in their seats for dinner. Merit was so relieved by the silence that she didn't even react when she noticed that one of them had colored on the table with Sharpie. There was a twisted sort of poetry in it, she decided as she ran her finger over the slick, clumsy scrawl. If this nicked and water-stained dining table was indeed the metaphor for their family life she'd always thought it was, an ugly scribble in black permanent marker in the center of it seemed about right.

She dished up soggy pasta and store-bought sauce and poured glasses of milk. Jude and Nash devoured their portions. Jude informed her that the noodles were disgusting. Nash pronounced it the yummiest thing she'd ever cooked. Merit pushed penne around on her plate. She wasn't hungry, hadn't been hungry, since she got back from her trip.

She fought the distraction. She fought the impulse to withdraw. It was difficult; the memories of Jane were magnetic, and that hidden place in her mind was a compelling retreat. It took effort to remember these two small humans, her sons, shoving food in their faces, dropping noodles on the floor that she would later pick up—this was her real life. A life she would have to reconcile with the hidden place eventually. But not yet.

"I love you guys," she said to them at one point. "So much."

Merit reached out to ruffle Jude's hair, a gesture she was sure he'd come to hate very soon. *Would he also come to hate her? Would she deserve it if he did?*

"Can we still have ice cream?" he asked suspiciously.

"Definitely," Merit said, and stood to gather their plates.

IT WAS AN eternity to Friday night. And then, suddenly, it arrived, and Merit was scrambling to make the five-thirty ferry to Sausalito. It seemed impossible that it'd only been five days since she and Jane parted in baggage claim at SFO with a pally fist bump that was both perfect and awful. Merit had wanted Jane to take her face in her hands and kiss her the way they'd kissed in bed that morning. But of course she couldn't, they couldn't, so close to home.

Her stomach was in knots as she walked toward Jane's blue Tesla, idling at the curb. It was unfair that Jane was able to watch her cross the sidewalk while she couldn't see Jane at all through the tint. Merit had offered to take an Uber up to the house, but Jane wouldn't hear of it. She'd insisted on meeting her at the terminal when her ferry got in. Merit couldn't remember the last time Cory had picked her up at the airport, if he ever had.

Jane rolled down the driver's side window and stuck her head out. "Hi, beautiful girl," she called, pushing her sunglasses off her face.

"Hey," Merit called back, and touched her hair self-consciously. She'd spent a good ten minutes in the bathroom at work trying to zhuzh it up, as if some extra volume in her tresses might turn her back into the dauntless woman she'd been on that ledge in Mexico instead of the antsy bundle of nerves she'd become. "It's good to see you."

(Were there any truer words than these?)

"Get your ass in here," Jane said, and blew her a kiss before she rolled up the window.

Any worries Merit had about their new dynamic evaporated when she got inside the car. Mostly because she was unable to assess the vibe between them after they started kissing, which happened approximately four seconds after she shut the passenger door. When had they become people who kissed each other in a car like teenagers? As she took hold of Jane's black T-shirt, pulling her in closer, it struck her that maybe the better question was how they'd navigated two years of friendship without doing exactly this.

(It did not occur to Merit to ask herself how she had never once in thirty-nine-and-a-half years considered the possibility that she might enjoy kissing a girl.)

"I told myself I wouldn't do this until we got to the house," Jane said at some point. Had it been five seconds or five minutes? Merit had no idea.

She smiled and kissed Jane again. "Oh yeah? How's that working out for you?"

"Not so well, I'd say."

"To be fair, it *has* been an eternity since we've seen each other."

"At least." Jane sat back in her seat and looked at her. "I was worried it'd feel different," she said finally.

"Me, too."

"It doesn't, though."

Merit shook her head.

Jane pulled her sunglasses back down on her face. "We're in trouble, you know."

Merit nodded. She was terrified. She was completely unafraid. "I know."

f o u r t e e n

M ERIT?"
     She didn't know how many times her husband had said her
name. She suspected it was many.

She blinked and turned her head toward him, shading her face with her
hand. She'd left her beach hat in their hotel room; she was probably getting
too much sun.

"So? Do you want to come with us?"

Come with you where?

Although she'd been sitting two feet from Cory for the past several
hours, sipping the too-sweet piña colada he'd ordered her and turning
pages of the paperback she'd bought at the airport gift shop, she hadn't
heard a single word he'd said. Her mind was somewhere else. It was back
in Jane's bedroom, with Jane.

They'd seen each other three times in the three weeks before she left for
Hawaii with Cory and the kids. Each time for dinner, on a Friday, at Jane's

house. That first night Jane had roasted a chicken, and they'd eaten the entire thing with their hands, pulling the crispy skin off the legs with their teeth, washing it down with buttery chardonnay, the whole time talking, really talking, about everything and nothing at all. It had felt so decadent. Merit had never felt so deliciously full.

They'd made love on Jane's white linen sheets after that.

When Merit had finally looked at her phone, it was eleven-thirty. They'd been in bed for three and a half hours. It felt like a fraction of that.

"You could stay the night," Jane had said when Merit reluctantly dragged herself out of bed at eleven forty-five and put on her bra.

"And tell Cory what? 'Jane and I are fucking now, so, you know, I'm gonna sleep over.'" Merit fished around the sheets for her underwear.

The light had gone out from Jane's eyes in that moment.

"What an awful thing to say," she'd said quietly.

"What?" Merit knew exactly what.

"We aren't 'fucking,' Merit."

"I know that."

"Do you?" Jane had squinted a little in the dark and Merit had felt like a child in detention. It wasn't an entirely unwelcome feeling. She'd wished, suddenly, wildly, to be spanked.

"Don't be mad at me," she'd said, and then she'd crawled across the bed on her hands and knees in the same lacy bra and underwear she'd worn the night she got pregnant with the baby she lost and climbed on top of Jane. *What is my life?* she'd asked herself as she flicked her tongue inside Jane's mouth, watching this beautiful woman's back arch in pleasure as she pinned her wrists against the bed.

Their next two outings were a lot like that, except they weren't outings because they never left Jane's house. Should she call them innings? Jane's belly button was an innie; there was a café au lait birthmark on the inside of her right thigh. Innings, innie, inside. Being with Jane was an experience of in-ness, Merit decided, the sensation of being *in*, of being *let inside* another person. It was literal. It was metaphoric. It was sexual and it wasn't. It was everything she and Jane had ever been to each other. It was nothing she had ever experienced before.

And now there was an ocean between them.

As she watched Cory walk the boys down the beach from her lounge chair by the pool, where she sat in the frumpy black one-piece she'd bought the week before because she couldn't go on a family vacation with the same bikini she'd started her affair in, Merit wondered what would become of her life.

They'd been in Oahu for three days. The first day and a half had been fun; the novelty of a new place, a nice hotel, four gigantic pools, a swim-up bar. But the novelty had worn off the second night when Cory had gotten in the shower with her at nine o'clock, already hard and buzzed from the two mai tais he'd had on their balcony while Merit put the boys to bed on the pullout couch. "I've been wanting to do this all day," he'd said in her ear as he'd pushed into her from behind. It was the first time they'd had sex since she got back from Mexico, and gratefully, it was fast. Water from the shower ran down her forehead, hiding her tears. She didn't want to cheat on her lover with her husband, but there weren't gold stars for that.

The whole thing was a head trip; not just the affair, but the fact that she was on a family vacation less than a month after her weekend away with Jane. She felt as if she'd been slingshot into an alternate reality. In this universe, she blew up swim floaties and cut room service hamburgers into bite-size pieces and had perfunctory sex with her husband in the shower while their kids slept. In the other, she drank tequila and slept naked and made love to a woman who made her feel like she had electricity in her veins. Which one was the real Merit? But she knew that wasn't the right question. It was her in both places. She was in all of it. She was right here.

She wouldn't let herself pretend she wasn't conflicted. She was, deeply, more now than she had been at first. She'd betrayed Cory—no, she was betraying Cory, present tense. She was aware of it every Friday when she got on the ferry. It took all of her effort not to sob every Sunday morning in church. But if her affair with Jane was a mistake—and surely it was, had to be, could an extramarital affair ever be anything other than that?—it was one she would make again and again. Every time she felt herself starting to spiral—which happened at least once a day now, though she hadn't breathed a word of it to Jane, and was happening now as she sat on her lounge chair in the blazing sun, fighting coconut-syrup-and-infidelity-induced nausea— she reminded herself that the only alternative to doing what she was doing was never doing it at all. And there was nothing as unfathomable as that.

When Cory and the boys got back from the beach, Merit put her book in her bag and stood up. "How was it?" she asked brightly. She heard the falsity in it. She didn't want to be the sort of person who had to pretend to be happy at a beautiful island resort with her well-meaning husband and two healthy kids. But in this moment there was no one else to be.

"It was awesome!" Jude said, grinning. He hadn't had a haircut in ages. His dark hair was curling around the ears, the way hers had when she was a kid.

"Oh yeah?" She sat down on her heels so she was eye level with him. Nash came up beside them and flung his arms around her neck.

"We saw a turtle!" he squealed, his face lit up with delight. *When had he stopped looking like a baby?* She didn't know. She'd spent the majority of his third birthday party in December texting with Jane about plane tickets for their trip.

Jude's face darkened. "Nash! I said *I* was gonna tell her!"

"You can both tell me," Merit said, sliding her free arm around Jude's sun-warmed body. He was lanky and olive-skinned like his dad. He was a rule follower like Cory, too, and it frustrated him to no end that his younger brother didn't give two shits about protocol, a trait Nash had clearly inherited from her.

"It was so big," Nash said, and Jude shot him another dark look.

"It wasn't *that* big," Jude retorted, knocking his brother's sand bucket out of his hand.

"My bucket!" Nash shrieked, and then dissolved into tears on the ground.

"I have an idea," Merit said cheerfully, as though one of her offspring hadn't just behaved like a bullying asshole and the other wasn't thrashing on the pool deck like a wild beast. "Why don't you guys take me to this waterslide you love so much?"

"Wait, really?" Jude asked. "You'll go on it, too?"

"Sure," Merit said easily, and stood up.

"Did you hear that, Dad? Mom's going on the waterslide!"

"Why do you sound so surprised?" she asked Jude.

"Because you never do fun stuff."

"That is so not true!"

"Whatever. Can we go now?" He was impatient like his father, too.

"For the record, I am very fun," she told Jude. *Just ask my friend Jane.*

"Let's go, Mommy," came Nash's voice beside her, the tears gone as fast at they'd come. He jumped up and down. "Let's go, let's go!"

She looked at Cory. "You coming?"

"You guys go ahead," he said. "I'm gonna order some lunch."

"But it's so early," she said. "Why don't you wait until we get back, and we can all eat together?"

"Nah. No need. I'll just grab something now." Cory signaled for the waiter.

"You can't wait?"

Cory looked at her. "Mer, I'm just going to order something from the pool menu, which you can do just as easily when you get back. Why does it matter if we all eat at the same time?"

"It doesn't," she said, and, taking the boys by their hands, left.

As they made their way to the main pool, it occurred to Merit that Jane would never order lunch without her, and maybe that was the thing she'd fallen in love with first. From the very beginning of their relationship, when they were still basically strangers and Jane invited her to a pitch she didn't need her for, and brought her a latte the next morning, and took her out for oysters and champagne that afternoon, Jane had made it clear that she wanted Merit around. The Monday-morning gossip sessions, the afternoon coffee breaks, their Friday lunches out—all the little rituals that followed, none of them necessary or efficient or remotely productive, each one instigated by Jane. Her affection for Merit was immediate and unequivocal, and it was the antidote to the loneliness Merit had felt for so long she'd stopped identifying it as loneliness. It wasn't simple, but it wasn't that complicated either. Jane had shown up for her. Before the attraction, before the overwhelming desire that clouded everything else. Merit had stopped feeling alone in her boat.

That didn't explain their chemistry, the undeniable magnetism, the sensation of waking up from a deep sleep to an amplified sort of consciousness that felt like the very definition of being alive. But the experience that came before all that, the experience of togetherness, was the thing that made Merit feel safe enough to eventually acknowledge the rest of it. More than Jane's beauty (god, she was beautiful), or her talent, or her brilliant mind and the way it tackled problems like a bird devouring a fish, Merit had fallen in love with the thing that happened when they were simply *with* each other, when she and Jane became *MeritandJane*. It was miraculous, really. She'd found togetherness with someone she wanted to be together with.

There was a hint of that same sensation now, standing in line at the waterslide with Jude and Nash, holding their hands. Merit inhaled and tried to hang on to it: the scent of sunscreen and chlorine, the sun on her shoulders, her sons' exuberant, uncomplicated grins.

In front of them, a child let go of the handles at the top of the slide and disappeared down the flume. Merit's breath escaped with a short, frenzied *whoosh*. Time was like that slide, sucking the moments right from under her as she just stood there with her bathing suit riding up her butt and a vague background headache, waiting for something spectacular to happen.

Except, she realized suddenly: It already had.

"You're up," the attendant called to them.

"Mommy," Jude said, yanking her arm forward. "It's our turn."

Beside her, Nash bounced on his toes, shivering with excitement and fear.

I know how you feel, she wanted to tell the little boy beside her, whose body she'd carried for forty-one weeks in her womb, a week past his due date because he always did everything on his own terms. Instead, she sat down in the freezing water and lifted her youngest son onto her lap. Jude sat between her legs, palms grazing her knees.

This is my life, she thought. These two little boys. Her middle-aged body. The water rushing past them. The bathing suit wedged up her rear. All of it was symbolic. All of it was exactly what it seemed. She felt both the movement and the inertia: the pull of the water, nudging them forward; her thighs against smooth plastic, keeping them put. Then, the combination of instinct and decision that lifted her hips up, the precise moment the current caught them, the surge of adrenaline when gravity took over and it was no longer hers to control.

Love is like this.

It didn't answer any of her questions. It didn't make anything easier, or simpler, or right. But for one infinite second, Merit saw beauty in the mess she'd made of her life. She knew she couldn't hang on to it—it was slipping through her fingers like the water rushing past. While it lasted, though, it was magnificent: the gratitude, the awe, the wholeness, the peace.

THAT NIGHT, AFTER Merit put the boys to bed, Cory went out on the balcony with his iPad and a beer from the minibar to catch up on emails. "Want to bring your book out here and sit with me?" he asked, glancing over his shoulder at her. "I think there's some canned rosé in the fridge."

"Uh—" she faltered. No, she didn't want to sit out there with him and pretend to read a book she didn't care anything about. She wanted to be alone so she could call Jane before it got too late. But this was Cory making an effort, offering his version of a moment together. And yes, there would be a screen between them and none of his attention would be on her, but there was a time when an invitation to do something separate right next to him would have seemed like the most romantic gesture in the world. "I was actually thinking of going down to the beach," she said finally. "I'm still a little full from dinner and thought a walk might help."

"Okay," Cory said, and smiled. His dark hair was mussed and he had three-day scruff on his chin. She liked him best like this, disheveled and relaxed. It was the way he'd been in college, back when nothing ever seemed to stress him out. She could still see that twenty-one-year-old boy in her husband's forty-year-old face, and she missed him. Even now, as she was itching to get out the door and out of earshot so she could call her lover in California, she wanted to reach inside Cory's fit middle-aged body and yank out the boy she married.

"I won't be gone long," she said, and left.

Jane picked up on the second ring.

Merit grinned into the phone when she heard Jane's very particular hi, which wasn't actually hi but *hej*, the Danish word for hello. Merit whispered it to herself sometimes when she was alone in the car, trying to get the intonation exactly right.

"Hey," Merit said back. "How are you?"

"Desperate for you to come home to me," Jane said. "How's Hawaii?"

"Beautiful. Lonely."

"Are you and Cory fighting?"

Merit shook her head and then remembered Jane couldn't see her. "No. We're fine. It's all fine. I just miss you. A lot."

"I miss you, too."

Merit plopped down on the sand and looked up at the sky. "I don't think I realized how lonely I was in my marriage," she heard herself say. "For years."

"I get it," Jane said quietly. "I was, too."

"Except you're not married anymore."

"No. I'm not."

"Lucky you."

"You love Cory," Jane said. "And you have two gorgeous kids."

Merit didn't say anything.

"Cory is a good father," Jane added. "And you know he loves you."

Merit squeezed her eyes shut. All of these things were true but she didn't want Jane to say them. She wanted her to say something else. "But what if I'm only in love with you?"

In the excruciating moment of silence that followed, Merit wished she could take the words back.

"Merit," she heard Jane say finally.

"Jane."

"I'm in this with you."

Tears sprung to Merit's eyes. "Okay."

"I mean it."

"Okay." She choked back a sob she didn't understand.

"Merit."

She was crying now, but she didn't want Jane to know that.

"Little bird. Talk to me. What?"

"You're in this with me," Merit repeated. "I don't know what that means."

"Honey? It means I'm in love with you, too."

fifteen

IT'S A FUND-RAISER for the western pond turtle," Cory explained one Tuesday morning in April, as Merit was speed-scrambling eggs for the boys. "Greg's on the board." Greg was the CEO of Cory's company, a thirty-two-year-old man-child who wore gray joggers and a Brooks Brothers blazer to work.

"It's an entire fund-raiser for one species of turtle?"

"Not just any turtle," Cory said. "The only native freshwater turtle on the Pacific Coast. Do you know where my travel mug is?"

"Dishwasher," Merit said. "They're clean." She said this as though there was a possibility Cory might put all the dishes away.

He pulled out his mug and poured himself some coffee. "So, anyway, it's this Friday. It's at Yerba Buena Gardens so I figured you could just go straight from work. It starts at six."

"I can't on Friday," Merit told him, dumping undercooked eggs onto two plates. "I have dinner with Jane."

Cory looked at her. "Can't you move that to Saturday?"

She could, certainly. Jane would understand. But their Friday dinners were sacred, and Merit didn't want to mess with their routine. They'd seen each other nine times since Mexico, eight dinners at Jane's house, plus one coffee on a Wednesday afternoon at their old spot, which was lovely and terrible and ruined Merit for the rest of the day. She'd made a rule after that, that they could only see each other on Friday nights. It was brutal, the apartness, but Merit understood that five-and-a-half hours a week was all she could give this thing between them unless she was ready to give it her whole life.

"It's not just the two of us this week," she lied. "It's a big group. A networking thing." She turned her head to avoid eye contact and raised her voice to a shout. "Nash! Jude! Come eat your breakfast! It's getting late!"

Cory frowned. "At Jane's house?"

"Yep. She's having it catered." This detail was completely unnecessary and another brazen lie. Merit busied herself with wiping the counter, which was already clean.

"Oh," Cory said. Merit winced at how disappointed he sounded.

"I'll just tell Jane I can't make it," she said.

"No, no, it's okay," Cory said quickly. "If it's a networking thing, you should go. The fund-raiser will probably be boring anyway."

Merit swallowed her guilt and smiled. "If you're sure," she said, planting a dry kiss on his face. She'd been doing this a lot lately, treating him like someone's kindly grandfather: pats on the arm, pecks on the cheek. "I'll make sure Sierra can stay late."

"Eggs! I hate eggs!" Jude was standing by his plate with his arms crossed.

"Great," Merit told him. "Don't eat them, then."

"Can I have pancakes?"

"I want pancakes!" Nash parroted.

"No pancakes," she said. "I have to get ready for work."

"But I'm hungry!" Jude yelled as she left the kitchen.

"There's cereal in the pantry!" she called from the stairs. "Knock yourself out!"

She let herself imagine that Cory might run some interference, until she heard the front door open and close, and then the very distinct sound of Jude dropping the entire gallon of milk.

"Mommy!"

She sighed and went back downstairs.

She didn't raise her voice, not even when Jude blamed her for the spill, or when Nash tried to help and dumped the rest of the jug on the floor. It wasn't the boys' fault their mother was running late because she'd let herself stay in bed for a full seventeen minutes after her alarm went off that morning, her hand between her legs, getting herself off.

Now the piper was coming to collect, and Merit would sop up one hundred and twenty-eight ounces of milk without losing her shit if that was the price. But how much sin would this penance cover? Just the fact that she'd laid in bed fantasizing about her lover while her husband showered and shaved in the bathroom ten feet away? What about the fact that she'd lied to him about a networking event that didn't exist just so she could live that fantasy out?

It was madness, this thing she was doing. It was also madness how easy it was to pull off. She spent six and three-quarter days every week working through her to-do list, capably performing the role of the Woman She'd Always Been. Then, on Fridays at five-thirty, she got on the ferry to Sausalito and forgot everything but Jane.

Her mother called as she was walking into work.

"Come see us for Easter," she said. "The church is doing an egg hunt on the beach. The boys will love it."

"We can't," Merit said automatically. She told herself she was thinking of Cory. Taking a day off work to fly across the country for a weekend with her parents was a hassle he didn't need.

"We haven't seen you in over a year," her mom said pointedly, a jab at Merit's decision not to come to Florida for Christmas.

"We'll come for a week this summer," Merit promised.

"What will you do for Easter?" her mom asked.

"Go to church. Eat a honey-baked ham." *Fantasize about the woman I'm sleeping with.* "Honestly, Mom, I haven't thought about it. It's three weeks away."

"Your 'radically inclusive' church?" Only her mother could make this sound derogatory.

"That's the one," Merit said. The redbrick building in which Merit had sat, Sunday after Sunday, clutching the pew Bible with two hands, waiting for God to tell her she'd made an unfathomable mistake.

"Hm." It was a familiar sound, the one her mother made every time her daughter did something questionable, like take an art class instead of calculus, or date the one Muslim kid at her high school, or wear a red jumpsuit to senior prom. Merit had trained herself not to react to it, but hearing it now was almost enough to unleash the gurgling truth inside her in one triumphant, irreverent shout: *I AM IN LOVE WITH A WOMAN AND I TRULY DON'T CARE WHAT YOU THINK.*

"Yep," she said instead.

Merit half-participated in the remainder of their conversation, which ended when she got in the elevator and pretended to be surprised when the service cut out.

When did I become this person? she wondered as she made herself a coffee in the office kitchen. A person who could hang up on her mother and cheat on her husband and still make small talk with her co-workers about her kids. The mug she'd pulled out of the cupboard read, ADULTING IS HARD. There was a comforting simplicity in this.

Her workday was like every other: busy and mostly unfulfilling and punctuated by unproductive thoughts about Jane. Time was intermittently fast and slow. She forgot to eat lunch.

She stopped at the grocery store on her way home and put taco shells and turkey meat and red licorice in her cart. Her phone buzzed as she was checking out.

LEENA: are u here?

Merit frowned at her screen.

"Do you need bags?" the girl at the register asked.

"Yes, thanks." Merit was distracted now by the text.

here where? she wrote back.

LEENA: the art auction!

"Fuck," Merit swore. The girl at the register flinched. "Sorry," Merit said quickly. "That was really aggressive, I'm sorry. Also, I don't need any of this stuff anymore. Well, except the licorice. I'll take that." She fumbled for her credit card. "My son's school is having a fund-raiser tonight, and I completely forgot about it. Hence the swearing. Sorry, I can't find my credit card, I—"

"It's in the machine," the girl at the register said, pointing. "You already paid."

"Oh!" Merit stared at her AmEx, which was, in fact, in the machine.

(Was it bad that she had no recollection of how it got there? How much of a person's life could be executed on autopilot? Apparently, a big fucking chunk.)

Merit yanked her card out of the reader and shoved it into her purse. She would regret that later, when she'd open her wallet and assume her credit card was lost. "Well. I guess I'll take everything, then."

The girl at the register just nodded. The woman in line behind Merit inched her cart forward, a passive-aggressive signal that Merit's time at the register was now up.

"Great," Merit said, to no one in particular. She took her bag, which she only now realized was not actually a complete meal for anyone other than a frat boy, and left.

She called Cory from the car, while shoving fistfuls of licorice into her mouth.

"We forgot about the art auction," she said as soon as he answered. She used the word "we" even though she knew her husband maintained a state of zero awareness of all school-related events.

"What art auction?" he asked.

"The first-grade parent fund-raiser."

"Fund-raiser for what? It's a public school."

"The art program," Merit said impatiently. "Anyway, it started at six. I'm on my way there now."

"We live in California," Cory said. "We get state funding for the arts."

"Cool." She didn't know why she'd called him. What had she expected him to say? "I'll have Sierra feed the boys. You should probably pick up something for yourself."

"No problem," Cory said, which was his way of being agreeable but, as always, annoyed the crap out of her because why would it ever be a *PROBLEM* that he didn't have to keep track of anything or show up anywhere and the only thing expected of him was to occasionally feed himself?

"'Kay. Bye." She hung up. She wanted to turn her car around and drive across the Golden Gate to Sausalito. She inhaled the rest of the bag of licorice instead.

The elementary school parking lot was crowded with mid-range SUVs.

Merit parked her Subaru in a spot marked CLEAN AIR COMPACT VEHICLE ONLY and sprinted inside.

She could've easily skipped it. She could've told her mom friends that something came up at work. But the story she was telling herself was that her relationship with Jane wasn't making her any less present in the rest of her life. This narrative was utter horseshit; she was aware of this every night at seven forty-five as she read bedtime stories to her children without registering a single word. But during daylight hours, Merit endeavored to believe that having an affair that occupied every waking thought wasn't making her a less-engaged mom, and that meant showing up at the first-grade art auction with her game face on.

The cafeteria was crowded with the usual assortment of parent types. The working moms gulped plastic cups of wine while staring blankly at their stay-at-home counterparts who had fresh makeup and cute outfits they hadn't been wearing all day. The working dads hovered near exits clutching smartphones they checked incessantly. The stay-at-home dads spoke passionately about the selection of art.

Leena beelined over as soon as Merit walked in. She was wearing a confusing combination of dressy black pants and a gray sweatshirt with more than one stain on the front.

"Why do you look so good?" she demanded.

"I don't," Merit said. She was scanning the room for the nearest jug of wine.

"Shut up. Did you get filler?" Leena was eyeing her suspiciously.

"I can't afford filler," Merit replied with a laugh. *Was this true? How much did filler cost?* She still hadn't located the wine.

"Well, you look great," Leena said, "whatever you're doing."

I'm in love, Merit felt like saying. But this wasn't an acceptable explanation, not when the person she was in love with wasn't her husband or one of her kids. "So what's new with you?" she asked, bringing her attention back to Leena. She hadn't seen her friend in months. "How's work?"

"Work is fine," Leena said. "I'm bored as shit. Dev thinks I need antidepressants."

"Are you depressed?" Merit asked.

"No, I'm fucking bored," replied Leena, many decibels too loud. Merit wondered if she was also drunk. The cup in her hand was empty, yet Leena kept taking intermittent sips. "Tell me how you are. You've been very off the grid lately. How's work, how's Cory, how are the boys?"

"Everything's good," Merit said. She didn't want to go into any details. She didn't want to accidentally confess the whole thing. "So what's the deal with the auction? How does it work?"

"They're asking everyone to bid on at least one piece, and it's not supposed to be your own kid's," Leena replied, taking another swig from her empty cup. "Which is good, because my girls have zero artistic talent." Merit decided that her friend was, in fact, quite drunk. In six years of friendship, she'd never heard Leena say anything that wasn't unequivocally complimentary about her twins.

Another mom approached. Merit seized the opportunity for escape.

"I'll find you in a bit," Merit told Leena.

Leena nodded. "I'll be here. Bored as shit."

Merit arranged her face in a pleasant but preoccupied expression and set off through the crowd. She wasn't particularly worried that anyone would talk to her. Leena and Dev were the only people in the room she knew. She had a list of faceless names and email addresses in her head; Jude's room parent, the dad who ran the booster club, the mom who always replied-all to messages from the teacher with excessive punctuation and a puzzling use of initial caps. Merit supposed the right thing to do would be to attempt to meet these other parents, to introduce herself with the appropriate exchange, "You must be Wesley's dad. I'm Jude's mom!"

Instead, she would fill a cheap plastic tumbler with grocery store merlot and peruse first-grade art by herself.

The school had done a great job with the pieces. Every canvas was mounted in a floating wood frame that the kids had made themselves. Merit moved slowly from section to section, sugar buzzed from the licorice, surprised by how well put together it was and inordinately happy that she'd come.

She was still smiling over Jude's painting—a self-portrait with a very intense facial expression that the placard on the wall indicated was meant to be reminiscent of Van Gogh—when her eyes caught a brightly colored canvas across the room. It was a painting of two girls, sitting side by side, holding hands. There were oversize hearts painted on their chests, connected by a single looping line. Merit knew even at a distance that this was a little girl's take on Frida Kahlo's *The Two Fridas*, a piece she'd studied in art history but hadn't thought about in years. She refilled her cup and moved toward it. She would've paid an excessive sum to take it home.

As it turned out, fifty bucks was all it took.

Later that night, while the boys slept and Cory ate takeout on the couch, Merit took the painting she'd won upstairs and propped it up on the dresser by her bed. She stared at it until she fell asleep, thinking about the two Merits she held inside her, swept up in a compassion for herself she couldn't have explained.

"IT'S NOT SOME amazing piece of art," she told Jane on Friday. There was salmon in the oven and they were standing at Jane's kitchen island, snacking on olives and brie. "A first-grader painted it."

"But it spoke to you," Jane said.

Merit nodded. "Something about the two girls' faces. One is smiling, one looks so sad. I don't even know the little girl who made it. Did something happen in her family? Did her parents get divorced?"

Jane frowned a little at Merit's mention of divorce.

"Where are you going to hang it?" she asked.

"I'm not sure. My office maybe." Merit popped an olive into her mouth. "Enough about my art collecting. How are you? I missed you a lot this week."

"I miss you a lot every week," Jane said. "And I'm good. Work is finally picking up."

"I suppose you can't hire me now."

"I *could*," Jane said. "We just wouldn't get anything done."

Merit smiled at her. "Oh, we'd get plenty done. It just wouldn't be work related."

Jane turned and kissed her. Merit wrapped her arms around Jane's waist and caught her own elbows. She could never hold a man like this.

"I'm glad I'm here," she said against Jane's lips. Jane's hands were in her hair.

"Mm. Where else would you be?"

"Cory wanted me to go to a fund-raiser with him tonight."

Jane pulled back. "Why didn't you go?"

"Because Fridays are our night," Merit said. Her grip on her elbows slipped. Jane stepped back.

"What's the fund-raiser for?"

"An endangered turtle. His boss bought a table, I guess. Who cares?"

"What time does it start?"

"Why?"

"Because I think you should go."

Merit blinked. "What?"

"If his boss bought a table, then it's a work thing, and if he asked you to be there, then you should go," Jane said. "It probably starts at seven, right? I'll drive you into the city. You can borrow a dress."

"You're joking."

"I'll make you salmon next week."

"Jane."

"Merit."

"I don't want to go to a fund-raiser for a turtle! I want to stay here and make love to you." It was the first time she'd called it that out loud. It felt funny on her tongue.

"We have to be sensible," Jane said. She walked over to the ceramic bowl where she kept her keys.

"But this is our night," Merit said. She hated how silly it sounded. How needy she felt. There was a sharp tingling in her chest, like frozen fingers under hot water. Or a heart dropped in an ice bath.

"We'll have other nights," said Jane.

"You know what?" Merit heard herself say. Her voice was the ice bath now, as cold as she could stand. "You're right. I should go. But I'll just get an Uber."

"I don't mind driving you, birdie."

Merit was already on her phone, ordering the car. She felt like a marionette, her movements jerky and stilted and controlled by someone else.

"It's the two Merits." Jane's voice was uncharacteristically small.

Merit stopped. "What?"

"I know there are two Merits," Jane said quietly, fiddling with her keys. "And I know it's hard for you. Harder than you let on."

"Then don't make it harder," Merit said.

"I don't want you to feel like you have to choose."

"But I did choose. I'm here. I chose you."

Jane looked away.

"Honestly, I don't understand," Merit said. "Cory doesn't even care that I'm not there. You're making this so much more complicated than it has to be."

"It's beyond complicated, little bird, and I'm endeavoring to make it simpler. The man you're married to has priority. If he has a work thing, you go."

"Got it. Are there any other rules I should know about?"

Jane sighed. "You are not easy."

"Neither are you."

"We agreed we'd be careful."

"We *are* being careful."

"The stakes are higher for you. You have more to lose."

"Why do you always do this?"

"What exactly?"

"Defend Cory."

"I don't give two shits about Cory," Jane retorted. "I just don't want you to do anything you'll regret."

"Then don't make me go to a fund-raiser for a fucking turtle!"

"Okay."

"Okay?" Merit repeated.

Jane nodded. "Okay." She tossed her keys onto the island. "If you don't want to go, don't go. You're a grown woman."

Merit set her phone on the counter. "I am."

"But for the record, I was trying to be sensible."

"Noted." Merit pulled her sweater over her head and dropped it on the kitchen floor. She watched Jane's eyes drift down her torso.

"If you'd done that earlier, we could've skipped the drama," Jane said. Neither of them moved. The distance between them was agonizing and delicious. Merit felt her nipples harden in her bra.

"What's the status of that salmon?" she asked.

"Who the fuck cares."

"So we're clear," Merit said, slowly unbuttoning her jeans. "Fridays are our night. Do you understand?"

Jane nodded. "I do."

"Good."

As she sauntered across Jane's kitchen in the pink lingerie she'd bought online and hidden in the bottom of her drawer until today, Merit felt in her body all the things Leena had noticed in her on Tuesday night but hadn't been able to name: her own power, a sense of possibility, and most of all, a sheer, unbridled glee.

sixteen

FOUR DAYS BEFORE her fortieth birthday, Merit decided she was having a heart attack. It started with a creeping tightness in her chest, then the sensation of not being able to take a full breath. When was the last time she'd had a physical? She hadn't been to a doctor that wasn't her OB in years. Women had heart attacks at forty. She wasn't in great cardiovascular shape.

When she told Cory, he laughed.

She stared at him. "Truly. What the fuck?"

His smile dropped. "What?"

"I tell you I might be having a heart attack and you *laugh*?"

"You're not having a heart attack, Mer." He was using his patient voice. "I laughed because you said the exact same thing right before you turned thirty. Remember? You made me take you to urgent care."

The memory came catapulting back. The stabbing pain in her back, the shortness of breath, the feeling of being too big for her skin. Cocaine-induced cardiac arrest, that's what she'd thought, from the one and only time she'd tried it, two days before her thirtieth birthday. The fact that she was having a heart attack at twenty-nine hadn't surprised her; she'd been told her whole life that drugs were evil and that if you were dumb enough to try them, you should expect God to strike you down. Except, it turned out, her heart wasn't failing; her psyche was. A panic attack, the friendly doctor at the twenty-four-hour urgent care explained, at which point Cory told him how anxious his wife was about turning thirty, and both men agreed that they'd figured it all out. Merit hadn't argued with them, even though she knew it wasn't getting older that terrified her, but the fact that she could no longer see herself when she looked in the mirror. She saw someone who resembled her, but the girl in the glass was vapid and flaky and snorted cocaine in bathrooms with people she'd just met.

"This is about you turning forty in four days," Cory told her now. "It'll pass. You're fine."

His certainty was irritating, but Merit knew as soon as he said it that he was right, because really, her current circumstance wasn't so different from the one she'd been in a decade before. Sure, now she was reliable and socially responsible and only consumed legal drugs laced in homemade baked goods, but the woman she saw in the mirror every morning was four months deep into an extramarital affair and enjoying every second of it. It was a different version of the same existential what-the-fuck.

"Are you sure you don't want me to throw you a party?" Cory asked as Merit was attempting—and failing—to suck in a full breath without her lungs feeling like they might explode in her chest. "Or organize a dinner at least? It's just so unlike you not to want to celebrate with friends."

He was right about this, too. It *was* unlike her. But she'd been replaced by that woman in the mirror, a woman who didn't want the attention a birthday celebration would bring. That woman was walking a tightrope between deception and confession and if too many people started paying attention to her she might crash to one side.

She exhaled sharply.

"I'd rather just have a nice dinner with you," she said, light-headed now. *And spend the next night with Jane.*

Her birthday was on Thursday, and she and Cory had reservations at a fancy new seafood place in the Marina that night. On Friday, she was sleeping over at Jane's. They were going out for the very first time since Mexico, to a tiny restaurant in Mill Valley. They joked that it was their second date. Merit was debating wearing a dress.

She was looking forward to the dinner, but the sleepover was the real gift. She'd told Cory there was a breakfast place in Sausalito that Jane wanted to take her to Saturday morning, did he mind if she just stayed the night? She knew he'd be fine with it, and he was. He'd always been a big fan of Jane.

"As long as you're sure," Cory said now, returning to his Sunday-night emails. "I don't want you to get mad at me later for not planning something for you."

"Got it," Merit said, and went upstairs to take a bath.

She still had that creepy-crawly feeling on her skin and thought about medicating with a very tall glass of wine, but she hadn't eaten much at dinner and couldn't afford to be hungover the next morning at work. She poured lavender bubbles in the bath water and tried to take deep breaths.

How did she feel about turning forty?

(How did she feel about anything other than Jane?)

She asked herself these questions as she sat in scalding hot bathwater and stared at her knees.

No answers came.

Her mind drifted to the fan of fine lines beside the exquisite blue eyes that dilated every time Jane was turned on. How could she dread turning forty when she was wildly attracted to a woman who'd be sixty in September? Every time Jane tugged at the skin on her cheekbones or lamented the sunspots on her chest, Merit wanted to scream at her, *YOU'VE NEVER BEEN MORE BEAUTIFUL THAN THIS!*

The water had gone cold. Merit sighed and pulled the drain up.

BY THE TIME her birthday arrived on Thursday, the tightness in Merit's chest had mostly subsided. She got up early that morning and went to a Pilates class, then stopped at her favorite coffee shop on the walk home and bought herself a fancy latte and a scone. The air was clear and brisk, and whether it was the endorphins from the workout or the sugar from the scone or the fact that her ass looked better at forty than it had at thirty-five, Merit was happy when she came through the front door.

Cory and the boys were in the kitchen with grins and balloons. "Happy birthday!" they shouted in unison, Nash tripping over himself to get to her first. Cory was in pajama pants and a faded Cornell T-shirt, making her fried eggs. She felt like a jerk for eating the scone. She crumpled the pastry bag and shoved it into her purse.

"What's all this?" she asked, smiling at the spread of hand-drawn cards and presents on the table.

"Daddy got you coffee!" Jude said, pointing at a coffee cup identical to the one she was holding in her hand, from the same coffee place she'd just stopped at on her way home.

"It looks like Mommy got herself a latte," she heard Cory say.

"Wait, you had this delivered?" she asked, going toward the cup, feeling even more like a jerk now.

"And a scone," Cory said, flipping the eggs. "I just put it in the oven to warm it up."

"So sweet," she said, moving toward him to wrap her arms around his waist. "Thank you." She laid her cheek on his back and felt the muscles moving beneath his shirt as he tended to the eggs. She was struck by how wide his shoulders were, how narrow his hips. He switched off the burner as soon as he'd turned the eggs over, his signature method for perfectly runny yolks, and bent to kiss her shoulder. His scruff scratched against her cheek.

"Happy birthday, babe," he said.

She felt the urge to kiss her considerate and clueless husband deeply on the mouth, the way they used to, the way she now routinely kissed Jane. Instead she pecked the back of his neck and went to the oven for her second blueberry scone of the day, which she didn't want but would absolutely eat.

"Open your presents, Mommy!" Nash exclaimed, jumping up and down. "Mine first."

He'd made her a telescope out of a paper towel roll. Seeing his little face on the other end as she held it to her eye, Merit ached for the moment when she'd held him as a newborn, when she thought she'd never want anything more than what she already had.

"I'll give you my present at dinner tonight," Cory said after she'd opened the I LOVE MOM! mug Jude had made her for Mother's Day the previous year and repurposed as a birthday gift.

"Fun," she said, and to her surprise, meant it. The dread she'd been feeling about their evening together had mostly disappeared. Cory was still Cory, her husband, the man she'd spent the past nineteen birthdays with, the one person in the world who knew exactly how she liked her eggs. They weren't *that* unhappy. Maybe they weren't unhappy at all.

Jane called her on her way to work. "Happy birthday, love," she said as soon as Merit picked up. "Can I come take you to lunch?"

"Really?"

"Yes, really. Why do you sound so surprised?"

"I don't know. Because I'm seeing you tomorrow night for our sleepover. Because it's an annoying drive."

"First of all, I'll take the ferry in, obvs. Second, it's your fortieth birthday. I don't care if I'm seeing you tomorrow. I want to see you today."

Merit felt her rib cage expand with breath and space and delight. "You're good at this," she said.

"Good at what?"

"Me. Us."

"It helps that you're irresistible," Jane said. "I couldn't stay away if I tried."

Merit thought about all the times she'd asked Cory if he wanted to come into the city to meet her for lunch. There was always some reason why it didn't make sense.

"So where am I taking you?" Jane pressed. "Birthday girl's choice."

Merit hesitated.

"It's okay if you can't," Jane said then. Merit heard how casually she said it; she also heard the effort it took for her to sound that way.

"I want to," Merit said.

"But you can't. It's fine."

Merit wanted a real excuse, a party they'd planned at work, a lunch with a girlfriend, anything other than the truth.

"I can't see you for lunch and have dinner with Cory five hours later," she said finally. She couldn't lie to Jane.

"Two Merits," Jane said. "I get it."

"I love you." Merit choked on all the other things she wanted so desperately to say.

"Love you, too. Enjoy your birthday, lovely girl."

"WE'LL BOTH HAVE champagne," Cory told the bartender at the restaurant that night. They'd decided to meet an hour before their reservation to have a drink at the bar. "The nicest one you have by the glass. And maybe the grilled artichoke?" He looked at Merit. "What do you think?"

"Perfect," Merit said. She did not let herself think that champagne was the perfect metaphor for how her body felt every time she was with Jane. Instead, she thought of the bubbly she and Cory had drunk in the limo that took them from the church where they got married to their wedding reception on Pensacola beach. They'd finished the whole bottle in ten minutes, cheap champagne in cheap glasses, and kissed sloppily in the parking lot of her parents' beach club until one of her bridesmaids made them get out.

"To the next forty," Cory said now, fourteen years later, raising his glass.

He was talking about her life, not their marriage. But Merit could not find her next breath.

His words were obvious, meaningless, profoundly trite. So why did Merit suddenly feel like she had an anvil sitting on her chest? Light-headed, she lifted her drink. The crisp *clink* of their glasses felt like a gong, or a gavel coming down, or the door of a jail cell slamming shut.

She was being dramatic. She still wanted to be in this marriage. She wasn't stuck.

She gulped her champagne.

Cory drank half of his then set the glass down and ordered a beer. "Now let's talk about your present," he said with a mysterious smile.

"Okay," she said, signaling to the bartender for more champagne. How many liters would it take to drown the panic out? She focused on Cory's eyes, the warm brown irises she'd looked into as she pushed both their babies out. The eyes she'd looked at across so many tables, so many rooms, at weddings and funerals and birthday parties. He loved her. She loved him.

"There's something I haven't told you," he began, and for one wild second she thought he was going to tell her he'd been having an affair. But this was her birthday dinner and he was smiling like the cat that ate the canary, so, no, she decided, infidelity probably wasn't it.

"I got a promotion," he announced. "To chief technology officer."

"What! Cory! That's amazing! Congrats!" She slid forward on her seat to hug him. "I'm so proud of you, babe."

"Thanks," he said, smiling even wider now. "I was pretty shocked. I knew there was talk of creating a CTO position, but I figured Greg would bring an outside person in."

"And you just found out today? How exciting." The bartender hadn't refilled her glass yet. She picked up what was left of Cory's champagne for another toast.

"No, actually," Cory said casually, "I've known for a while."

She put the glass back down. "How long is 'a while'?"

"Since right before Christmas."

It was May sixth.

She blinked.

"You got a promotion before Christmas and you're just telling me now?" She stared at him. "But why? I don't understand."

"I'm getting to that," Cory said, and Merit understood that there were more revelations to come. She tried to make eye contact with the bartender. She needed that champagne.

"I got a pretty significant salary bump with the promotion," Cory was saying. "And that gave me the idea for your birthday present. But it meant I couldn't tell you about the raise."

"How significant are we talking here?"

"Double my salary."

"Wow," she said. At least the last-minute trip to Hawaii now made sense.

"The increase was effective January first. That gave me five months to save up."

She did the math. Five months of his salary wasn't an insignificant amount. What could he possibly have bought her? Diamonds? A car? Oh god. A minivan?

"Cory. Enough with the buildup. What did you get?"

He grinned. "Happy birthday! I bought you a house."

A hammer slammed down on the anvil. Merit felt her smile drop.

"*What?*"

"It's a tear-down, so technically it's a lot for a *future* house," Cory said, beaming like a maniac now. "*Our* future house. You always said you wanted to design our 'forever home' and now you can. Putting aside the fact that 'forever home' sounds like a euphemism for a mausoleum." He laughed and pulled out his phone. "Here, you can scroll through the photos. The house is pretty run-down, but check out the lot!"

Merit's vision was blurred with confusion and fury. Her brain tried to catch up.

Cory got a big promotion that he hadn't told her about.

Cory had been secretly saving money.

Cory bought a house without consulting her.

And he felt good about this?

She stared blankly at his phone without touching it. She didn't want to take it. She didn't want to scroll through photos of a property she already knew she didn't want.

"I don't understand," she said finally. She still hadn't taken his phone. His screen had gone dark. Her heart was racing. There was a metallic taste in her mouth.

"Which part?" he asked.

"All of it."

Cory sighed. For a moment Merit felt bad about the fact that the news of his promotion was being overshadowed by her reaction to this. Then she remembered that he'd gotten the promotion five months before and kept it to himself.

"I thought you'd be excited about it," he said.

"Excited," she repeated. "About a house I don't want."

"How do you know you don't want it? You haven't even seen it yet!"

"Where is it?"

Cory rubbed his forehead wearily.

"Cory. Where's the house?"

"Redwood City."

She felt like she wanted to throw up. Redwood City was thirty miles south of the city. An hour from Sausalito, at least.

"I need to stand up," she said, and jerked to her feet. Her elbow knocked her empty champagne flute. The glass broke when it hit the bar. "Sorry," she mumbled at the bartender. She abruptly sat back down.

"No worries at all," the bartender said smoothly, quickly wiping up the mess. "You wanted another of the same, right?"

"Yes, please," Merit said. *I'll take the whole bottle, thanks.*

"There are a bunch of contingencies," Cory said when the bartender finally left them alone again. "Including your approval. If you don't want it, we can get out of it."

"I don't want it."

"Yeah, I'm picking up on that," Cory said, his voice tight. "Can you tell me why? You haven't even looked at the pictures yet. It's a corner lot."

"Well, for starters, I don't want to live in Redwood City. We live in San Francisco. I work in San Francisco. Our kids go to school in San Francisco."

"Redwood City has great public schools."

"I don't want to live in fucking Redwood City!"

Cory's jaw clenched. "Got it. So I'm just supposed to commute an hour for the rest of my life."

"Your commute is never an *hour*, Cory. You leave before traffic and come home after it."

"I wouldn't have to do that if we lived in the South Bay," Cory pointed out. "I'd be able to spend more time with you and the kids."

"By 'spend more time' I assume you mean sit on our couch with your laptop for longer every night?"

"Don't be a bitch, Merit. It doesn't become you."

She wanted to throw her champagne in his face. Instead, she guzzled it then swallowed back a very unbecoming burp. Cory had never used the word "bitch" and her name in the same sentence before this. She was proud of him for saying so clearly what he meant.

His face changed as soon as he said it, and she could tell he felt bad about calling her names. *I AM NOT THAT DELICATE!* she wanted to shout.

"I'm sorry you don't want the house," he said finally. "I thought it'd be a fun surprise. But like I said, we can get out of it. The money isn't in es-crow yet."

"How could you think that I would want you to *buy a house* without involving me? Even if it weren't in an awful suburb where I have no desire to live. Buying a home is something couples are supposed to do *together.*" How could he not see that what he'd done was actually the exact opposite of what she wanted, the inverse of togetherness, the quintessence of being apart?

"I wanted it to be a surprise," he said defensively. "And I knew I was getting a tear-down so you could draw the plans for the exact house you want, so I didn't think it mattered all that much what the house looked like."

"Do you hear yourself?"

His jaw clenched. "It's not like we've never talked about this, Mer. When you were pregnant we agreed we needed more space."

"Right. When we thought we were having a third kid."

"So now that we're not, you want to rent a two-bedroom apartment for the rest of our lives?"

"I didn't say that." She was getting into dangerous territory, the realm of her desires and the future and what she really wanted to do with the years of life she had left. "I don't want to move to Redwood City," she said finally. "Let's just start with that."

"Yep. Message received." He reached for his beer. She realized she didn't want any more of the champagne. She didn't want to amplify the emotion of this moment, or bring her inhibitions down. She didn't want to say the things a drunker version of her might say.

She pushed her glass away.

"I think we need to talk about what we want for our future," she heard herself say.

The next forty years.

Cory gave her a look she couldn't read. "Meaning?"

"Exactly what I said. I'm not the person I was when you married me. I'm not the person I was five years ago." *Or five months ago.*

"Okay, so what does the person you are now want?"

She couldn't tell if he was being snarky. In a way, it didn't matter, because her answer was the same. The truth bubbled up like the champagne she'd swallowed down.

"Honestly? She doesn't know."

seventeen

Y OU SAID YOU wanted him to go big," Jane said.

It was the night after Merit's birthday, and they were on Jane's deck drinking gin lemonade, her latest cocktail concoction, before leaving for their dinner reservation in Mill Valley, which they'd made late on purpose to avoid a crowd. Merit had decided against a dress and instead was wearing a short red romper that probably should've come with an age limit on the tag.

"I never said I wanted him to go big," Merit replied. "Like, ever."

"But didn't you sort of want him to?" Jane asked, putting her bare feet up on Merit's chair. She was wearing white jeans and a blue silk tank. *Please let me look that good when I'm almost sixty,* Merit thought.

"Did I want him to buy me a tear-down in the suburbs? No."

"Okay, maybe not that specifically. But haven't you wanted him to do something grand?"

"Nope. And after nearly twenty years together, he should know me well enough to know that."

"Cut the man some slack, little bird. You're not the easiest to decipher."

"Why are you defending him again?" Merit demanded. "The house is in Redwood City. Do you know how far away that is?"

"I'm not defending him! I'm just offering an alternative point of view. If the point is to Cory-bash, I can get on board. It's your birthday, honey. Whatever you want."

"I want *you*," Merit said, pulling Jane's bare foot into her lap. It was taking more effort than she wanted for her to be in this moment and nowhere else. Her mind kept leaping back to Cory's face at the bar the night before. The misguided good intentions. His warm brown eyes.

"You have me," Jane said, wriggling her toes. "Look, I painted them just for you." The polish was a pretty pale pink.

"Is that my birthday present?" Merit brought Jane's foot to her lips, kissing her arch. Even this made her think of Cory. His feet were covered in calluses from his cycling shoes.

Be here with her. Don't think about him.

"You told me I wasn't allowed to get you a present," Jane said.

"Mm-hmm," Merit said, moving her lips up to Jane's ankle, and then her calf. Jane's eyes fluttered as she flexed her foot. "What time is our reservation?" she murmured against Jane's leg. Cory's face was fading from her mind.

"Soon," Jane said. "We should go before we decide not to go."

Merit nodded and released Jane's foot. Part of her would've been content not leaving the house, peeling Jane's clothes off layer by layer, spending the time they had in bed. But she was hungry, and distracted, and something else she couldn't name. She wanted to go out.

They kissed like teenagers in Jane's foyer while they waited for the Uber to pick them up. Merit was already feeling the gin.

"Do you want your gift now or after dinner?" Jane asked at some point.

"I thought you didn't get me one."

"You know I did."

"After," Merit said, putting her hand on the back of Jane's neck as she kissed her. She wanted to disappear into this, into them. She didn't want to be a middle-aged woman with a husband who made her feel like the best part of her life had already passed. She opened her mouth hungrily, tugging on Jane's lips with her teeth. "How much time do we have?" she murmured, unbuttoning Jane's jeans.

"Not enough," Jane said, catching her hand.

"Nonsense," Merit said, and dropped to her knees.

Jane didn't fight her after that.

At some point, Jane's phone buzzed. Neither of them noticed.

Eventually, they called another Uber. They held hands as they made their way down the front steps. Merit was giddy with the privilege of this. They'd never been out in the world as a couple, not even in Mexico, where the closest they'd come was dancing together in a seedy bar. Jane opened the car door for her. Their driver was playing Barry Manilow. They made out in the back seat.

The restaurant Jane had chosen was perfect; intimate and inviting, half-filled with no one either of them knew. The hostess took them to a table in the back. Merit had dropped Jane's hand, instinctively, when they walked in the restaurant, but as they made their way across the restaurant she felt the urge to grab it back. *WE ARE TOGETHER!* she wanted to shout. She felt exhilarated and reckless. She didn't care who saw them. She wasn't afraid of being found out.

They sat beside each other in a corner booth and ordered French fries and mussels as an appetizer. Jane picked out an expensive bottle of red wine. Merit sipped hers slowly. She treasured the feeling of Jane right beside her. She didn't want the night to end.

"What are we doing?" she asked at some point. They were splitting a filet mignon. Jane was feeding Merit little bites of meat and creamed spinach with a cocktail fork. Briefly, Merit wondered how they appeared to others in the restaurant, these two women with nearly twenty years between them, the older one feeding the younger one steak.

"Other than making a spectacle of ourselves?" Jane's cheeks were pink from the wine. "We're enjoying a fabulous meal. The food's really good, don't you think?"

"Yes," Merit said.

"But that's not what you meant."

"No."

"We're taking it as it comes, I guess," Jane said. She put the fork down and reached for her wine. Merit watched Jane's hands on the glass. Her lover kept her nails very short now, and dark.

"Am I having a mid-life crisis?"

"Quite possibly," Jane replied.

Merit sat back and pushed her hands through her hair. She felt hot suddenly. Flushed. "When I think about it, it seems so completely insane—I mean, honestly, what the actual fuck?"

Jane frowned. "Are you having second thoughts?"

"Jane!"

"Merit."

"How can you even ask me that?"

"Because I know how complicated it is for you," replied Jane. "I've been saying that from the beginning."

"No." Merit shook her head. "That's the whole thing. When we're together, it doesn't feel crazy at all. Or complicated. Or wrong, even. It feels . . ." She inhaled with the enormity of it, fumbling for the words she didn't have.

Jane took her hand. "It feels like everything there is."

Merit kissed her.

(Could they do this? Could they kiss in a restaurant?)

Jane kissed her back.

"I love us," Merit murmured against Jane's lips.

"We're pretty great."

Merit closed her eyes and breathed Jane in. "Also? I think kissing you might be my favorite thing ever."

"You might be a little gay, then," Jane said in a low voice.

"You think?" Merit kissed her again.

"Let's go to Denmark," Jane said.

"Will you kiss me like this in Denmark?"

"Fuck yes."

"Then let's go and never come back."

Jane smiled against her lips. "Can I give you your present now?"

"If you insist."

Merit settled back into her seat. The restaurant was still half full, but no one was paying any attention to them. She pushed her leg against Jane's. She felt like some other person. She felt completely like herself.

Jane reached behind her chair and pulled a small box out of her bag.

"I am one hundred percent uncertain about this gift," she said, setting the box on the table. "So if you don't like it or won't wear it, I promise it won't hurt my feelings."

Merit saw the bird first. An intricate gold hummingbird with an emerald eye. It was perched on a thin branch that wrapped around three times, forming a layered band with paper thin gold leaves.

It was a ring. A delicate and beautiful and perfect ring.

"I love it," she breathed.

"Really?" Jane asked. "I know you don't wear a lot of jewelry, but the stone is an emerald, and it seemed so serendipitous when I saw it. A little bird with your birthstone. Anyway. We can get something else if you don't think you'll wear it."

"It's perfect," Merit said, examining it in the palm of her hand.

"You're wondering what finger to put it on," Jane said with a wry laugh.

"Maybe." She was.

"I sized it for your second finger, figuring you could wear it on your middle if it doesn't fit."

Merit nodded. She wanted to wear it on her fourth finger, on her left hand. She wanted to tell the world she belonged to Jane. But there was already a ring there, a princess-cut diamond on a platinum band.

"Thank you," she said when she'd put the ring on, laying her hand on Jane's cheek. "I love it. And I love you."

"I love you, too," Jane said, turning her head to kiss Merit's palm. "And I'm glad you like the ring. Does the birthday girl want dessert?"

"I want you," Merit said.

"You have me."

Merit nodded. It was what she wanted to hear, but it wasn't enough. She heard her mother's voice in her head. *It's wrong to want more than you have.*

"I want this to be my life," she heard herself say. She'd never accepted her mother's view of things anyway.

"Honey. This *is* your life."

"We spend five hours a week together."

"So let's see each other more," Jane said. "You're the one who made the once-a-week rule."

"I want to see you every day."

Jane smiled a little. "Your husband might take issue with that."

"Maybe I don't want a husband anymore."

Jane frowned.

Merit made herself smile. "It's your fault for being so irresistible," she said lightly.

Jane gave her a look she couldn't read. "Merit."

"You don't want me to leave Cory," Merit said. "I get it. It puts too much pressure on you."

"It's not that."

"What is it, then?"

"Honestly? I don't feel as if I'm entitled to an opinion on it."

"You realize that's crazy."

"It isn't, actually," Jane said. "You're talking about breaking up your family. I can't weigh in on that."

"People get divorced all the time," Merit replied. She was surprised by her own casualness. Is this what she did now, talk of divorce in a flippant tone? "Maybe Jude and Nash would be fine with it," she added. "Happier, even. And maybe Cory would get remarried. Maybe he'd be happier, too."

"Those are quite a few maybes," said Jane.

Merit felt suddenly, ineffably, sad. Her own happiness, it seemed, would never be simple again. "So I'm supposed to just stay married and see you once a week."

"You're not 'supposed' to do anything," Jane said gently. "There is beauty and loss in every direction. That's all I'm saying. And I guess what I want you to know most of all is that I don't expect anything out of you. Or out of this. You give me everything I need already." She smiled in her way. *"Det är lagom."*

"It's so hot when you speak Danish words I don't understand." Merit kissed the inside of Jane's wrist. "Translation?"

"Just enough," Jane said, and laid her hand on Merit's cheek. "Perfect as is."

Merit nodded a little.

Jane's smile faded. "That makes you sad."

"It's okay," Merit said. "We're allowed to want different things."

"We don't want different things, birdie. I'm playing the long game here."

Merit looked at the woman she loved and finally understood.

"You think I'm going to change my mind about us."

"I think this is very early stages," Jane said carefully. "And I think the further in we get, the more certain you'll be that this is what you really want."

"Mm-hmm. And if I ignore this sage advice and get divorced anyway?"

"Bitch, if you get divorced I'll have you at a courthouse in a white tux immediately."

For a moment, Merit could see it, vaguely. Standing with Jane, holding her hand, promising to do things she'd do anyway, but saying the words just the same because being with this woman made her want to take vows.

"To be clear, I am not wearing a tux to our wedding," she told Jane. "And I'm marrying your ass in a church."

"That seems reasonable," Jane said.

Merit bit her bottom lip. She wanted to bite Jane's. "How about we go back to your house, and I have you for dessert? Does that seem reasonable, too?"

Jane's eyes flickered with the exact same desire Merit felt. "So reasonable," she said, and she signaled for the check.

THE CLOCK ON Jane's bedside said it was 2:02 in the morning. They'd dozed off in each other's arms just after midnight, naked and clammy with sweat, but now Merit was awake again, her mind pawing at the edges of a dream she'd just had but now couldn't quite recall. A snowstorm; Jane in a black dress; the Collegetown Bridge in Ithaca; an enormous diamond ring.

She could tell from Jane's breathing that Jane was awake now, too.

"Hey," she said softly in the dark.

Jane rolled over to face her, pulling Merit's body against her. It was startling, still, how perfectly their bodies fit together. How there was never a need to shift or rearrange.

But something else was on her mind, too.

"Do you have any old pictures of you?" Merit asked as Jane pushed her leg between Merit's knees. "Like from when you were younger?"

"Sure, in a box somewhere." Jane slid her hand down Merit's back, sending a ripple up Merit's spine. "Why?"

Merit pulled away and sat up. "Can I see them?"

"Now?"

"Is that weird?"

"A little," Jane said, but she was sitting up, too. "Is there a particular reason you want to look at old pictures of me in the middle of the night?"

"I just do," Merit said. She leaned over and kissed Jane deeply.

Jane took Merit's face in her hands. "Can you be deterred? I can think of a few other things we could do that would be more fun and won't make me feel a thousand years old."

Merit smiled against Jane's lips. "Nope."

"You're very stubborn."

"I am."

Jane turned on the bedside lamp. "I might need an aquavit for this little walk down memory lane. Will you have one with me?"

"I don't know what that is, but whatever you want," Merit said, smiling. It was the middle of the night and she was exhausted and dehydrated and deeply conflicted about so many things, but at this moment there was nothing she wanted to be doing other than exactly this.

"It's a Scandinavian spirit," Jane said, pulling Merit's T-shirt over her head. "Like vodka on crack, if crack were made of caraway seeds. Anyway, it's delicious. Be right back."

While Jane headed out for the aquavit and to hunt down the box, Merit went into the bathroom to brush her teeth. As she sat on the edge of Jane's vintage tub, completely naked, every trace of makeup washed from her face (one of the many benefits of sleeping with a woman, she'd learned, was that nighttime beauty rituals were always observed), dragging her toothbrush across her teeth the way she had every night of her adult life, she appeared to herself as pretty as she'd ever been.

Ever since Jude was born she'd been at odds with her appearance, and it'd only gotten worse after Nash. The creeping fine lines, her deflated chest, the way the skin on her stomach wasn't as taut as it'd been before. She'd promised herself that she wouldn't be one of those women who obsessed over aging or lamented what childbirth had done to her body, but she had been, for years, dodging mirrors and sucking in her abs and never taking off her bra. Not anymore. Sitting bare assed on Jane's tub in a position no one would find attractive, hair mussed and lips pink from activities that made her cheeks blush the same shade, Merit didn't want to change a single thing. This was who she was. A forty-year-old woman with a body that finally understood what it wanted and a face that didn't have to work at looking happy anymore.

"Where'd you go?" Jane called from the bedroom.

"In here," Merit called back, mouth full of toothpaste. "One sec." She stood up to spit and saw in the mirror how her brown eyes sparkled, just like Jane had always said. "Happy birthday," she whispered to herself.

"Oh my god," she heard Jane say from the bedroom, followed by a giggle that made her smile.

"What?" Merit asked, still smiling as she came back into the bedroom and took the tulip-shaped glass Jane had brought her, aquavit and a fresh lemon twist even though it was two in the morning. She held it carefully as she climbed into bed and snuggled up next to Jane, who had a shoebox of faded photographs in her lap and one in her hand.

"My sixteenth birthday," Jane said, handing the photo to Merit.

"When I could legally buy alcohol at the supermarket, which was quite the milestone for me."

The girl in the photo was indisputably Jane. The way she was standing, the subtle tilt of her head. "You're adorable," Merit said, aware as she said it that it was exactly what Jane always said about her.

"I was probably drunk in that picture," Jane said, and laughed. "Off some cheap supermarket beer."

"Who took it?" Merit asked.

Jane shrugged, but she was still smiling. "My mum, I guess. Honestly, I have no recollection, and can't imagine why I would ever wear those hideous trousers."

"Do you have any pictures of her?" Merit asked. She could count on one hand how many times they'd talked about Jane's parents. All she knew about Jane's mother was that she'd died of breast cancer when Jane was twenty-seven, and that she'd hated cats.

"Somewhere in here," Jane said, riffling through the other photos. "She despised having her picture taken, so there won't be many. But there was a period when Fred fashioned himself a photographer, and she could never say no to him, so let's see what we've got."

Merit sipped her aquavit, which tasted like vodka and rye bread, and watched Jane flip through old photographs. She thought about her own box of pictures, stacks of glossy prints she kept in a wooden crate under her bed, memories from high school and college that had seemed so important to capture in the moment but would probably make her cringe now. All the important moments since then, the births of her kids and their birthday parties and first days of school and all their Christmas mornings, those were all digital, thousands of images she'd intended to make albums with but never had. If she'd made them—photos neatly organized by year, pithy captions for every shot—would she have a better picture of her life?

Nowhere in those hypothetical photo albums, Merit realized now, would there be any pictures of her and Jane. There couldn't be, because they'd never taken any. She had the ones she'd gotten of Jane that afternoon in her bedroom before everything started, and a few of Jane by the pool in Mexico wearing that ridiculous straw hat. But there wasn't a single shot anywhere of the two of them together. Not a print in a box, not an image in the cloud. If her life were ever summed up in photographs, her relationship with Jane would be entirely out of frame.

"Here's one," she heard Jane say. Merit blinked, bringing the room back into focus as Jane handed her a photograph. "This was right before she died."

Merit looked at the faded image. The woman in it was very thin but still beautiful, and looked strikingly like Jane. "She's gorgeous," Merit said, willing herself not to cry. She was overcome with an emotion she couldn't name. It felt like nostalgia, but for a past that never was; an alternate history in which she met Jane earlier, before it was too late.

"She really was," Jane said, examining the image. "Even when she lost her hair, she turned heads." After a moment, Jane dropped the photo back into the box and picked up another stack. "So what can I show you to satisfy this little desire of yours, birdie?"

"A picture of you at forty," Merit said.

Jane turned to look at her. "Really?"

Merit nodded. It was, after all, why she'd asked.

"Because you want to see if you look better right now than I did?"

"Exactly."

"What's the real reason?"

"I want to imagine meeting you back then. I want to be able to picture it in my head."

"Why?"

"Because you hadn't met Edward yet and I hadn't met Cory," Merit said. "So, there's a chance, if we'd met that year—"

"We might've ended up together instead."

Merit nodded.

"You forget that I was decidedly straight back then," said Jane with a smile.

Merit kissed her shoulder. "Mm-hmm. So straight."

Jane set the box aside and reached for her drink. "Okay, so, at forty, I was working for Andrew Skurman and living . . . here, in fact. In this house. And you were . . . where? At Cornell?"

"San Francisco, actually," Merit replied. "The summer before my senior year, I was out here for eight weeks, interning at Gensler and Associates."

Jane's eyebrows shot up in surprise. "Really?"

"Yep. Living in cheap UCSF housing in the Inner Richmond."

"How chic. Okay, so where might we have run into each other?"

"A networking event," Merit said immediately. She'd thought about it before. Many times, in fact; trying to imagine the exact scenario in which she and Jane would've met, ignoring the fact that the girl she was at twenty-one would never have been brave enough to recognize what the woman she'd been at thirty-nine hadn't been able to ignore.

"A networking event," Jane said. "Nineteen years ago. You think that was our moment."

"I'm just saying it could have been. In theory."

"It wasn't," Jane said firmly. "I was a hot mess at forty and you were practically a child. And if we'd gotten together back then, you wouldn't have the boys." Of course, Merit had thought about this before, too. It was the one thing that made the whole what-if break down. Having kids—*her* kids, the two very particular creatures she'd made with Cory—was something she would never want to undo. She had a sudden flash of longing for their little-boy bodies. She wanted to hold them close and breathe them in and remember how gloriously alive being their mother made her feel. It wasn't so different from the hum of aliveness she felt now, really. The crackle of human connection. The sensation of not being the only one awake.

Jane set her glass on the bedside table and turned to face Merit. "This is our moment, little bird. Not nineteen years ago. Not any time other than right now."

"You're not going to show me a picture of you at forty, are you?"

Jane smiled. "And have you realize how much I've aged? Not a fucking chance."

THEY WOKE WITH the sun the next morning, but it was past nine before they got out of bed. She'd told Cory they were going to brunch, so Merit figured she had at least until noon before she had to head home. She wondered briefly what he was making the boys for breakfast, but resolved to just let him handle it. If the roles were reversed, he wouldn't feel compelled to check in.

"Want coffee?" Jane asked when they finally went downstairs, Jane in Merit's T-shirt, Merit in one of Jane's robes, her hair damp from the shower she'd reluctantly taken. She didn't want to wash Jane off, but she couldn't go home smelling of sex. She settled for Jane's hand-milled lavender soap and her coconut shampoo.

"I'd love some," Merit said. "Can we drink it outside on the deck?"

"Of course we can. Want to grab the papers at the front door?"

"You still get a physical newspaper?"

"So many physical newspapers, I am single-handedly keeping American print media alive. If you're nice, I'll let you read the riveting *Marin Independent Journal* first."

The morning air was dense with fog as Merit gathered the heap of newspapers at the bottom of Jane's steps, four total, and carried them inside, passing a trail of her belongings from the night before: heels, purse, phone, wrinkled red romper, bra. They'd talked about opening a nice bottle of wine and taking a bubble bath when they got home from the restaurant. They'd gotten creative on the stairs instead.

Merit was smiling to herself as she dropped the papers on Jane's kitchen island. Yes, she was playing house a little bit, but so what? She would go home soon and spend the afternoon with the boys. She would be relaxed and undistracted with them. Even if they misbehaved, she wouldn't raise her voice. She carried on this little negotiation with herself as she pulled the newspapers out of their plastic wrappings. She would be a great mom today. She would make up for the hours she'd been away.

But for now, she would let herself be here, in Jane's kitchen, with Jane. She would leave her phone on the floor in the foyer for another hour at least. She would give herself permission to enjoy every second of this.

Her eyes caught her new ring in the morning light. The bright emerald, the elongated beak, the intricate gold wings. It seemed to her the most exquisite piece of jewelry ever made.

"Did I thank you properly for your absolutely perfect gift?" she asked, twisting it on her finger.

"Mmm. I can't remember. You might need to demonstrate your gratitude again after our coffee."

"I think that can be arranged," Merit said. She was still admiring the ring.

"Let's send a pic to Lise," Jane said. "She wants to see it on you."

"Um. You told *Lise* about us?"

"Of course. She's my oldest friend. Though I didn't have to tell her. She guessed. Have you seen my phone?"

"By the front door. And what do you mean, she *guessed*? She's never even met me!"

"I told her I was involved with a friend and she immediately knew it was you." Jane disappeared into the next room.

Merit smiled to herself. "Involved, huh?"

"It felt like an appropriate euphemism!" Jane called from the other room. "Also, to be clear, I didn't say the friend was a woman, which leads me to wonder if I'm the only person in my life who ever thought I was straight?"

"Or maybe she thinks I'm your only American friend?" Merit called back.

"Fuck," she heard Jane say. A moment later she reappeared in the kitchen, frowning at her phone.

Merit felt her smile drop. "Is everything okay?" she asked.

"Cory called me," Jane said slowly. "Six times."

"What? When?"

Jane looked at her. "Midnight. And there's a text, too. Asking you to call him right away." She held out her phone.

"Shit," Merit mumbled, mind racing, terror rising, *something happened to one of the boys*, as she took Jane's phone and called him back.

"What is it?" she demanded as soon as he answered. "Are Nash and Jude okay?"

"They're fine," Cory said, and the vise grip on Merit's chest released. *Thank you, God.*

But only for a second. Then Cory spoke again.

"It's your dad, Mer. He—he had a heart attack."

eighteen

THEY FLEW TO Pensacola on Sunday morning. Her dad's funeral was scheduled for Tuesday, at her parents' church.

They couldn't be certain it was a heart attack without an autopsy, but her father had been on beta-blockers and blood pressure medicine for years, and her mom didn't want to cut up his body, so they'd gone with the coroner's best guess. Merit supposed it didn't matter anyway. Whatever the cause of death, her father was gone.

As their plane took off from SFO that morning, with Nash beside her clutching her hand and Cory and Jude three rows behind them because they couldn't get four seats together, Merit pressed her head against the headrest and prayed. She knew, intellectually, that her brazen infidelity hadn't caused her dad's heart to fail. But her first thought when Cory told her that her father had passed away was that her life was quite literally falling apart.

Jane had insisted on driving Merit back into the city on Saturday morning. Merit cried into her neck the whole way. When they got to Merit's building, Jane parked illegally and walked Merit inside, her arm around Merit's waist. There was an awkward moment at her front door when Merit felt like a package being handed off, from her lover to her husband, *Here, you take her.* It couldn't have been smoother if they'd choreographed it; Jane pulled her arm back and Cory reached his forward, and Merit passed from the universe she inhabited once a week in Sausalito into the other one where she lived the rest of the time.

She spent the rest of Saturday in a numb daze. She made travel arrangements. She went to an overpriced children's boutique and bought two dark blue suits. They couldn't show up looking like wayward Californians, not to this. Merit decided to wear the dark blue dress she'd bought for her first day of work at Jager + Brandt. She'd had it dry-cleaned right after to get the milk stains out. She hadn't worn it since.

She tried the dress on at midnight on Saturday night after taking three doses of melatonin in a misguided attempt to sleep. It fit, probably better than it had when she bought it, and in it, she looked a lot like the woman she'd been back then, when she thought the only thing going back to work full-time would give her was a salary and some of the dignity she'd lost. But she wasn't that woman anymore, not even close. Had she evolved into someone truer or was she losing herself completely? Looking at herself in the bathroom mirror that night, her eyes bloodshot from crying and lack of sleep, she didn't know. The voice in her head she'd always attributed to God told her it was too soon to tell.

So the prayer on the plane was for clarity, and forgiveness, and peace. She wasn't sure she deserved the second two, but her dad had always told her that God liked it better when you asked for what you really wanted. God already knew she wanted Jane. She didn't know if she was devastated or relieved that her father never would.

Her cousin Mitch met them at the airport. Cory had wanted to rent a car but Merit knew that would be perceived by her relatives as ungrateful and rude. So, they all piled into Mitch's SUV and rode the fifteen minutes to her parents' house in Gulf Breeze. A hotel was also out of the question, not that Merit would've even considered it with her mom being all alone in the house.

"How are you doing?" Cory asked her as they turned in to the driveway.

"Not great," Merit said.

"What can I do?"

She shook her head. He couldn't give their sons a second grandpa. He couldn't take away the guilt she felt about how long it'd been since she'd been home. He couldn't shield her from her mother's grief.

She fiddled with her new ring. If Cory had noticed it, he hadn't said.

"You'll get through this," she heard him say. She wondered what the "this" was.

Her mom was in the kitchen when they came in, sitting at the table with Merit's aunt and a cup of tea she hadn't touched.

"Hey, Grandma," Jude said solemnly. Nash was less clear on the decorum following a death and ran to jump in his grandmother's lap.

"Hi, Mom," Merit said softly. "Hey, Aunt Carol."

"Hey, darlin'," her aunt Carol said.

"How much does this suck?" her mom asked wryly, which was so unlike her that Merit almost laughed.

"So much," Merit said, and instead of laughing, started to cry.

"I'm glad you're here," her mom said.

Merit nodded a little. "Me, too."

She wanted to climb into her mother's lap the way Nash had, to make herself as small as his three-year-old body and be held by someone else.

"Y'all must be starving," Carol said, rising from the table. "I'll reheat the barbecue the Sunday school class brought over. Viv, you want some?"

Merit's mother shook her head.

As Carol started pulling food out of the refrigerator, Cory took the boys upstairs to get settled in. Merit sat down at the table with her mom.

"How was your flight?"

Merit shrugged. "Fine. Long."

"How long are you staying?"

"Cory and the boys will fly back on Saturday," Merit said. "But I can stay as long as—"

"Don't be silly," her mom said, waving her off. "A week is long enough. You have your life in California. Your career."

"Mom."

"Let's just get through Tuesday," her mom said wearily, rubbing her eyes. "Okay?" She looked older than she ever had to Merit, every bit of sixty-five. Merit realized, for the first time ever, that her mother was only six years older than Jane.

"Sure," Merit replied. But she knew they wouldn't talk about it again. Next Saturday would come, and Merit would leave with Cory and the boys. Her mother would never let her stay. That wasn't how their relationship worked. Her father had met all her mother's needs; there had never been anything left for Merit to do but wander, and disappoint.

"I like that ring," her mom said, nodding at the bird.

"It's a hummingbird," Merit told her. *It's from the woman I'm in love with, Mom.*

"It's nice. Cory's always had good taste."

Merit twisted the ring on her finger. She had nothing to say next.

"What time is it?" Her mother squinted at her watch. "Is it too early for bourbon?"

Merit was already on her feet. The bourbon was an unspoken tribute to her father, who drank it every night. Her mom only ever drank white wine. "You having some, Aunt Carol?"

"Yes," her mom answered before Carol could.

Merit pulled out three glasses and her dad's favorite bottle of Kentucky rye and brought them back to the table, where she gave them each a hefty pour. She didn't know how to show up for her mother right now, but this, at least, she could do.

"To Dad," she said hoarsely, and raised her glass.

THE FUNERAL WENT as well as it could have. The church was packed. Merit's mother wore a black Diane von Furstenberg dress Merit bought the day before at Nordstrom Rack. She seemed pleased that her grandsons were in suits.

Merit sat next to her mom in the front row during the service. Cory and the boys sat near the back, in case the boys misbehaved. Cory's decision, which Merit didn't fight. Tears dripped down Merit's cheeks as the pastor read Psalms she knew by heart. She noticed at some point that she was holding her own hand.

After the burial, everyone went back to her parents' house for lunch. Merit slipped upstairs to her old bedroom to call Jane.

"How is it?" Jane asked.

"Surreal," Merit said. She felt wobbly, like she'd stood up too fast. She stepped out of her shoes and laid down on her old bed. It was the same mattress she'd slept on in high school, in the same white wicker frame. The girl she'd been back then had worn a silver purity ring they'd given her at church. The woman she was now wore a diamond on one hand and an emerald on the other and no longer believed in black and white.

"I'm sure," Jane said. "Death is such a fucking shock to the system. How's your mum?"

"It's hard to tell. She's swearing for the first time in her life, which feels positive?"

Merit heard Jane smile. "And how are you, my love?"

"Sad."

"Oh, honey," Jane said softly. "Talk to me. Were you and your dad close? You haven't told me much about him. Other than the fact that he was an upstanding Floridian who loved Jesus and cruises."

Merit felt herself smile. "He also liked Tom Petty, jalapeños, and golf. And he adored my mom. But no, we weren't very close."

"Was he a good father?"

It was a question very few people would ask on the day of a man's funeral.

"I think he did the best he could," Merit said finally. "He made excellent French toast."

"That counts for a lot," Jane said.

"Yes."

"I miss you."

"I miss you, too."

"I wish I could be there with you," Jane said. "Holding your hand through all this." Her voice got quieter. "I know it could never happen, but it's what I keep thinking about."

Merit wanted to tell Jane it could happen; they could absolutely sit in the living room of her childhood home with her family and the brown leather Bible on the bookshelf and hold hands.

"Me, too," she said instead.

"I almost bought a plane ticket, actually," Jane said then. "To be there for the service today. But then I decided it would probably make you uncomfortable."

"Oh," Merit said, because she didn't know what else to say. She tried to picture Jane in a funeral dress, sitting in her parents' church, singing "Amazing Grace." Where would she have been seated? On the front row next to Merit, or in the back with Cory and the boys? What was the protocol when your lover was your mother's age and also your closest friend?

Just thinking about it made her nauseated with relief that Jane hadn't come.

"Merit?" It was Cory's voice, from the stairs.

"I should go," she said quickly into the phone. This was the first time since Mexico that she felt like a person hiding an affair. The irony of this didn't elude her. This was her least incriminating act. But she didn't want Cory to know she'd snuck away to call Jane.

"Call me anytime," Jane said.

"Love you," Merit whispered hurriedly, and hung up.

Cory appeared in the doorway. "Hey. You okay?"

She nodded and sat up. It was easier to lie if she didn't speak. "How's it going downstairs?"

"Your cousins are arguing about NASCAR. Your mom is pounding the bourbon pretty hard."

"And Nash and Jude?"

"They're in the backyard on their iPads."

"Awesome."

"I figured you wouldn't care."

"I don't."

Cory studied her. She could feel him trying to read her.

"I'm fine," she told him. "I just needed a sec."

He came into the bedroom and sat on the bed beside her. "I want to say the right thing," he said finally. "I don't know what that is."

"If it makes you feel any better, I don't, either," she said.

They sat in silence for a few minutes. She searched for a true thing to say.

"Want me to sneak you a piece of your aunt's pecan pie?" Cory asked eventually. "I heard a rumor someone brought ice cream, too."

Merit smiled a little. "I can't hide up here all day." She pecked his cheek and stood up from the bed. "I should go check on Mom."

"Mer."

She turned.

"You're a good daughter," Cory said.

She didn't believe this but it was kind of him to say. "Thanks."

He held out his hand and she pulled him to his feet. She stepped back quickly before he could hug her. His arms around her in this moment would put her over the edge. "C'mon," she said, taking his hand. "You can be my moral support."

Her mom was in her dad's leather chair in the living room, pushing chicken salad and wilted crudités around a paper cocktail plate while her siblings and their children made small talk around her. There was a rocks glass on the side table beside her, half-filled with bourbon and melting ice, sweating on the wood because the only person who would think to put a coaster under it was preoccupied with pretending to eat the plate of food someone had put in her lap.

Merit dropped Cory's hand and went over to her.

"Don't you dare take my drink," her mom said, reaching for it.

"Never," Merit said. "I was just raised to use a coaster." She pulled open the skinny drawer on the front of the table and pulled one out, not letting herself get teary over the handful of butterscotch candies that were also hidden inside because that's where her dad kept his sugar stash.

"My compliments to your mother," her mom said. "Have you eaten?"

Merit shook her head.

"You should eat."

"Uh-huh. So should you."

"Or we could just drink bourbon and try to get to the other side of this day."

"Let's do that," Merit said. "Want to go out on the deck?"

Her mother arched an eyebrow. "What, you don't want to sit in an overcrowded living room that still smells like your father's aftershave and listen to your cousins blabber on about politics and rednecks in race cars?"

"We heard that," Mitch said from the couch.

"I just don't want to share the bourbon," Merit said, and everyone laughed.

Her mother pointed at an empty spot on the couch. "Sit down and be social with your family. You, too, Cory. Grieving widow's orders."

They sat.

"So how are things on the left coast?" someone asked.

There was literally no place Merit wanted to be less than in her parents' living room, on their microfiber couch, making stilted conversation with people she had nothing in common with beyond some shared DNA, on the day her father was buried at a cemetery Merit would never visit. But here she was.

"Cory got a promotion," she announced.

While Cory attempted to explain his job function with words of one syllable, Merit let herself imagine walking out the front door and never looking back. It was what she'd done when Nash was an infant, night after night, when she'd lie on the floor beside his crib with her hand through the slats trying to shush him back to sleep. She'd fantasize about driving off and becoming someone else.

"Mommy?" Nash was in the doorway, his cheeks flushed from the backyard heat.

"You hungry, peanut?" Merit asked, sitting up. "I can make you a plate."

Nash shook his head. "I don't feel good."

"What hurts, buddy?" Cory asked.

Nash shrugged.

"I'm sure he's just overheated," Merit said. "Come sit in here where it's cool," she told Nash. "Want me to get you some water?"

"I'll get it," Cory said, getting up.

Nash climbed into Merit's lap and put his head on her shoulder. His forehead burned against Merit's neck. The heat of his skin on hers was sharp and unexpected, like a slap across the face.

She gripped him tighter and stood up.

"Hey, Mom, do you have a thermometer in the house? He feels like he has a fever."

"In the medicine cabinet in my bathroom. I probably have some Children's Tylenol somewhere, too." Her mother was already getting up.

"I can look for it," Merit said, waving her mom back down, as Cory returned with a cup of water.

"Look for what?"

"Tylenol," Merit said. "I think he has a fever."

"Oh no." Cory frowned. "Do we have a thermometer?"

"Medicine cabinet in Mom's bathroom," Merit replied.

"I'll get it," Cory said. "You guys sit."

"I'm gonna take him upstairs," Merit said. The air-conditioning was pumping, but the living room was suddenly unbearably hot.

"Good idea," Cory said. "I'll meet you up there."

Merit's heart pounded as she carried Nash up the stairs, down the hallway with the faded floral wallpaper, past the framed photograph of her in her wedding dress on the front steps of her parents' church, and into the bedroom where twenty minutes before she'd been on the phone with her lover in California, letting herself believe there was a universe other than this.

"Mommy," Nash said weakly, pressing his head against her neck.

His little voice. *Mommy.* Shame slammed into her like a runaway truck and nearly knocked her into the wall. She hadn't been behaving like any-one's mother for months.

"I'm here," she said, holding him tighter. "Mommy's right here."

She sat on the bed and rocked back and forth the way she had when he was a baby and wouldn't sleep. His forehead was sticky against her neck. He was burning up.

"Got the thermometer and the Tylenol," Cory said, coming through the doorway.

Merit watched as Cory knelt in front of the bed and brushed Nash's damp hair from his face. The gesture was so tender her breath caught in her throat. *This man, this little boy, this life.*

Merit couldn't take her eyes off her husband's face as he carefully put the thermometer in their son's mouth. She was outside this moment, ob-serving it. She was present, viscerally, within it. She couldn't put words around what she was feeling, other than the sensation of being fire hosed with impossibility and disgrace.

The thermometer beeped: 101.9.

"Am I sick?" she heard Nash ask, his mouth turning the *s* into a *th*. His preschool teacher had suggested they call a speech therapist months ago. But this, like everything else on the list Merit hadn't been keeping for the past six months, had never been done because it didn't involve Jane.

"Not too sick," Cory assured Nash. "Nothing Mickey Mouse and lem-onade won't fix."

Merit watched as Cory measured out the Tylenol and brought the little cup to their son's lips. This man she'd known for two decades. The person she'd become a family with long before they had kids. Her anchor and her harbor when she'd been an orphan boat.

She kept watching as Nash drank the medicine, a tiny bit dribbling down his chin. Her little boy with brown eyes and flushed cheeks who'd handled a grown-up thermometer like a champ but had no idea how complicated grown-up relationships were.

The tears came fast, and were hot on her cheeks.

"Hey, now," Cory said gently, rising to his feet. "It's just a fever. A virus, probably, that he picked up on the plane. He's fine."

The five-hour flight during which she'd held her three-year-old's hand and thought about nothing but herself. Grief and guilt swirled in her stomach. She wanted to throw up.

"I'm okay, Mommy," she heard Nash say. "Don't cry." His little hands cupped her cheeks. Merit managed to nod.

"Let's give Mommy some space," Cory said, lifting Nash off her lap. He carried him over to the other side of the bed and propped him up with pillows so he could see the TV.

"I should've noticed he wasn't feeling well," she whispered hoarsely. What she meant was *I should've remembered I was his mother* and also *I should've been someone other than who I've been.*

Cory came back around the bed and put his arms around her. "Don't be silly. There was nothing to notice. This is what happens when kids get sick. You know how it is."

Merit wished she could disappear into his certainty, the way she had when they first met, when he'd decided who she was, and she'd been so relieved she hadn't thought to question it.

"It's been a really terrible week," Cory said against her hair. "But it'll end eventually, and Nash will be better soon, and we'll go home. Okay?"

She nodded. She understood that he thought it was grief she was feeling, and she realized he wasn't entirely wrong.

"Do you want to lie down for a while?" Cory asked. "You could stay up here with Nash. Your mom would understand."

Merit shook her head. If she tried to be still she would explode into a million pieces.

"Do you want to call Jane?"

He gave her a look she couldn't recognize.

"No." She stood up abruptly. "I think I'll go for a drive," she said.

Cory nodded.

"Will you stay up here with Nash?" she asked. "Text me if anything happens, or the fever gets worse?"

He nodded again. "Of course."

She looked over at her son's fever-flushed cheeks and hesitated. Cory saw it.

"He's okay, Mer. Take your drive. We'll be right here when you get back."

"I won't be long," she said. She had no idea if this was true.

She didn't know where she would go, just that she needed to experience the sensation of moving forward through space. If it were an option to put herself into a catapult and be hurled into the air, she would've done it without hesitation.

She didn't tell her mother she was leaving. She took her dad's keys from the ashtray in the kitchen and snuck out the side door to the carport where his Buick was parked next to the blue Ford Mustang convertible he'd bought his wife for her sixtieth birthday because she liked feeling the wind in her hair. Merit remembered how her mom's face had lit up when she opened the box that held the keys, the little squeal she'd let out that made everybody at the party Merit and Cory had flown in for laugh. Was there a version of her life where she'd reacted that way when Cory told her he'd bought her a house?

She drove across the toll bridge to Pensacola beach with the windows of the Buick down. The air outside the car was humid and hot; Merit felt sweat bead up on her thighs. She should've changed out of her dress. It felt like a sausage casing, or shrink-wrap.

She parked on the street and stumbled over the sand dunes in her bare feet. She could only imagine how insane she looked, red-faced and wild-eyed in a merino wool sheath.

It wasn't until she got to the water's edge that she understood why she had come to the beach. She was there to stand with her feet in the surf, the warm gulf gently lapping against her ankles, nothing before her but calm emerald water and a few distant boats, and let herself believe that there was a universe where no one got hurt, and choices didn't have consequences, and she lived happily ever after with Jane.

Then, when the sun finally began to sink in the sky, she turned and walked back to her car in the only universe that actually was.

nineteen

JANE PICKED MERIT up at the ferry terminal in Sausalito the Friday after the funeral. She had cut her blond hair short.

"I can't believe you didn't tell me," Merit said as they pulled away from the curb, grateful for something to talk about that wasn't the thing she knew she would eventually say but wasn't ready to yet.

"I needed to decide how I felt about it first," Jane said, raking through it with her fingers.

"And?"

Jane smiled. "It depends on how you feel about it."

"I love it," Merit said, swallowing the lump that had already formed in her throat. The haircut was sexy and chic and reminded Merit just how far out of her league this woman actually was. She wanted to press her face against Jane's neck and breathe in the scent of her, but she knew if she did she would start to sob and might never stop.

Jane glanced over at her and frowned. "You okay, little bird?"

"I'm great," Merit lied. She slid a hand inside Jane's thigh. "I just missed you," she murmured, touching her lips to Jane's shoulder.

"I missed you, too," Jane said.

"Why are you driving so slow?"

"Because I'm old."

"Well, speed it up, old lady. I need to be naked with you immediately."

She could do this. She could pretend her heart wasn't fractured into a thousand shards. She could hold it together for one night.

"What about the *stegt flæsk med persillesovs* I made you?"

"Whatever that is, I hope it keeps," Merit said, scratching Jane's shoulder lightly with her fingernail and wanting suddenly to scratch her hard; no, to be scratched by her, to feel something other than the ache in her chest. She tugged at Jane's tank top.

"Hey, now," Jane said, catching Merit's hand. "I am not the best driver under pristine conditions. You're not allowed to distract me with your minx-y ways."

"Who's calling who a minx?" Merit asked coyly. The more she hid inside the role she was playing tonight, the safer she felt. "You're the one with the sexy haircut and the sexy shoulders."

Jane laughed. Merit couldn't fathom how she would live without that sound. She remembered so clearly making Jane laugh in her interview that very first day, how delighted she felt at having pleased her, this extraordinary woman who lit up the room. She'd been trying to please her ever since. She wanted to please her for the rest of her life.

She would do the opposite instead.

"I adore you," Jane said.

"I'm counting on it," Merit said back.

Merit kept her hands to herself for the rest of the short drive up to the house, but as soon as they were parked in the driveway, she climbed over the middle console like she'd done once when she and Cory were in college and borrowed a friend's car to drive up to Vermont. They'd had sex on the side of a snowy back road at midnight next to a covered bridge. Had she actually wanted to? She couldn't remember. She couldn't remember ever wanting anything as much as she wanted this.

She slid her knees beside Jane's hips and sat back on her heels. "Hi," she said.

"Hi," Jane said back.

"I have a present for you," Merit said.

"What kind of present?"

"Just a present. It's in my bag."

"When do I get it?"

"Later," Merit said. "After you kiss me a little."

"That sounds fair," Jane said, and she wrapped two hands around Merit's neck. She kept them there as their faces came together, open mouths hovering, the air between them electric and dense. *Don't hurry*, Merit thought as her lips brushed against Jane's. *We will never get this moment back.*

Time seemed to dilate then, the way it had that first night in Mexico, when every second held an eternity within it, and the universe paused its incessant rush. She felt a swell of gratitude, and then of grief, as she inhaled slowly, reverently, drinking every detail in.

She waited until she was so filled with the intensity of the present that she felt as if she might burst to finally surrender to the kiss. She savored the precise sensation of Jane's tongue against hers, the tiny hairs above Jane's lip, Jane's fingers on her neck.

"Let's go inside," Jane whispered at some point, and Merit nodded, and somehow they disentangled long enough to get out of the car and up the stairs to the house, but not long enough to make it to Jane's bedroom. They ended up on the living room couch.

"I really did make you an excellent dinner," Jane said as she pulled the tank top over her head. She wasn't wearing a bra. Her bare torso, backlit and shadowed, was more exquisite than any painting Merit had ever seen.

"Later," Merit breathed, and undid the button on Jane's shorts.

She thought of nothing after that but the immediacy of Jane. Her smell, how she tasted, the way her skin felt. It was dark when they finally came up for air. They were both naked and damp with sweat and saliva and it was difficult to tell whose limbs belonged to whom. It crossed Merit's mind that she wouldn't mind dying like this.

"Let's eat," Jane said, brushing the hair off Merit's face. "I'm starving, and you've lost some weight." This didn't surprise Merit. She hadn't been hungry since the night her father died.

"Do we have to get dressed?"

"Fuck no," said Jane. "That's the perk of being bougie enough to have a house on a hill. No one can see in."

She followed Jane into the kitchen. The subtle sway of Jane's naked hips as she walked reminded Merit of the water lapping against the rocks in Mexico, and then, of that first morning after, when she'd curved her body around the back of Jane's and slipped a hand between her legs. How she'd felt it in her own body, the rippling waves of sensation, as Jane came.

She was still thinking about Mexico as Jane melted butter and chopped parsley for their sauce. Would the picture always be this clear in her head?

"Want your present now?" Merit asked suddenly.

"And here I thought you already gave it to me," Jane said lightly. "Back there on the couch."

"That was all bonus content," Merit said, hopping off the stool. "Be right back."

Her bag was by the front door where she'd dropped it, the gift for Jane wrapped in brown paper inside. Her heart hammered as she carried it into the kitchen. It was one thing to give the woman you loved your heart. It was another to give her your art.

She'd started working on it the day she got back from Florida, and she'd taken the whole week off from work to finish it. She hadn't told Cory, and she'd asked Sierra not to say anything, either. Every afternoon she'd showered and put on work clothes just before the boys got home from school, like she'd been at the office all day. She promised herself it would be her very last lie.

"It's okay if you hate it," Merit said as she held out the gift.

"What a winning endorsement," Jane said with a laugh.

Merit held her breath as Jane slit the brown paper with her paring knife and pulled the small canvas out. It was a painting of Jane's face, the first watercolor portrait Merit had ever attempted. She wasn't certain Jane would like it, but she was proud of how it had turned out. It looked how she wanted it to look. She'd gotten the eyes right.

"Oh, Merit," Jane breathed when she saw it. "It's stunning."

Merit let herself smile. "It's my favorite thing I've ever done."

"If I'd known you were this talented, I would've fired you years ago and forced you to go back to art," Jane declared. "I mean, I assumed you were good, but this is extraordinary." She leaned across the counter on her elbows to kiss Merit's hand. "Thank you for my painting. I love it."

"Good," Merit said. "Now I can regale you with my bad poetry."

"Yes! But you have to eat first before my sauce gets lumpy and I disgrace my home country with bad *persillesovs*."

"Mmm. I love it when you talk dirty."

They ate crispy pork and potatoes with parsley sauce at the kitchen island. Jane opened a nice bottle of red wine.

"I bought it for your birthday," she said. "We were going to drink it in my bathtub after we got back from dinner that night." She smiled. "But we did other things."

"Let's take a bath tonight," Merit said.

"Can you stay over?" Jane asked.

Merit shook her head. *If I do I will never leave.*

"Well, we'll do another sleepover eventually," Jane said. "And we have to plan our trip to Copenhagen! Now that you've had *stegt flæsk med persillesovs*, you're practically a native."

Merit managed to smile.

Jane frowned. "What is it?"

Merit shook her head quickly. "Nothing. Just bummed I can't stay over." She took a long sip of wine and willed the boulder in her throat back down to her chest where it would sting like fire behind her sternum but not make her choke.

"You know you don't have to pretend with me," Jane said. "It's okay if you're not okay." She put her hand on Merit's knee.

"I'm fine."

"How are things with Cory?" Jane asked.

"Fine."

"But?"

"There is no but."

"You sure?"

"Yes. But can we not talk about my husband right now?"

"Whatever you want," said Jane.

"Good. I want you."

Merit slid forward and slowly opened her legs. Her eyes were on Jane's as she took Jane's hand and moved it up her thigh. She watched blue irises eclipse into black as she eased Jane's fingers inside her and held them there as she rocked against Jane's palm. Merit pushed her heels into the rung of the stool and lifted her hips. She heard Jane moan and then felt herself come. She wondered if it was possible to orgasm tears.

"Let's take that bath," she whispered.

They brought the bottle of wine with them but forgot the glasses, so they passed the bottle back and forth as they sat with their backs against opposite ends of Jane's giant claw-foot tub, soapy bubbles between them and a flickering candle on the window ledge beside them.

"I've never been as happy as I am right now," Jane said, fishing for Merit's foot under the water. She caught it and held it with two hands. *"Mit livs kærlighed."*

"Translation?"

Jane smiled. "Love of my life."

Tears pooled in Merit's eyes. She hoped Jane couldn't see them in the dark. "Rob will be so disappointed," she joked, trying to keep her voice light.

Jane smiled a little. "Right?"

She let go of Merit's foot and dipped her head back into the water. Watching Jane's blond hair swirl around her face, Merit was reminded of her own baptism at thirteen; of dipping back in a glass tank filled with water, of sinking beneath the surface. She remembered the sensation of weightlessness, the taste of chlorine in her mouth. *You'll go into the water one thing, and come back up another*, the pastor had told her, and she'd looked at him with raised eyebrows and teenage doubt. *It's not the water that changes you*, he'd said then. *Only love can do that.*

"I didn't know it could be like this," Merit heard herself say to Jane now, her voice thick with emotion. "I didn't know love could be so . . ." She struggled to find a word big enough to hold all she wanted to convey.

"Complete," Jane said, like it was obvious, and Merit's tears spilled over.

"Yes," was all she could manage to say.

Jane sat back up and held out her hand for the wine bottle. Merit passed it to her, then splashed some water on her face. She couldn't fall apart yet.

"I wish you'd tell me," Jane said after a minute. Merit studied her hands.

"Tell you what?"

"Whatever's on your mind." Jane took another sip from the bottle. "Not that I don't enjoy your distraction techniques. That move in the kitchen was pretty epic." She set the bottle on the window ledge and laid her hand on Merit's thigh. "But there's nothing you can't tell me," she said. "Truly."

Merit nodded a little.

"So what is it?"

Merit shrugged. It was getting late but she couldn't bring herself to say what she had come there to say. She wanted to sink under the surface of the water and scream.

"Is it Cory?" Jane asked gently. "Did he find out?"

"About us? No." She wasn't sure this was true.

Merit played with a soap bubble on her knee. "He's been really great, actually. Since my dad."

"Good," Jane said, and it sounded as if she meant it. "You deserve that. You deserve everything, *mit livs kærlighed.*"

"What do you love about me?" Merit heard herself ask. She was still looking at her knee.

"Do you want a list?"

Merit smiled faintly. She felt herself nod.

"Your perfect ass is high on the list. But not above your kindness, and your generosity, and your feisty little heart."

She raised her eyes to Jane's. "In an alternate universe, do we end up together?"

Jane caught her ankle under the water again and squeezed it. "Bitch, we end up together in *this* universe. Just give us time."

Merit came forward as if propelled. She was sitting back and then she was on her knees and then her legs were wrapped around Jane in the center of the tub and they were kissing with such intensity that Merit lost all awareness of where her mouth ended and Jane's began.

This is what I want, was echoing over and over in her head. *I want this.*

But she wanted other things, too. She wanted to be a good mother. She wanted to do the right thing. She didn't want to be selfish. She didn't want to disappoint her own mother. She didn't want to break her husband's heart.

"Honey, honey, honey," she heard Jane say. Her voice sounded so far away, but she was right there, her lips against Merit's ear, her thighs against Merit's back, her fingers brushing the hair from Merit's face, which was soaking wet not from bathwater but from tears. And then Jane was lifting her from the tub and carrying her into the bedroom, where she laid Merit on the bed and pulled the duvet up around her like a baby's swaddle.

"Honey, honey, honey," Jane said again, stroking her face. "Don't cry. Everything will be okay."

Merit shook her head. She was sobbing uncontrollably. She couldn't see through her tears.

"Talk to me, love."

Merit forced herself to meet Jane's eyes. Those exquisite, intelligent, miraculous eyes. There were oceans inside them, infinite depth. There was so much she hadn't uncovered yet.

"I can't do this anymore," she finally managed. "I can't—be two Merits at once. And I can't leave Cory. I thought I could, but—I can't."

Jane sat back on her heels. An eternity passed.

Merit reached for her hand. "Say something."

Jane smiled, but her mouth twisted a little. "I don't suppose I could talk you out of it?"

Merit didn't trust herself to answer this. She closed her eyes and shook her head.

"You've made up your mind, then."

"I'm so sorry." Merit was crying again. Her whole body shook with it.

"There's nothing for you to be sorry about." Jane was crying now, too, but with composure and resolve, the way she did everything else. Her face was a watercolor in the rain, ravishing even in the ravaging, beautiful even as she was coming undone. "It was a complicated situation from the start. We both knew that."

"It was spectacular," Merit said hoarsely. "The most spectacular thing."

Jane nodded. Tears dripped from her chin. "But you have a husband. And two beautiful kids." Her voice broke. "I get it. I do."

"Jane."

"Merit."

"You're the love of my life."

Jane smiled faintly. There was agony in it, and grace. "Don't ever forget it, bitch."

Tears poured from Merit's eyes. She wanted to drown in them, to be suffocated by sorrow, anything to stop the crushing sensation in her chest. "I wish things were different," she wept. "I wish *I* were different. I wish I were the kind of person who could just burn it all down and—"

Jane cut her off. "No. You wouldn't be you." She unwrapped the duvet and tenderly kissed Merit's collarbone, and then her sternum, and then each of her breasts. "My darling girl."

"I don't know if I can do it," Merit whispered. She was trembling under Jane's touch. "Live without you. Honestly. I don't know if I can."

Jane gently parted her legs. "Who said anything about living without me?"

"Stop," Merit said. She didn't want her to stop. "If you do that, I might never leave."

"I won't do anything," Jane said. "I just want to look at you. My pretty bird. One last time."

"And then what?" Merit couldn't see past this moment. She couldn't see anything other than Jane.

"Then we get dressed and you let me put some makeup on you so your husband won't suspect that you had mind-blowing sex with your lady lover before breaking her heart."

"Jane—"

"Sssh. And then you go home to your family and you call me tomorrow and we make plans for the next time we'll hang out. Platonically. And it'll be brutal at first but we'll figure it out."

Merit sat up. "Do you really think we can do that? Be just friends again?"

"Oh, honey," Jane said, laying a hand on her cheek. "We'll never be just friends."

Merit searched Jane's eyes. "What will we be, then?"

"What we always were," Jane said, and then she smiled the smile Merit would spend the rest of her life trying to capture in paint. "We'll be everything there is."

five years later

M OM?" NASH WAS hovering at the edge of the living room. "Jude and I are hungry. Can we order pizza or something?"

She'd exiled her sons to their bedrooms when the photographer showed up. That was at noon. It was now almost five.

"Dad will be here any minute," Merit said. "Let's wait and see what he's thinking for dinner, okay?"

"When will you be done?" Nash asked.

"Soon," Merit said. She glanced at the photographer; she had no idea if this was true. "I think?"

"Twenty minutes, tops," the photographer said. "I'd like to get a couple more of you by that gorgeous fireplace, and a few of Jude and Nash on the couch if we can?"

Nash perked up. "You want pictures of us?"

"Absolutely," the photographer said.

Nash pumped his arm in the air, a gesture he'd picked up at baseball camp the summer before and now used any time he got excited about something. Everything seemed to delight him these days, from his fourth-grade reading list to the wild roses in their new front garden to the secret compartment he'd found under the floorboards upstairs.

His thirteen-year-old brother, meanwhile, was irritated with everything lately. He would definitely not be thrilled about having his picture taken. "Will you ask Jude to come down, too?" Merit asked Nash. "Tell him I'll let him surf for an extra hour this weekend if he does it without complaining."

"Jude!" Nash yelled from the doorway. "Mom wants you!"

"Nash, sweetie, can you please go upstairs and get him? And also brush your hair."

They'd both gotten haircuts in anticipation of this photoshoot, part of a five-page spread in *Architectural Digest*. Merit could still remember sitting in the lobby of Jager + Brandt nine years before, ambivalent about going back to work in architecture, thumbing through an old issue of the magazine that would one day feature her house on the cover. Her house. On the cover!

It was hard to believe, still.

That, and everything else.

"What an exquisite painting," the photographer said now, lowering his camera to admire the canvas on the wall over the couch. It was a watercolor of a rainstorm over the ocean. The rainstorm that afternoon in Mexico, the day that altered the course of the artist's life. Merit painted it in two days, the weekend after that night in the bathtub with Jane. It stayed under her bed for years after that. There hadn't been a place for it, until they bought this house. Merit liked it, but it wasn't her favorite piece. That one was in their bedroom upstairs, hanging over the bed.

"Who's the artist?" the photographer asked.

"A friend," Merit said. *The person I used to be.*

"Well, it's really something," the photographer said, snapping several pictures of the painting. "She's quite a talent."

Merit bit back a smile. "I'll tell her you said so."

"Why do we have to be in them?" Jude was scowling in the front hall. The past couple years had been hardest on him, Merit knew. The only time he seemed happy was when he was surfing, so Merit had started taking him down to the breaks at Linda Mar on Saturday mornings. The weekend before, she'd rented a board and gotten in the water with him, and they'd laughed so hard they both got side cramps. He'd let her hold his hand when they walked back to the car, his board under his other arm like a pro. She'd felt herself holding her breath, not wanting to risk him pulling away. The past few years had felt a lot like that.

"You don't have to," Merit told her teenage son now, coming over to where he stood in his board shorts and faded Hurley T-shirt. It crossed her mind to tell him to change into something nicer, but that wasn't who she was anymore. They could wear what they wanted. They could be themselves.

Jude's eyebrows shot up. "Really?"

"Really." Merit shrugged. "I'd love it if you would, because this is your house, too, and if they're writing about us in a magazine, it feels like you should be in the pictures? But it's your choice. I won't make you do it if you don't want to."

"Can I be in them by myself?" Nash asked the photographer. "It doesn't have to be both of us, does it?"

"I'll do it," Jude said before the photographer could answer. "Whatever. It's fine."

Merit touched his shoulder. She'd learned to dial back the mom hugs. "Thank you. I really appreciate that, Jude."

"Such well-mannered kids," the photographer said, and Merit laughed out loud.

"I'm glad we've fooled you," she said.

The boys behaved long enough for him to get a few shots of them side by side on the couch, smiling at the camera in their mismatched clothes and bare feet. They were almost finished by the time Merit realized they'd never brushed their hair. She was amazed at how little she cared. These were her sons, disheveled and unruly and full of grace for their mother. There was no way to improve upon this.

Through the front window, she saw Cory's black Prius pull into the driveway and had a brief memory of that awful night at 720 Steiner when the owners changed the plans at the last minute because of a window angled just like the one she now had. Regina and Allie sold their Painted Lady four months after the renovation was complete. Rumor was they'd gotten divorced. It occurred to Merit now that they'd ripped out a beautiful piece of history to make way for a future that didn't actually exist. It was tragic, and really fucking funny.

"Dad's here, you guys."

"Dad!" Nash yelled, jumping up from the couch.

Merit turned her head to watch him at the door and heard the *click* of the camera. She wondered what the photographer had seen on her face in that moment, and if it at all matched what was going on in her mind, that swirl of emotions she no longer tried to resolve into something orderly, because love wasn't orderly, and love was her only compass these days.

"Hey," Cory said, coming into the house. "Wow, look at you. Great dress."

"It's a loaner," she said. "But thanks. I like it, too."

"How's it going so far?"

"Really well, I think. We're wrapping up."

"Can we have pizza for dinner?" Nash asked. "Please?"

"Sure, bud." Cory ruffled his hair. "Pizza sounds great."

"Can we go now?" Nash looked at Merit. "Is it over?"

"I think so," Merit said, looking at the photographer for confirmation. "We're finished, right?"

"Almost," he said. "I just need a few shots of the whole family together."

Merit felt the discomfort in her stomach, but she didn't let it show on her face. She'd known this was coming. She'd seen it on the shot list. And of course the editor wanted one of all of them together. That was part of the story, how this very particular family had come to live in this very particular house, a one-hundred-and-fifty-year-old formerly dilapidated Victorian in the Lower Haight that Merit and her business partner had painstakingly renovated and brought back to life. "It's a metaphor for my own experience," Merit told the reporter writing the piece during their phone interview the previous week.

"Are you the house being renovated, or the architect doing the renovating?" the reporter had asked.

Merit hadn't hesitated. "I'm both."

"I was thinking we set it up on the front stairs," the photographer was saying now. "We can get the light coming in from the skylight in the foyer. I think it'll be really lovely, just the four of you sitting on the steps." Merit saw his eyes drift over to Cory and then back to her. Cory wasn't looking at them. He'd picked up a framed photograph of the boys that was on the console by the front door. He'd taken it, on that vacation to Hawaii. Nash at three, Jude at seven, covered in sand on the beach.

"Cory?" she asked gently. He looked up. "Are you okay with that?"

He held her gaze for a second before answering. She would never know for sure because she would never ask him, but she sensed in that moment that he was asking for her recognition. For her to acknowledge how much she had asked of him already; how audacious it was for her to ask him for this. She nodded a little as they looked at each other. If they'd been alone she would've said *I know* and *thank you* and *I'm sorry*. He nodded a little also. "Do your thing," he finally said. "I'll be out front."

She waited until the man she'd once been married to was outside the house before she leaned over the stairwell and yelled up to the bedroom. "Jane!"

a c k n o w l e d g m e n t s

This is not a novel I ever thought I would write. But here we are, and I couldn't be more grateful for the lovely humans who helped bring this story to life. Thank you in particular to:

My extraordinary agent, Kristyn Keene Benton, who always believed I had an adult novel in me and understood what I was trying to do from the very first draft.

My smart and insightful editor, Gabriella Mongelli, who made this story so much better with her careful and wise notes, and Sally Kim, for saying yes. My experience at Putnam has been nothing short of wonderful.

My marketing and publicity team at Putnam, and the art department who created a truly spectacular cover.

My honest and smart friends, Ceara Donnelley, Kayli Weatherford, Noel Salyer, Jordanna Fraiberg, and Katherine Pope, who read early drafts and told me everything that wasn't working and delighted me by telling me everything that was. And in particular to Lindsey Bayman, who never once acted bored during that period when I talked incessantly about Merit and Jane as if they were real people, and to Tyler Mann, who, as always, read the earliest draft and gave the most extensive notes. Thank you for telling me that I'd finally written a book that you'd buy even if you didn't know me. What better praise than that?

And finally, to my family, who didn't balk when I told them I was publishing a racy book about intimacy and infidelity under my maiden name. I'm indebted to your constant love and unwavering support.